a&b

The Secret Journals of Sherlock Holmes

JUNE THOMSON

Allison & Busby Limited
12 Fitzroy Mews
London W1T 6DW
www.allisonandbusby.com

First published in Great Britain in 1993.
This paperback edition published by Allison & Busby in 2012.

A CIP catalogue record for this book is available from the British Library.

10 9 8 7 6 5 4 3 2

ISBN 978-0-7490-1109-3

Typeset in 11/16 pt Sabon
by Allison & Busby Ltd.

The paper used for this Allison & Busby publication has been produced from trees that have been legally sourced from well-managed and credibly certified forests.

Printed and bound by
CPI Group (UK) Ltd, Croydon, CR0 4YY

TO

H.R.F. KEATING

FOR AGAIN GIVING SO GENEROUSLY

OF HIS TIME AND EXPERT ADVICE

My thanks also to Bill and Daphne Mellors and to
Mr, Mrs and Miss Barber of St Albans Music Centre for
their help in setting up the experiment with the metronome.
I am also grateful to Mr James Pratt for his expert
knowledge of diamonds, both real and synthetic.

I should again like to express my thanks to
June Thomson for her help in preparing this
third collection of short stories for publication.

Aubrey B. Watson, LDS, FDS, D. Orth.

CONTENTS

FOREWORD

by

Aubrey B. Watson LDS, FDS, D. Orth.

Readers of the two earlier collections of hitherto unpublished accounts of adventures, supposedly undertaken by Sherlock Holmes and Dr John H. Watson, will be familiar with the circumstances under which they came into my possession.

However, for the benefit of new readers, I shall give a brief account of the facts.

They were bequeathed to me by my late uncle, also a Dr John Watson, although his middle initial was 'F' not 'H' and he was a Doctor of Philosophy, not medicine. Struck by the similarity of his own name to that of Sherlock Holmes' illustrious chronicler, he had studied widely in the Holmes canon and had become an acknowledged expert.

It was for this reason that, in July 1939, he was

approached by a Miss Adeline McWhirter, who claimed to be a relative of Dr John H. Watson on his mother's side of the family. Finding herself in straitened circumstances, Miss McWhirter offered to sell to my late uncle a battered tin despatch box with the words 'John H. Watson, MD, Late Indian Army' painted on the lid which she said she had inherited. It was, she alleged, the same box which Dr John H. Watson, Sherlock Holmes' companion, had deposited in his bank, Cox & Co. of Charing Cross,[1] and contained records in his own handwriting of those adventures which the great consulting detective had undertaken and which for various reasons had never appeared in print.

Having examined both the box and its contents, my late uncle was convinced they were genuine and was planning to publish the latter when he was prevented from doing so by the outbreak of the Second World War.

Anxious about their safety, he made copies of the Watson papers before depositing the originals in their despatch box at his own bank in Lombard Street, London EC3. Unfortunately, the bank suffered a direct hit during the bombing of 1942, which reduced the papers to charred fragments and so blistered the paint on the box that the inscription was indecipherable.

Left with only his own copies of the original manuscripts and unable to trace Miss McWhirter, my late uncle decided very reluctantly not to publish in case

[1] Dr John H. Watson refers to this despatch box in the opening paragraph of 'The Problem of Thor Bridge'. Dr John F. Watson.

his reputation as a scholar might be called into question. On his death, he left the papers, together with his own footnotes on them, to me.

As I pointed out in the Forewords to the two earlier volumes, I am an orthodontist by profession and, having no academic reputation to protect and no one to whom I can bequeath the papers in my turn, I have decided to offer them for publication although I cannot guarantee their authenticity.

Among them were several monographs which my late uncle had written on various matters pertaining to the published canon. Readers will find one of these, that on the subject of Dr John H. Watson's second marriage, included in this volume as an appendix.

THE CASE OF THE MILLIONAIRE'S PERSECUTION

I see from my notes that it was on Thursday, 21st April 1895, only a few days before the arrival of Miss Violet Smith with an account of her singular adventures in Surrey,[1] that a telegram was delivered at our Baker Street lodgings.[2]

While it was not unusual for my old friend Sherlock Holmes to receive such communications, requesting his assistance in some urgent case or other, few had summoned him in quite so peremptory a manner.

---

[1] An account of this case was later published under the title of 'The Adventure of the Solitary Cyclist'. Dr John F. Watson.

[2] On Mr Sherlock Holmes' return to England in the spring of 1894, after the unsuccessful attempt on his life by Professor Moriarty at the Reichenbach Falls, Dr John H. Watson again shared lodgings with him at 221B Baker Street, his wife, the former Miss Mary Morstan, having died in the meantime. Dr John F. Watson.

Having read it and raised a quizzical eyebrow at its contents, Holmes passed the missive to me with the comment, 'Well, Watson, what do you make of that?'

It was a lengthy message which read: HAVE RECEIVED A SERIES OF ANONYMOUS LETTERS THREATENING MY LIFE STOP AS LOCAL CONSTABULARY QUITE INEFFECTUAL AM PLACING THE CASE IN YOUR HANDS STOP SHALL SEND MY CARRIAGE TO MEET YOU AT MAIDSTONE STATION OFF THE 2 23 TRAIN FROM CHARING CROSS STOP YOU MAY NAME YOUR OWN FEE STOP JOHN VINCENT HARDERN

'He is clearly a man for whom money is no object and who is used to having his own way,' I remarked.

'A wealthy American, would you say?' Holmes suggested. 'A millionaire, perhaps, who has made his fortune from tobacco?'

Although I was used to my old friend's remarkable powers, I was nevertheless startled by his comments, for I had read nothing in the telegram to warrant such precise conclusions.

'How could you possibly have deduced all that, Holmes?' I enquired, at which he burst out laughing.

'There is no mystery,' said he. 'The plain fact of the matter is that John Vincent Hardern was the subject of a short article in *The Times* three weeks ago when he arrived in this country in which his wealth and background were remarked on. It is his first visit to England and he is here, it seems, for a year, principally to introduce his only daughter, Edith, to English society. For that purpose, he has taken the lease of a country residence as well as a house in Belgravia. As the Dowager Lady Wroxham is to chaperone the young lady for the London season and as her ladyship has an eligible son, I think we may safely assume that the next notice to appear in *The Times* of the two families will be the announcement of an engagement between Miss Hardern and Lord Wroxham. So marriages are made, Watson; not in heaven but by society hostesses in the drawing-rooms of Park Lane and Grosvenor Square.

'That being said, I think I shall accept Hardern's summons, little as I care for its high-handed tone.'

'He says you may name your own fee,' I pointed out.

Holmes waved a negligent hand.

'Oh, the money is of no consequence! I have refused wealthy clients before when the cases they presented were of no particular interest. But threats to Hardern's life! Now that is no trivial matter. We shall catch the 2.23 train, as Hardern specifies, and trust that in the course of our enquiries in Kent we shall find the solution to one aspect of the case which strikes me as particularly curious.'

'The identity of the villain who has threatened Hardern's life?'

'That, too, my dear fellow. What interests me far more is the sequence of events.'

'I do not follow you, Holmes.'

'Then consider the facts such as we know them. According to *The Times*, Hardern arrived for the first time in England a mere three weeks ago and yet he has already received what he describes as a series of threatening letters. It seems too short a space of time for Hardern to make so mortal an enemy in this country, unless I gravely underestimate his talent for arousing hatred.'

'So you do not think his correspondent is English?'

'I said nothing of the sort. I merely expressed doubts about one aspect of the case.'

'But if he is not English,' I persisted, 'must he not be American, someone who bears Hardern a grudge and who has followed him to England?'

'That is possible but once again there is the matter of dates. Why wait for Hardern to come to England? Why not strike him down at home? It would seem the logical course, would it not?'

'Perhaps the conditions over there made it impractical.'

'That, too, is another possibility. However, until we are in possession of all the facts, any discussion of the matter is pure speculation. I have remarked before on the danger of basing a theory on insufficient data.'[3]

He refused to say another word on the matter, not even on the train to Maidstone where we were met at the station by Hardern's brougham. After a journey of some three miles past the blossoming orchards of Kent, we arrived at our client's residence, Marsham Hall, a noble Queen Anne mansion set among extensive grounds.

Here the butler, a dignified, middle-aged servant with

---

[3] In 'The Adventure of the Speckled Band', Mr Sherlock Holmes makes the following comment: '"I had," said he, "come to an entirely erroneous conclusion, which shows, my dear Watson, how dangerous it always is to reason from insufficient data."' Dr John F. Watson.

a face as long and as pale as a church candle, conducted us into a large drawing-room where Hardern was waiting to welcome us.

He was a tall, heavily built man in his fifties, of an overbearing and autocratic manner, who gave a powerful impression of suppressed energy waiting to erupt, like a kettle about to come to the boil. His broad, ruddy features and shock of reddish hair spoke of a choleric nature.

No sooner were the introductions over, than he plunged straight into his account.

'Now, see here, gentlemen,' said he, 'I am a man of few words and I don't propose wasting your time or mine. I shall lay before you the facts of the case as briefly as possible. I received the first threatening letter within a few days of my taking up residence in the house.'

'So soon?' Holmes murmured, giving me a sideways glance. 'I find that quite remarkable.'

'So do I, sir! So do I! Why, I had barely set foot in this country when some blackguard had the audacity to tell me to clear out or take the consequences.'

'You have no idea of his identity?'

'No, I have not, sir! If I had, I should not have asked for your assistance. I would have sought the ruffian out myself and given him a good thrashing.'

'I think such action would be unwise,' Holmes remarked coolly. 'May I see the letters? I assume you have kept them?'

'Not the first one. I took it to be so much trash and I burnt it immediately.'

'In your telegram, you mentioned a series of letters. How many were there?'

'Four altogether. The other three are here.'

Striding across the room, Hardern jerked open the drawer of a bureau and took out a small bundle of papers which he handed to Holmes.

'All posted in Maidstone, I see,' my old friend remarked, examining the envelopes. 'And all addressed in capital letters by the same hand. Now what of the contents?'

Taking out the letters, he read them through in silence before passing them to me with the comment, 'Note the quality of the paper, Watson, as well as the spelling. You will not need me to draw your attention to the imprint of a finger at the bottom of each page.'

Indeed, these marks were impossible to overlook. At the end of each message, where normally a signature would be found, was the impression of a single finger made in black ink, amounting in all to the three middle fingers of someone's hand, presumably the mysterious correspondent's.

They stood out, stark and sinister, against the white paper which was of a cheap quality, the type which could be bought at any stationer's. I could make nothing, however, of Holmes' comment about the spelling which was unremarkable, except perhaps in its correctness.

As for the messages themselves, they were printed, like the envelopes, in neat capital letters in the same black ink which had been used to produce the finger-marks.

The message of the one signed by the ring finger read:

'You have been warned once, Hardern. Clear out of the country while you can.'

The second, which carried the impression of the middle finger, expanded on this theme: 'Your life is in danger while you remain. This is no idle warning.'

It was the last, the one bearing the print of the forefinger, which was the most threatening.

'You are a fool, Hardern,' it read, 'but you do yourself no favour by being stubborn. I shall not wait much longer. Pack up and leave at once or, on my oath, you are a dead man.'

Hardern, who had waited with considerable impatience while we read, could contain himself no longer.

'Well, Mr Holmes,' he burst out. 'What conclusions have you come to? Who is this villain? And why is he persecuting me in this manner?'

'My dear sir, I am not clairvoyant,' Holmes answered, a gleam of amusement in his deep-set eyes. 'I cannot put a name to your unknown correspondent. That will need much further enquiry. However, I can furnish you with a few details I have deduced. He is undoubtedly male, about thirty years of age, right-handed and a clerk by training if not by profession. He is, moreover, a British citizen.'

'Not an American, Holmes?' I interjected, a little dashed that my earlier theory regarding his nationality had been dismissed.

'No, Watson, decidedly not. When I advised you to note the spelling, I had in mind the word "favour" which is written in the English manner. An American would have omitted the *u*. As for the rest of my conclusions,' Holmes continued, turning to Hardern, 'I have made a study of the various styles of handwriting and I can assure you that my deductions are correct. I see from your expression, sir, that my description means nothing to you.'

'No, it does not, Mr Holmes!' our client exclaimed. 'Since my arrival, I have met no one who at all resembles it. In fact, the only acquaintances I have so far made in this country are the Dowager Lady Wroxham and her son, neither of whom would have any reason to threaten me. Why, it was on Lord Wroxham's invitation that my daughter Edith and myself decided to make the trip to England in the first place.'

'Under what circumstances was that?' Holmes enquired.

'I first met Gerald – Lord Wroxham – about eighteen months ago when he was in the States visiting some of his American kinsfolk. An aunt of his had married one of the Brightleys, friends of mine and of old Virginian stock who can trace their ancestry back to Tudor times. My daughter and I were invited to a reception given by the Brightleys in honour of their English relation and it was there that Edith and I were introduced to Gerald Wroxham.

'To cut a long story short, Mr Holmes, the young couple took a shine to one other immediately. The possibility of marriage was hinted at but I objected on the grounds that they had not known each other long enough. It was then that Gerald Wroxham suggested I brought my daughter to England to meet his mother and to be introduced into English society. If they felt the same about one other on longer acquaintance, their formal engagement would be announced at the end of the season.

The Dowager Lady Wroxham approved of the arrangements and undertook to find suitable residences in London and in the country where Edith and I could stay during our visit. By great good fortune, this house came unexpectedly on the market. It had belonged to an elderly gentleman, Sir Cedric Forster-Dyke, whose relatives decided to admit him to a nursing-home. He was extremely deaf and had become increasingly bedridden. His family were delighted to find a tenant willing to take the house for the whole year and to retain the domestic staff.

'From my point of view, it was particularly fortunate for two reasons. Firstly, Lady Wroxham's residence, Whitehaven Manor, is a mere three miles away which meant the young people could meet easily and Edith could get to know Gerald's family and friends. Secondly, the lease on a house in Sussex which Lady Wroxham had arranged for us had to be suddenly cancelled when fire broke out in the servants' wing, causing considerable damage.

'All of this happened when Edith and I were on board the ship bringing us to England and it was only when we arrived in London and were met off the train by Gerald Wroxham that we learnt of the fire in the Sussex house and the unexpected vacancy of Marsham Hall.'

At this point in our client's narrative, Holmes broke in to exclaim, 'Well, Mr Hardern, your account has effectively put paid to one possible explanation.'

'And what was that, Mr Holmes?'

'That one of your enemies in the States had engaged an English accomplice to send the threatening letters on his account. But as you yourself learnt only on your arrival in London that your country residence was to be in Kent, not Sussex, then he could hardly have arranged for your persecution in advance. But I interrupted you, Mr Hardern. Pray forgive me and continue your account.'

'There is very little else to relate, sir. On Gerald Wroxham's advice, we stayed a few days in a hotel in London while Marsham Hall was made ready for our arrival. He then accompanied us here and saw that we were comfortably installed. The first threatening letter arrived shortly afterwards; four days later to be precise.'

'Bearing, I assume, the mark of a little finger printed in black ink?'

'Indeed so, Mr Holmes!'

'You notified the police?'

'Only on the receipt of the second message. An Inspector Whiffen of the Kent Constabulary called at the house and examined that letter as well as the subsequent correspondence but could offer no explanation. He seemed to consider the whole affair was an elaborate hoax.'

'Oh, it is a great deal more serious than that,' Holmes said. 'I believe your anonymous adversary is in deadly earnest. I also believe that you will receive a further letter, bearing this time a thumb-mark, thus completing the five prints of a whole hand. A black hand, Mr Hardern. Does that have any significance for you?'

'I am totally at a loss, Mr Holmes. A black hand! What action do you advise me to take?'

'To pay heed to the warnings and leave before that last letter arrives for, once it is delivered, your safety cannot be guaranteed.'

'You suggest I return to the States? No, sir!' Hardern exclaimed. 'I refuse to be hounded out of this country.'

'Then at least retire to your house in London.'

Hardern, whose anger had been simmering just below the surface, could contain it no longer. His blue eyes blazing, he brought his fist crashing down on the arm of his chair.

'I will not, Mr Holmes! That would be capitulation and no man living has ever got the better of John Vincent Hardern!'

'There is not only your safety to consider,' Holmes reminded him quietly. 'There is also your daughter's.'

'I am well aware of that, sir. She is at present out riding with Gerald Wroxham and his sister. As soon as they return, I shall ask if Edith may be allowed to move to Whitehaven Manor. I am sure Lady Wroxham will agree. She and her son are aware of the threats made against me. Indeed, it was Gerald Wroxham who recommended you, Mr Holmes. As for myself, I intend remaining here.'

'Then I strongly advise you stay indoors and make sure the windows and doors are securely locked and barred at night. You have a revolver?'

'A Colt, Mr Holmes.'

'Then keep it with you at all times,' Holmes said, rising

to his feet. 'And as soon as you receive the fifth letter, the one bearing the thumb-print, you must inform me at once.'

'You really think Hardern's life is in danger?' I enquired when, a little later, having taken leave of our client, we set off in the brougham for the return journey to Maidstone station.

'I fear so, Watson,' Holmes replied, his expression grim. 'As he has refused my advice to leave Marsham Hall immediately, we can only trust that, when his unknown enemy chooses to strike, we are at hand to deflect the blow. What an abstruse case this is proving to be! I refer not just to the matter of its sequence. There is also the motive to consider. Why should anyone wish to force Hardern to leave this country when he has only just arrived in it? Then there is the curious business of the Black Hand signature. It suggests a connection with an unlawful fraternity. And yet I know of no gang which operates under such a *nom de guerre* although I pride myself on keeping informed of all underworld activity.

'I shall ask discreetly among my criminal acquaintances. In the meantime, I propose returning to Maidstone tomorrow to start making enquiries at the hotels and inns for a stranger answering my description.'

'Do you wish me to accompany you?'

'Thank you, but I think it would be better if I went alone. If we are to discover this man's identity and whereabouts, we must go about it circumspectly. Two of us asking questions might arouse suspicion.'

The following morning, Holmes left for Maidstone by an early train, not returning to Baker Street until late that evening.

'You have found out nothing?' I enquired, seeing his morose expression as he entered the sitting-room.

'Not a trace,' he replied, seating himself wearily by the fire. 'I believe I have visited every likely hostelry in the town and have drawn a complete blank. There remain, of course, the lodging-houses, of which there must be dozens but where I shall be forced to continue my enquiries tomorrow. To be frank, my dear fellow, it is like looking for one particular pebble on a beach. But I see no other alternative if I am to run this scoundrel to earth.'

In the event, there was no opportunity for him to return immediately to Kent as he had planned. The following day, Saturday, Miss Violet Smith arrived from Charlington in Surrey with her own remarkable account of her pursuit by an unknown cyclist, and begged for Holmes' assistance. Reluctant though he was to take on another inquiry while he was so deeply immersed in the Hardern affair, her plight and the singular nature of the story she laid before him finally persuaded him to accept the case, even though I urged against it.

'My dear Watson, I could hardly turn her away,' he protested. 'She is a solitary female with no one to protect her. I admit it will be a distraction. However, as I expect to hear nothing from Hardern for several days until the fifth and last letter is delivered, then I should have time to pursue this other investigation.'

'But your enquiries in Kent!'

'I shall continue those on Monday. If in the meantime you could assist me with the Sussex case, I should be infinitely obliged.'

'Of course, Holmes; in any way I can,' I assured him.

Therefore, on the Monday, when Holmes set off once more for Kent, I was despatched to Charlington in order to make enquiries there on his behalf, quite unsuccessfully according to Holmes who criticised my methods.[4] Although at the time I was deeply hurt, I could make allowances for his strictures. His own investigations in Kent, as well as those among his criminal acquaintances, had still come to nothing and, in consequence, he was in a state of high nervous tension.

The Surrey adventure was satisfactorily resolved on the following Saturday, 30th April, when Holmes and I were in time to prevent the abduction of Miss Violet Smith and to effect the arrest of a certain Mr Woodley who had been attempting, by means of a forced marriage, to seize the young lady's fortune.

It was a singular triumph for my old friend who now had the leisure to turn his full attention to the Hardern affair.

---

[4] According to Mr Sherlock Holmes, Dr John H. Watson chose the wrong hiding-place from which to observe Miss Smith's unknown pursuer and made the mistake of enquiring about the occupants of Charlington Hall at a London house agent's rather than at the nearest inn where he would have heard all the local gossip. *Vide:* 'The Adventure of the Solitary Cyclist'. Dr John F. Watson.

In the meantime, he had heard nothing from the American millionaire and it was this period of uncertainty which plunged him into the deepest gloom. He was fearful that, despite his confident assertion that the Black Hand would not strike until after the receipt of the fifth letter, he might be mistaken and his client's life was therefore in immediate jeopardy.

It was not until the following Monday, 2nd May, that Holmes at last received the long-awaited communication from Hardern which arrived by the second post.

As soon as it was delivered, Holmes eagerly tore the envelope open.

It contained two sheets of paper, the first a letter from Hardern himself which Holmes set to one side while he hurriedly scanned the second missive, before passing it to me.

As he had anticipated, it bore at the bottom of the page the thumb-print of the Black Hand while the message itself was as chilling to the blood as that sinister imprint.

It was dated Saturday, 30th April, and read: 'I have waited long enough, Hardern, but time is running out. Leave at once, for your days are already numbered.'

'A charming note, is it not, Watson?' Holmes asked with a grim smile. 'But at least we know that the villain has not yet struck, as I had feared.'

'Perhaps Hardern will at last take the matter seriously and decide to leave,' I suggested, although without much hope, I must confess.

Holmes confirmed my doubts.

'Out of the question, Watson! The man is as stubborn as a mule. Instead, he proposes in his letter that we catch the 3.17 train to Maidstone this afternoon and stay overnight at Marsham Hall, although what he imagines we can achieve is beyond my comprehension. We are no nearer establishing the identity of the Black Hand, let alone apprehending him. Apart from standing guard over our client, we can offer little else.' Rising to his feet, he began to pace restlessly about the room. 'This is a most damnable affair, Watson! An unknown adversary and a client who declines to take my advice! I can think of no worse combination.'

'You could refuse to continue with the case,' I pointed out.

'And risk putting Hardern's life in danger? Never! Besides, it would be admitting defeat,' Holmes cried, at which last exclamation I had to admit a wry amusement, despite the gravity of the situation, for my old friend was proving as obstinate as his client.

Under the circumstances, there was nothing Holmes could do except comply with Hardern's instructions, however unwillingly, and consequently we caught the afternoon train to Maidstone, fully expecting our journey would be wasted, although, as a precaution, Holmes insisted I packed my army revolver.

However, as soon as we arrived at Marsham Hall, we were made aware that, since our receipt of Hardern's letter that morning, something of a much more dramatic nature had occurred. Hardern himself was impatiently awaiting us, pacing up and down the terrace with the restlessness of a caged lion.

Hardly had the carriage halted than he came rushing down the steps to meet us, calling out excitedly, 'The villain has sent me another of his damnable threats, this time inside the house itself! Come and see for yourselves.'

As he hustled us into the hall, he continued over his shoulder, 'It must have happened last night or in the early hours of the morning . . .'

He broke off to address the butler, who had come forward to take our coats.

'Be quick about it, Mallow,' he ordered in his hectoring manner. 'And then bring Inspector Whiffen to me at once. You know where to find him.'

Hurriedly divesting ourselves of our outer garments, we turned to hasten after Hardern, who had gone charging ahead of us with the energy of a steam locomotive down a series of corridors and passages which led at last to the kitchen quarters.

Here, our client unlocked a door which he then flung open with one sweep of his arm, at the same time announcing dramatically, 'Take a look at that, gentlemen!'

We found ourselves in a narrow pantry equipped with shelves and a sink with wooden draining-boards, above which a small casement window, less than three feet square, was swinging open upon its hinges.

Below it, stamped in black ink on the whitewashed wall, was a single handprint, its fingers splayed out and so clearly delineated that, even from the doorway, it was possible to make out the individual lines and whorls which marked the surface of the skin.

It was accompanied by a message in the same neat capital letters which the Black Hand had used in all his communications.

'Your time has come, Hardern,' it read. 'Beware the terror that strikes at night.'

'You see, Mr Holmes!' the American millionaire was expostulating. 'The infernal scoundrel has had the audacity to force his way into my house. It is not to be tolerated!'

Holmes stepped forward to examine the casement, first shutting and then opening it again.

'The window is loose in its frame,' he announced. 'It was simply a matter of inserting the blade of a knife, or a similar instrument, into the gap and lifting the catch. Was anyone disturbed by the intrusion?'

'I heard nothing,' Hardern informed him. 'As for the servants, they sleep on the top floor of another wing. Inspector Whiffen questioned them earlier but they, too, were not aware that anything was amiss.'

'Then who discovered the pantry had been broken into?'

'The housekeeper. Fortunately, she is a sensible woman and came straight to me. After I had examined the scoundrel's handiwork, I ordered her to lock the door and say nothing of her discovery on the threat of instant dismissal. I have no intention of allowing my affairs to become the subject of servants' gossip. I then sent for Inspector Whiffen. Ah, I believe I hear him coming now!'

All three of us turned at the sound of footsteps approaching along the stone-flagged passage to see a thick-set, blunt-featured man, accompanied by Mallow, the butler.

It was obvious that Whiffen had already examined the black handprint and the message, for he hardly troubled to glance at them as Hardern introduced him to Holmes and myself.

It was Mallow who was the more deeply affected. He had come to a halt in the passageway just behind the inspector and was staring fixedly over his shoulder, his pallid features even paler than usual and his eyes nearly starting out of his head in horrified consternation.

'Oh, Mr Hardern!' he gasped out involuntarily. 'What a dreadful outrage, sir!'

Hardern seemed aware for the first time of the butler's presence.

'Now you know why the police have been sent for,' he said brusquely. 'But, if you value your place, not a word to the other servants. It is none of their business. As far as they are concerned, an attempt was made last night to break into Marsham Hall; nothing more. That is why Inspector Whiffen and his men are here. You understand? Then you may go.'

'Very good, sir,' Mallow replied, his features resuming that expression of polite deference which a well-trained servant learns to maintain under all circumstances.

'And now,' Hardern continued, as the butler departed, 'I suggest we lock this place up again and retire to discuss what is to be done. And I warn you, I expect action to be taken!'

It was a demand which he repeated when, a few minutes later, we took our seats in the drawing-room.

Hardern remained standing in front of the fireplace, glaring down at us with considerable disfavour.

'So,' he barked out, 'exactly how do you propose laying this villain by the heels? Inspector Whiffen?'

'Well, Mr Hardern,' the inspector began, a little apprehensive at being called upon to speak first. 'At present, I have my sergeant and a constable searching the grounds for the place where the man entered.'

'But they cover several acres,' Hardern protested. 'It will take hours!'

'I think not,' Holmes interjected. He was sitting at ease in his chair, his legs crossed, not at all intimidated by our client's blustering manner. 'As all the letters were posted in Maidstone, I think we may safely assume that the Black Hand is residing somewhere in or near the town. I therefore propose that we begin our search in that part of the estate which adjoins the Maidstone road. Inspector Whiffen, if you and your colleagues would care to assist us, our task will be made lighter.'

'What shall we be looking for, Mr Holmes?' Whiffen enquired.

'Any signs that someone has recently entered – a fresh footprint or newly disturbed undergrowth. In the meantime, you, Mr Hardern, will remain in the house.'

'Now, see here, Mr Holmes . . .' Hardern began in protest.

'No, sir; you shall not accompany us,' my old friend said sternly. 'I cannot guarantee your safety. At this very moment, the Black Hand may be lurking somewhere nearby, waiting for you to emerge into the open. You have refused to take my advice in the past, Mr Hardern. This time I fully intend you shall obey my instructions.'

It was quite clear from the millionaire's expression that no one had ever before had the temerity to address him in this manner. But he offered no further objection and shortly afterwards the three of us, Holmes, Inspector Whiffen and I, left the house and, having collected the sergeant and the constable, who were poking about ineffectually in the shrubbery with sticks, we set off for that part of the estate which abutted the main road into Maidstone.

On Holmes' instructions, we spread out, each of us taking a separate stretch of the boundary hedge. It was Inspector Whiffen who found evidence of the intruder. 'Over here, Mr Holmes!' he called out.

When we joined him, we found him pointing excitedly at some bushes, where there were clear signs in the disturbed foliage and the trampled earth below that someone had recently forced a way through the undergrowth.

With the eagerness of a bloodhound hot upon the trail, Holmes threw himself down on his knees to examine the bush and the surrounding soil, subjecting both to a minute scrutiny, at the same time commenting aloud on each fresh discovery as much for his own benefit as ours.

'See the way the leaves are broken! The twigs, too! As for the boot-marks, they are highly significant.'

'Of what, Mr Holmes?' Inspector Whiffen enquired in a baffled tone.

'Of the fact that our quarry has broken *into* the grounds but has not yet broken out again. All the foliage is bent inwards. The footprints, too, point in only one direction. It means, gentlemen, that the Black Hand must be lying low somewhere in the grounds.'

'Then should we widen the search, Mr Holmes?' Whiffen asked, clearly depending on my old friend to make the decisions.

'There is not time for that. We must use another stratagem,' Holmes replied briskly. 'We now know not only where he has made his entrance but where he will make his exit when he is in need of one. The man may be as cunning as a fox but, like all wild creatures, he will come and go by the same familiar path.'

'So you think he will strike soon, Holmes?' I asked.

'Without a doubt; probably this very evening. The black hand and the message upon the pantry wall with its warning of terror by night suggest that the man is growing desperate. I fully expect this affair to come to a head very shortly and, when it does, we shall be ready with our trap in the shape of Inspector Whiffen here and his colleagues.'

Turning to address the officer, he continued, 'As soon as it grows dusk, I suggest you and your men conceal yourselves in the shrubbery, near to this bush, ready to arrest the Black Hand the moment he appears. Dr Watson, who is armed, will stay close to Mr Hardern in order to protect him while I shall also remain in the house in case of any attack in that quarter, although I do not expect the Black Hand to strike until much later tonight when everyone is in bed.'

As events were to prove, Holmes was too sanguine in making this assertion.

We returned to the house where the plan was put to our client, who listened attentively, only objecting to that part of it which concerned his own safety when he again showed that obstinacy of character which we had experienced before.

'Now, see here, Mr Holmes!' said he, bristling up at once. 'Do you expect me to sit idly by, looked after by you and Dr Watson like a child by its nursemaids? No, sir! I have a gun and, by thunder, I mean to use it! I'll have you know I am reckoned to be the best shot in the whole of West Virginia.'

Once more, Holmes overrode him.

His voice as cold and as cutting as steel, he replied, 'I do not doubt it, Mr Hardern. However, I, too, have a reputation to preserve and that is to protect my client's life at all costs. And now, sir, it will soon be growing dark. I suggest you make arrangements for Inspector Whiffen and his men to be given supper before they leave to set up their ambuscade.'

His brow contracted, Hardern stalked across the room to ring the bell for Mallow to whom he conveyed these instructions and, shortly afterwards, Whiffen and the other officers were summoned to the servants' hall.

Our own meal was served in the dining-room, where the curtains had been drawn against the gathering dusk. At Holmes' request, it was a simple supper of soup and cold meat although Hardern, determined to play the host, had ordered the butler to serve an excellent bottle of claret.

Mallow was in the very act of filling our glasses when the blow was struck.

It was so sudden and unexpected that I was aware only of a sound like a shell exploding as the drawn curtains were blown apart and a shower of broken glass was sent flying across the room. At almost the same instant, something round and dark fell with a crash upon the table, scattering china and silver in every direction before finally rolling to a halt beside my plate. It was only then that I realised that the object was nothing more deadly than a large stone which had been hurled through the window.

Mallow, who was already on his feet, was the first to take action.

Dropping the decanter in his haste, he started for the door leading into the hall, closely followed by Holmes who, thrusting back his chair, sprinted after him. By the time I had sufficiently recovered from the shock to follow, they had disappeared through the front door into the garden.

It was a wild evening with a strong wind sending the clouds scurrying across the moon, so that the scene before me was alternately brightly lit or plunged into deep shadow.

As I halted at the top of the porch steps in order to

get my bearings, the sky momentarily cleared and the darkness lifted. In those few seconds of illumination, I saw the thin, stooped figure of the butler running across the lawn towards the shrubbery. Holmes, who was close on his heels, turned his head briefly to call out to me before the moon was again obscured.

'Keep Hardern in the house, Watson! This could well be a trap!'

The warning came too late. Hardern, who must have followed me out on to the porch, had already descended the steps and had set off in pursuit across the darkened garden, shouting out as he ran, 'By God, I'll lay that infernal villain by the heels myself!'

What happened next was over literally in a flash. The moon suddenly reappeared, its pale, cold light streaming down and throwing into silhouette a venerable cedar tree which stood in the centre of the lawn, its black branches threshing in the wind. Below it, I caught a glimpse of Hardern, head lowered and shoulders hunched as, bellowing like an enraged bull, he went charging forward.

At that same moment, a loud report rang out from the shrubbery, accompanied by a spurt of yellow flame, and I heard the whine of a bullet pass in front of me.

It was a sound familiar to me from the battle of Maiwand[5] but before I could draw my own revolver, I

[5] Dr John H. Watson, who was serving as assistant surgeon with the Berkshires, was wounded at the battle of Maiwand on 27th June 1880, at which the British were defeated by a superior force of Afghan rebels. Dr John F. Watson.

saw Hardern topple face forward to the ground.

My first thought was that he was dead, felled by the bullet, and I ran towards him, calling for Holmes who turned and came racing back. But even as we reached the inert figure, Hardern was struggling to his feet.

'I tripped over a d——d root and the bullet missed me!' he roared out. 'Go after him! He mustn't escape.'

'Brave words, Mr Hardern,' Holmes remarked in a tone of genuine admiration. 'But further pursuit on my part would be useless. The Black Hand has too long a start. We can only trust that either the butler or Whiffen and his colleagues can capture this villain before he escapes. In the meantime, I urge you to return to the house in case another attempt is made upon you.'

Hardly had he finished speaking than we were joined by the butler, who came towards us across the lawn, breathing heavily, his clothes and hair much dishevelled.

'You lost him?' Holmes demanded.

'In the shrubbery, sir,' Mallow replied, struggling for breath and visibly trembling with his exertions.

'Did you catch sight of him?'

'Only a glimpse. He's a big man, Mr Holmes; as tall as you but much broader across the shoulders.'

'Well done, Mallow!' Holmes exclaimed. 'At least we now know what the Black Hand looks like. And now, if you and Dr Watson would care to escort Mr Hardern into the house, I have a crucial piece of evidence I wish to retrieve.'

'What is that, Mr Holmes?' Hardern enquired.

'You shall see that, sir, when I have recovered it,' Holmes replied.

There was a strange note of jubilation in his voice which seemed out of keeping with the seriousness of the situation and, as Hardern and the butler set off towards the house, I deliberately lingered behind.

'I know that air of excitement, Holmes,' I announced. 'It means you are hot on the scent.'

'A mere whiff so far, Watson,' said he, his eyes sparkling in the moonlight which was now drenching the scene. 'But I believe it will lead directly to our quarry. Now be a good fellow and go with our client. After such a close encounter with the Black Hand, he will no doubt be suffering from shock and may need your ministrations.'

As I turned away to comply, I glanced back over my shoulder to see my old friend walking briskly across the lawn in the direction of the shrubbery.

The effect of the night's adventure on John Vincent Hardern manifested itself more in anger than in shock. Although I suggested he sit quietly until he had recovered, he refused my medical advice and stamped up and down the drawing-room, all the time inveighing against the Black Hand and the infernal persecution to which he had been subjected, while Mallow and I looked on helplessly.

'It is intolerable!' he exclaimed. 'I wish I had never set foot in this country. Law and order, sir! You English do not know the meaning of the words. As for Mr Holmes' much-vaunted reputation as a consulting detective, why he is nothing but a mere amateur!'

I was about to protest at this quite unwarranted attack on my old friend's professional skills, when the door opened and Holmes himself entered the room.

'I am quite willing to admit,' said he cheerily, 'that the inquiry has not been entirely successful until this moment. However, the case is now solved.'

'Solved! How?' Hardern demanded, coming to a halt and regarding Holmes with great astonishment.

'If you care to sit down, Mr Hardern, I shall explain. And I shall require your presence, too, Mallow,' he added, as the butler made as if to leave the room.

'Mine, sir?' Mallow had halted in the doorway, his long, pale face turned in our direction.

'Yes, yours. For you know more about this affair than you have admitted, do you not? Your mistake was to describe the Black Hand as a broad-shouldered man. By so doing, you put into my grasp the first loose thread by which this whole tangled affair may finally be unravelled.

'The Black Hand entered the house through the pantry window before leaving his mark on the wall; a small window through which only a man with narrow shoulders could have gained entry. This was my first piece of evidence in my search for the man's identity. The second is this.'

Putting his hand into his pocket, he took out a revolver with a stubby, rounded butt and a short barrel, not more than two and a half inches in length.

'This is the gun which was fired at Mr Hardern. When I was chasing the Black Hand across the garden,

I heard him throw the weapon away into the shrubbery, no doubt because it was used not only for tonight's attempted murder but for an even more serious crime. Consequently, he may well have preferred not to be found with it in his possession, should he be caught. I went back to retrieve it. It is a Webley, known popularly as the "British Bulldog".[6]

'A similar revolver was used last March in a daring robbery in which a police constable was mortally wounded. Before he died, however, he was able to describe fully both the gun and the man who fired it. He was tall and thin, in his early thirties, with long, pale features; a description which bears a remarkable resemblance to you, Mallow. Who is he? Your younger brother?'

Before the butler could reply, a loud commotion was heard in the hall. Moments later the door burst open and Inspector Whiffen and his fellow officers entered, bearing between them the struggling figure of a man, his wrists handcuffed.

At the sight of him, Mallow started forward. 'Victor!' he cried, his voice anguished.

To those of us observing the scene, the likeness between the two men was indeed remarkable. Apart from the

---

[6] This type of revolver was manufactured in 1878 by the English gun-makers, P. Webley and Sons. It had either a .450 or a .422 calibre. A later version of this weapon, with a .450 calibre only, was supplied to the Metropolitan Police and other police forces. It may be for this reason that the constable was able to describe it so accurately before he died. Dr John F. Watson.

difference in their ages, they might have been twins. Both had the same dark eyes and narrow, pallid features. But while the butler's bore an expression of agonised grief, those of his brother, whom we had come to know as the Black Hand, were twisted into an expression of such dreadful rage and depravity that I involuntarily shrank back.

'Keep your mouth shut!' the Black Hand shouted at Mallow. 'These fools know nothing!'

'It is too late,' his brother told him. 'This gentleman is Mr Sherlock Holmes and he is already acquainted with most of the facts.'

'Holmes! That interfering half-wit!' Victor Mallow screamed out, letting fly a string of oaths.

'And those facts I do not know may be assumed from a process of logical deduction,' Holmes said coolly, ignoring the outburst. 'I suggest, Inspector Whiffen, that your officers remove the prisoner from the room but that you remain to hear the rest of my account before charging Victor Mallow with murder and attempted murder as well as burglary and theft.'

Whiffen's eyebrows shot up but he quickly recovered from his astonishment and, on his orders, Victor Mallow was dragged out into the hall, still struggling and shouting, by the sergeant and the constable.

'Allow me to repeat for your benefit, Inspector, what I have already told these gentlemen,' Holmes remarked, when the door had closed behind them. 'The Black Hand, otherwise Victor Mallow and the younger brother of Mr Hardern's butler, took part in a robbery a little over a year ago. I learnt the details of the case from the newspaper accounts.

'The raid was on a bullion dealer's in London where Victor Mallow, using the alias of George Hallem, was employed as a clerk. It was he who had planned the robbery and, by using a set of duplicate keys, had let his accomplice, William Stone, a notorious burglar already known to the police, into the premises by the back door. One of those keys was also used to open the strong room, from where they removed a box of gold ingots which they carried out to an alleyway behind the building, where they had left a hired carriage. It was their intention to transport the bullion to a man Stone knew in Whitechapel who dealt in stolen property.

'It was while they were loading the heavy crate into the carriage that they were surprised by a police constable who was patrolling the area. Victor Mallow took a revolver from his pocket, the same gun which he used tonight in his attempt on Mr Hardern's life, and in cold blood fired at the constable, who fell to the ground, mortally wounded. Although a hardened criminal, Stone was nevertheless horrified by Mallow's action and promptly took to his heels.

'We know these facts, gentlemen, because Stone was later arrested and made a full confession, although he denied being responsible for the murder. He is now serving a long term of imprisonment.

'Stone's denial was corroborated by the constable who,

after he was discovered by a passer-by, was conveyed to Charing Cross Hospital. Before he died, he was able to give a description of the gun as well as of his assailant, which exactly matched Victor Mallow's.

'At this point, our knowledge of the facts fails us but I think we may imagine Victor Mallow's state of mind immediately after the robbery.

'Picture the scene, gentlemen, as he stood in that alleyway. His accomplice has vanished into the night. A policeman lies dying at his feet. Very soon the whole of Scotland Yard will be searching for him. Once found, he will certainly be hanged. It is essential that he conceals his booty as soon as possible before going into hiding. But where? It has to be somewhere he can easily retrieve it once the hue and cry has died down.

'It was then, I suggest, that he thought of Marsham Hall, where his brother was employed as butler. At the time, the house was occupied by an elderly gentleman, Sir Cedric Forster-Dyke, an invalid and, moreover, extremely deaf. It was unlikely he would be disturbed by any strange noises in the night. Neither would the servants whose quarters are on the top floor of a separate wing.

'I believe the case of gold ingots was conveyed here the same night that the robbery took place and was concealed somewhere on the premises with your assistance, Mallow.'

The butler, who had listened to this account with increasing distress, finally broke his silence.

'I refused at first, sir! I told him I would have

nothing to do with it! But I could not turn him away. If he had been caught, he would have gone to the gallows. He swore he had not meant to kill the policeman, only frighten him. I believed him, Mr Holmes! As a boy, he had always been wild but never wicked; or so I thought. It was only when he went to London to become a clerk that he fell into bad company and began to gamble heavily. It was then that he turned to crime in order to repay his debts, first fraud at a bank where he was employed and for which he served a term of imprisonment. It was after he came out of gaol that he changed his name to George Hallem and, with the use of forged papers, obtained the post of clerk at the bullion dealer's.'

'Who supplied a reference?' Holmes enquired.

Mallow looked crestfallen.

'I did, sir. Victor swore he had learnt his lesson and would go straight from then on. I wrote from this address, using Sir Cedric's name and stating that I had employed him for the past five years as my personal secretary. I know I was a fool to trust him and to agree to help him when he came to me that night with the stolen bullion.'

'I think', said Holmes, 'that you had better give us a full account of what happened.'

'He left the carriage a little way down the drive, sir, so that no one would hear the sound of the wheels. Victor then forced open the pantry window, the frame of which was loose, and came upstairs to wake me. I helped him carry the box down to the cellar, where we concealed it under the bricks in the floor.'

'From where your brother intended to recover it later,' Holmes interjected. 'However, his plans were thwarted by Sir Cedric's removal to a nursing-home and by Mr Hardern taking Marsham Hall for the whole year.'

'I could not warn Victor of Mr Hardern's arrival,' Mallow explained. 'He was in hiding and I had no address to write to.'

'Then he must have spied out the land and discovered the situation for himself. And so began your persecution, Mr Hardern,' Holmes continued, turning to our client. 'The purpose was not to drive you out of the country as we first thought but to force you to vacate Marsham Hall so that Victor Mallow could collect his booty. Unlike Sir Cedric, you are an active man and in full possession of your faculties. Had he returned and attempted to dig up the cellar floor, you might well have heard him. It was a risk he could not take. So he devised the scheme of sending you a series of threatening letters, fully expecting you would take heed of the warnings and leave the house; letters which you, Mallow, would have taken to your master. Did you not recognise the printing on the envelopes as your brother's?'

'No, sir!' Mallow protested, beads of perspiration breaking out upon his brow. 'I remember several letters arriving, addressed to Mr Hardern in capital letters, but I did not realise they were from Victor. I give you my word that I did not make the connection until I saw the open pantry window. Remembering my brother had entered the house before by the same means, I realised that it was he who had left the print of the black hand on the wall and the message threatening Mr Hardern's life.'

'You should have spoken up then and told everything you knew,' Holmes admonished him in a stern voice. 'Had it not occurred to you that your brother was now desperate? He had murdered once and was quite prepared to kill again in order to recover the bullion, which I have no doubt he would have done once Mr Hardern was dead and the police had left the premises.'

Mallow sank his chin upon his breast and said in a low voice, 'I am aware of that now, sir. I thought with you and Inspector Whiffen in the house, Mr Hardern's life was not in any real danger. I did not know Victor was still armed and would carry out his threat. When he came to me that night for help, he swore he had thrown away the gun. He is my younger brother, sir, and I trusted him. I could not believe he was capable of such black-hearted villainy.'

'That is all very well but it is no excuse in the eyes of the law,' Whiffen put in, asserting his official authority. 'You have committed several felonies, Mallow, including the withholding of information from the police as well as the more serious charges of receiving stolen property and aiding and abetting a known murderer. It is my duty to arrest you.'

Unlike his brother, Mallow went quietly, holding out his wrists for the inspector to snap on the handcuffs, his expression impassive.

It was only when he was about to be led from the room that he showed any emotion.

Halting in the doorway, he turned to address us, his voice trembling but still retaining that note of deferential respect.

'I am sorry, gentlemen, for the great trouble I have caused, especially to you, Mr Hardern. I offer you my most profound apologies for the betrayal of your trust.'

Even Hardern was struck dumb by the man's quiet dignity.

And so, on that sober note, the persecution of John Vincent Hardern was brought to an end.

There is little else I wish to add to my narrative, except to say that the box of gold ingots was recovered the following morning from the cellar and in due course was returned to its rightful owner. In payment for his services, Holmes accepted a substantial fee from his client but refused an invitation the following year to the wedding of his daughter Edith to Lord Wroxham.

By one of those strange coincidences which Fate sometimes contrives, the ceremony took place in the same month that Victor Mallow was hanged for the murder of the policeman.

But it is not for his sake, nor the American millionaire's, that I have decided not to publish an account of the Hardern case.

It is in order to spare the butler, Mallow, at present serving a long term in prison, from further public disgrace and humiliation that I have resolved to place this narrative among those other private and confidential papers which I profoundly trust will never see the light of day.[7]

---

[7] In 'The Adventure of the Solitary Cyclist', Dr John H. Watson makes no mention of Mallow but merely refers to 'the peculiar persecution to which John Vincent Hardern, the well-known tobacco millionaire, had been subjected'. Dr John F. Watson.

THE CASE OF THE COLONEL'S MADNESS

I

For reasons which will later become apparent, it will not be possible to publish an account of this adventure while the chief participants are still living. At the time, the affair attracted a great deal of publicity, particularly from the sensational press, which caused considerable distress to those concerned, and I should not wish to add to their suffering by raking over the ashes of an old scandal.

However, the case was one of the few[1] I had the privilege

[1] According to Dr John H. Watson, he introduced only two cases to Mr Sherlock Holmes, that of Mr Hatherley's thumb, an account of which he published under the title of 'The Adventure of the Engineer's Thumb', and that of Colonel Warburton's madness. However, an account of a third case was discovered by my late uncle, Dr John F. Watson, among Dr John H. Watson's alleged private papers, deposited at his bank, Cox & Co. of Charing Cross. This was later published in *The Secret Files of Sherlock Holmes* under the title of 'The Case of the Amateur Mendicants'. However, I cannot guarantee its authenticity. Aubrey B. Watson.

of introducing to my old friend, Mr Sherlock Holmes. It also possesses some remarkable features, not least the part I myself was called upon to play in its solution. For these reasons, I have decided to commit the following narrative to paper, if only for my own satisfaction.

It was, I recall, in July 1890, some time after my marriage and my return to civil practice, that a lady was shown into my consulting room in Kensington.[2]

As she was not one of my regular patients, I took particular notice of her appearance, using those methods of observation with which my long association with Sherlock Holmes had made me familiar. She was, I perceived, of middle height, approximately five-and-thirty years of age; married, judging by the plain gold band on the fourth finger of her left hand, but only recently so for the ring looked new. Although she was soberly dressed in grey, her attire was of a good quality and, while not striking of feature, she had about her a look of candour and quiet intelligence which I found appealing.

'Pray be seated, madam,' I said, indicating the chair which stood before my desk and picking up my pen in readiness to note down those particulars, such as her name and address, which I would need for my medical records.

---

[2] Shortly before his marriage to Miss Mary Morstan, Dr John H. Watson purchased a practice in Paddington. However, by June 1890, the date of the adventure involving Mr Jabez Wilson, he was practising in Kensington. *Vide:* 'The Red-Headed League'. Dr John F. Watson.

To my surprise, she remained standing and it was she who began by questioning me.

'You are Dr John H. Watson?' she enquired.

'I am.'

'May I ask if you once served in India with the Fifth Northumberland Fusiliers?'

'Yes; indeed I did. But is this relevant? I understood you were seeking my professional assistance.'

'Forgive me, Dr Watson, if my behaviour seems uncivil,' said she, sitting down at last. 'There are several Dr John Watsons listed in the Medical Directory and I had to make quite certain that I had found the right one, as it would appear I have. I believe you know my husband, Colonel Harold Warburton of the East Sussex Light Horse.'

'Hal Warburton!' I exclaimed, in even greater astonishment. I had first made his acquaintance several years earlier in India, before I was transferred to the Berkshires as assistant surgeon and posted to the Afghan border where, at the battle of Maiwand in June 1880, I was severely wounded.[3]

Although my association with Hal Warburton was of short duration, he and I had struck up a close friendship and I had regretted losing touch with him on my return to England after I was invalided out of the army. He was a most efficient officer, very just in his dealings with the men under his command, and of a thoughtful, not to say

---

[3] Dr John H. Watson was struck in the shoulder by a Jezail bullet but there are also references to his 'wounded leg'. *Vide*: *A Study in Scarlet* and *The Sign of Four*. Dr John F. Watson.

serious, turn of mind. He was, moreover, a confirmed bachelor. Hence my astonishment at learning that the lady was his wife.

'My husband has often spoken warmly of you,' Mrs Warburton continued. 'It is why I have come to seek your advice on his behalf. There is a question I must ask of you which may appear strange but to which I should like a frank answer. I should not make the enquiry were it not vital to Harold's well-being.'

'Then pray ask it, Mrs Warburton. I shall do my best to reply in as honest a fashion as I can.'

'The question is this: to your knowledge had my husband ever shown signs of madness?'

'Madness?' I reiterated, my astonishment by now so complete that I was utterly confounded. 'He was one of the sanest men I have ever met. Hal Warburton mad! The very idea is itself insane!'

'But I understand that you once gave my husband medical treatment,' Mrs Warburton persisted.

'For a fractured wrist sustained during a chukka of polo,' I replied a little abruptly, for I must confess I was growing somewhat uneasy at this imputation of madness against my old army friend.

'And that is all? He never confided in you that he was subject to fits?'

'Certainly not! Who on earth, may I ask, put that thought into your mind?'

'My husband,' she said quietly, regarding me with a steady gaze.

It took me a moment to absorb this extraordinary remark and then I replied as calmly as I could, 'I think, Mrs Warburton, that you had better tell me the whole story from the beginning.'

'I agree, Dr Watson, for the situation is most distressing and is as inexplicable to me as it evidently is to you also,' Mrs Warburton said. For an instant her control faltered and I saw that her eyes had filled with tears. However, with a gallant effort, she composed herself and continued. 'I should explain that I first met Harold a little over five years ago in India. Until that time, I had been living in England with my widowed mother. On her death, a very dear friend of mine, a Mrs Fenner Lytton-Whyte, who was about to sail to India to join her husband, a major in the Fourth Devonshire Dragoons, suggested that I accompany her as her lady-companion. As I had no close relatives left in England, I readily agreed. Her husband was stationed then at Darjeeling and it was he who introduced me to Harold.

'Later, Harold told me that he had fallen in love with me at that first meeting, although it was another eighteen months before he proposed marriage. As you will know, Dr Watson, having been closely acquainted with him, he is a reticent man who finds it difficult to express his feelings. He is also several years older than myself and, as a bachelor, was used to living a single life. It was for these reasons, he said, that he hesitated so long before asking me to marry him.

'On my part, I had grown first to like and then to love

him and, after I accepted his proposal, we were married quietly in the Anglican church in Rawalpindi. At his request, no notice of the wedding was sent to the London newspapers, not even *The Times*, and it was only on my special pleading that he consented to my writing to my godmother in England to tell her of my marriage. I give you these facts because they may be relevant to later events.

'About two years ago, my husband suffered a bad attack of fever which left his health seriously impaired. He was advised to resign his commission and retire to a country with a more temperate climate. I had imagined that he would wish to return to England, but he seemed strangely reluctant to do so and spoke instead of going to New Zealand, a country with which neither of us had any connection.

'While the matter was still under discussion, I received a letter which decided our future for us. It was from my godmother's solicitor, informing me of her death, news which I was most sorry to receive as I was very fond of her. The letter went on to explain that I was named as the main beneficiary in her will and stood to inherit her house in Hampstead, together with its contents and an income of £1000 a year, provided I agreed to certain conditions. I had to return to England and occupy the house with my husband. It is a charming Georgian villa where she herself had been born and brought up and she was anxious that it should not be sold and the family possessions dispersed.

'If I refused to accept these conditions, I should receive

a capital sum of £3000 but the house and its contents would pass to a second cousin's son, my godmother's only remaining relative but a virtual stranger to her.

'Although grieved by my godmother's death, I have to confess that the offer of the house and a settled income came at a most opportune time when Harold and I were concerned about our future. As you no doubt know yourself, Dr Watson, it is not easy for a man to support himself, let alone a wife as well, on half-pay.'

'Indeed not!' I interjected, remembering my own financial difficulties on my return to England from India.[4] 'But pray continue, Mrs Warburton. I assume you accepted the terms of your godmother's will?'

'Eventually, yes; although Harold was not at all eager to do so. However, as neither of us had much money, I myself not having come from a wealthy family and Harold's father having lost much of his capital through unwise speculation shortly before his death, it was finally decided, after much hesitation on Harold's part, to accept the offer. Consequently, Harold resigned his commission and we booked passages on the SS *Orient Princess*. Even then, when our tickets had arrived and our trunks were packed, he seemed on the point of changing his mind. He appeared very anxious about the prospect of returning to England although, when I pressed him for a reason,

[4] On being invalided out of the army, Dr John H. Watson received a pension of eleven shillings and sixpence a day. It was because of financial difficulties that he agreed to share lodgings with Mr Sherlock Holmes at 221B Baker Street. Dr John F. Watson.

he would say nothing more than that he had unhappy memories of the place.

'As you are a busy professional man, Dr Watson, I shall summarise the subsequent events as briefly as possible. We arrived in England and settled into my late godmother's house, where we were very happy together. My husband's health steadily improved and the only drawback to our complete contentment was Harold's steadfast refusal to take part in any social life outside the home, not even the occasional excursion to a theatre or a museum. He even refused to renew any former acquaintanceships, including yours, as I assume from your earlier remarks, even though he had often spoken most warmly of you.'

'I should have welcomed a visit from him,' said I, touched by this mark of Hal Warburton's continuing friendship. 'Had I known he was in London, I should certainly have written to him, suggesting a meeting. But pray continue, Mrs Warburton. You spoke of your husband's admission that he was subject to fits of insanity. Were there any signs of this during your time in India?'

'No, Dr Watson. Nor was there any reference to such a tendency until recently; two days ago to be exact. As was his habit, Harold had retired to the study after breakfast where he was engaged in writing a history of his old regiment. When the second post arrived, I took it to him myself as he preferred not to be disturbed by the maid. He was then in excellent spirits. There were only two letters, one which I assumed was the grocer's bill, and one other, the handwriting of which I did not recognise. As we receive little correspondence, neither Harold nor I having any close relatives or friends in England, I took particular notice of this second envelope, which was postmarked Guildford. I was a little surprised as we know no one living in Surrey.

'About half an hour later, at eleven o'clock, I again went to the study to take Harold a mid-morning cup of coffee. On this occasion, I found him greatly changed. He was pacing about the room in a state of considerable agitation, trembling violently and almost incoherent in his speech. At first, I thought he was suffering from a recurring bout of fever and was about to send the maid for the doctor when he broke down, begging me not to do so.

'It was then he told me that from childhood he had suffered from occasional fits of madness, the early symptoms of which he had been aware of for the past few days. For that reason, he had written to a private nursing-home, recommended by a medical friend of his, arranging to be admitted as soon as possible. He had not spoken to me of this before as he had not wished to distress me. He had also hoped that the symptoms would subside and he would be able to cancel the arrangements. However, as they had not done so, a carriage would arrive at midday to take him to the nursing-home. He expected the treatment to last for a fortnight. As it was essential that he had absolute peace and quiet, I was not to visit or write to him. He even refused to give me the name of the home or the doctor who recommended it. I assume it was not you, Dr Watson?'

'Certainly not!' I exclaimed. 'As I have already explained,

I did not even know that your husband had returned to England. But what an extraordinary state of affairs, Mrs Warburton! Had your husband shown any signs of these early symptoms of madness of which he spoke?'

'No, never. Until that moment, his behaviour had been perfectly normal.'

'Then were you not suspicious of his sudden attack and his decision to seek admission to a private nursing-home?'

'Not at the time, Dr Watson. I was too shocked to think rationally. Besides, I had my husband to consider as well as practical affairs to see to, such as packing his valise. Harold was in no state to be questioned either. He was still so greatly agitated that I did not like to press him for a further explanation. Nor was there time. A closed carriage arrived shortly afterwards and a man, whom I took to be a male attendant, escorted my husband to it. They then drove off immediately.

'It was only after the carriage had left and I had the opportunity to collect my thoughts that I began to have grave misgivings. As my husband's attack had occurred so soon after the arrival of the second post, I returned to the study to look for the letter from Guildford, wondering if its receipt could be the cause of Harold's sudden fit. Although I found the grocer's bill lying on his desk, there was no sign of any other correspondence until I noticed the charred remains of some paper lying in the otherwise empty grate. As it is summer, no fire had been lit there that morning. The letter was nothing more than ashes which fell to pieces as I touched them. But I found one small portion, unconsumed by the flames, which had fallen through the bars on to the hearth. I have brought it with me.'

'May I see it?' I asked.

Mrs Warburton opened her reticule and took out a plain envelope which she gave me.

'The piece of paper is in there together with a small sprig of myrtle which I also recovered from the hearth. I assume it was enclosed with the letter, although I have no idea why.'

Opening the envelope, I tipped the contents carefully on to my desk. They were, as Mrs Warburton had described, a spray of dark green leaves, partly burnt by the fire, accompanied by a small piece of paper, about the size of a florin, badly scorched, on which the only writing I could discern were the letters 'vy', followed a little further on by what appeared to be the word 'use'.

'You say this is myrtle?' I asked, touching the sprig of leaves gingerly with one fingertip. 'But you are not aware of its significance?'

'Not in connection with Harold's decision to enter a nursing-home. However, I recognised it as myrtle immediately. I carried a piece of it in my wedding bouquet.[5] In the language of flowers, it is said to represent maidenly love.'

---

[5] Queen Victoria's daughter, Victoria, the Princess Royal, carried a sprig of myrtle in her bouquet at her wedding in 1858 to the future German Emperor. It was from a cutting from this sprig that a bush was grown at Osborne which supplied sprays of myrtle for other royal wedding bouquets. Dr John F. Watson.

'May I keep these, Mrs Warburton?' I asked, coming to a sudden decision. 'With your permission, I should like to show them to an old friend of mine, Mr Sherlock Holmes. Have you heard of him, by any chance? He has a considerable reputation as a private consulting detective and would, I am sure, undertake on your behalf any enquiries you might wish to have made.'

I saw Mrs Warburton hesitate.

'As you know, Dr Watson, my husband is a very reserved man. He might not approve of his affairs being investigated. However, I have indeed heard of Mr Holmes and, as I am deeply concerned about Harold's welfare, I am prepared to give my consent, provided you can assure me of your friend's discretion.'

'Without any reservation!'

'Then pray consult him without further delay. I know that you, too, have my husband's best interests at heart,' Mrs Warburton said, rising to her feet and handing me her card. 'You may find me at this address.'

I called on Holmes at my old lodgings in Baker Street that very afternoon and found him in the sitting-room, engaged in pasting newspaper cuttings into his commonplace book.

However, as soon as I had explained the reason for my unexpected visit, he laid aside the brush and, settling down into his armchair, listened with keen attention as I gave him a full account of Mrs Warburton's extraordinary story.

'And I am afraid, Holmes,' I concluded, giving him

the envelope, 'that these are the only pieces of evidence I can offer you in the case of Warburton's sudden and, to my mind, totally inexplicable claim to be suffering from madness and his decision to enter this unknown nursing-home somewhere in Surrey.'

'Oh, the whereabouts of the nursing-home is a minor mystery which can easily be solved,' Holmes announced nonchalantly. He had taken the charred piece of paper over to his desk, where he had inspected it briefly with the aid of his pocket lens. 'We know from the postmark that it must be in the vicinity of Guildford and that part of its address consists of the word "House".'

'How on earth have you come to that conclusion?' I asked, greatly taken aback by this deduction after so cursory an examination.

'Because, my dear fellow, this fragment is clearly part of the top right-hand corner of a sheet of paper. Although badly scorched, it is still possible to see the straight edges in those positions I have indicated. As the back of the fragment is blank, we may safely deduce that it is not part of the letter itself but must form a portion of the address which is invariably written at the top right-hand side of the page. The word that appears to be "use" must therefore form the last three letters of the word "House", otherwise in such a position on the paper it makes no sense at all. The first half of the name ends with the letters "vy", an unusual combination. There are not many words ending in such a fashion which can be applied to the name of a house. Have you any suggestions, Watson?'

'I can think of nothing on the spur of the moment, apart from "navy" which is hardly suitable.'

'Quite so. For the same reason, we may also dismiss the words "heavy", "envy" and "gravy". But what of "Ivy House"? Does that not sound perfectly acceptable? I propose therefore going down to Guildford tomorrow where I shall make enquiries at the post office of a nursing-home of that name in the immediate area.'

'So you will take the case, Holmes?'

'Of course, my dear fellow! I have no other enquiries on hand at present and this one contains some most interesting features, not least the strange behaviour of your old army friend, Colonel Warburton. I am not referring merely to his recent actions. There is also his past conduct to consider.'

'In what way?'

'Why, his reluctance to return to England and his avoidance of all society once he arrived here. I find that highly pertinent. You knew him in India. Tell me a little more about him, Watson. Was he, for example, a drinking man?'

'Quite the contrary. He was most abstemious in his habits.'

'Then did he gamble?'

'Very infrequently and only for the smallest stakes.'

'Or keep an expensive mistress?'

'Certainly not, Holmes!' I cried, deeply shocked. 'He is of the highest moral standards.'

'A most exemplary life!' Holmes murmured. 'In that

case, let us turn our attention to the sprig of myrtle.'

'Mrs Warburton seemed to think that it signified maidenly love.'

Holmes burst out laughing.

'A mere sentimental fancy, my dear fellow! I am surprised that you, with your professional training, should set any store by such nonsense. A red rose for passion! Myrtle for maidenly love! Why not other more humble members of the vegetable kingdom, such as the carrot or the parsnip to show "The roots of my affection run deep"? No, my dear fellow, I think you will find, once we have solved this mystery, that the sprig of myrtle is open to a much more prosaic interpretation.'

'And what is that, pray?'

But Holmes refused to be drawn.

'The answer, which is quite simple, I shall leave to you to puzzle out. If you care to call here again tomorrow evening on my return from Guildford, I fully expect to have further information regarding Ivy House and its occupants.'

As my wife was away for a few days, visiting a relative,[6] I was not able to discuss the significance of the myrtle sprig with her and I was no nearer to solving the mystery when, the following evening, I again presented myself at Baker Street to find my old friend in a jubilant mood.

---

[6] The relative was almost certainly an aunt whom Mrs Watson had visited on other occasions. *Vide*: 'The Five Orange Pips'. Dr John F. Watson.

'Sit down, Watson!' cried he, rubbing his hands together with delight. 'I have excellent news!'

'Then your excursion to Guildford was a success?' I asked, taking the armchair opposite his.

'Indeed it was. With the assistance of a post-office official, I traced Ivy House to the small village of Long Melchett, two miles north of the town. Having established the exact location of the nursing-home, I then retired to the local inn, the Cricketers, where the landlord, a most garrulous fellow, entertained me over a simple luncheon of bread, cheese and ale to a full account of Ivy House and its inhabitants, in which he takes the most lively interest. It has, it seems, about fifteen inmates, some permanent, some temporary, and is owned by a Dr Ross Coombes.'

'Ross Coombes!' I interjected, much surprised.

'The name is familiar to you?'

'He is one of the most eminent neurologists in the country, who used to have a thriving practice in Harley Street. From what you say, I assume he must have retired, for he must be quite elderly by now. It is strange, though, that, with his reputation, he should choose to run a small private nursing-home in Surrey.'

'Indeed, Watson? That is most interesting. Perhaps in the course of our enquiries we shall discover the reason. As for the investigation, I propose setting about it in the following manner. On your advice as my doctor, I shall have myself admitted to Ivy House as one of your patients who is unfortunately suffering from some mental aberration. What would you suggest, my dear fellow?

Nothing too serious, for I do not wish to find myself locked away as a dangerous lunatic. Would melancholia suit the occasion, do you suppose?'

'Most apt, Holmes,' I remarked wryly, recalling my old friend's tendency to periods of low spirits which, in his enthusiasm, he himself appeared to have forgotten.

'Then let us sit down immediately and draft a letter to Dr Ross Coombes so that it can catch the last post tonight.'

Between us, we composed the letter in which Holmes, who was referred to as James Escott,[7] was described as a patient of mine in need of treatment for melancholia. As the matter was urgent, I proposed accompanying Mr Escott myself to Ivy House, of which I had heard the most excellent reports, in two days' time, on the morning of 14th July at twelve o'clock.

Would Dr Ross Coombes kindly telegraph to confirm the arrangements?

On Holmes' advice, I added a final paragraph suggesting that plenty of fresh air and exercise would help alleviate my patient's condition.

'A necessary addendum,' Holmes explained, 'if I am to have the opportunity of exploring the house and its grounds without arousing suspicion. I assume, by the

---

[7] Escott was the pseudonym used by Mr Sherlock Holmes when, disguised as a plumber, he became engaged to Charles Augustus Milverton's housemaid, Agatha, in order to gain entry to the house. *Vide*: 'The Adventure of Charles Augustus Milverton'. Dr John F. Watson.

way, that you will be free to accompany me? One of your medical colleagues will be willing to take over your practice in your absence?[8] Excellent, my dear fellow! Then I shall wait to hear from you that Dr Ross Coombes has agreed to your proposal.'

I took the draft letter home with me and wrote out a fair copy on my headed writing-paper which I posted in plenty of time to catch the last collection.

The following afternoon, having received a telegram from Dr Ross Coombes confirming the arrangements, I again set out by cab for Baker Street to pass the good news on to Holmes, quite forgetting, in the excitement of putting the final touches to our stratagem, to question him further about the significance of the sprig of myrtle.

---

[8] Dr John H. Watson had two medical colleagues who looked after his practice, presumably in Paddington, during his absence. However, in 'The Final Problem', dated 1891, by which time he had moved to Kensington, he refers to 'an accommodating neighbour' who was willing to oblige him in a similar manner. Dr John F. Watson.

II

The next morning, Friday, we caught the 10.48 train from Waterloo, Holmes carrying a valise containing those personal possessions he would need during his stay at Ivy House, I bearing in my pocket some medical records for 'James Escott' which I had drawn up the previous evening.

On our arrival at Guildford, we took the station fly to Long Melchett and, after a two-mile drive, approached on our right-hand side a high brick wall, topped with broken glass.

'The grounds of Ivy House,' Holmes remarked. 'Take note of the iron gate we are just about to pass, Watson. It is a side entrance. On the left, about halfway down, you will find a gap in the brickwork of the supporting pillar. I discovered it when I made my earlier reconnaissance. As communication may be difficult between us, I suggest you wait for three days to give me time to establish myself in the nursing-home and then collect any instructions I may have left for you there.'

The gate was tall and made of strong metal bars, the tops of which were spiked and bent over at an angle to prevent anyone from climbing over them. As a further precaution, it was secured by a stout padlock and chain.

A little further on, we came to the main entrance, a pair of double gates this time, guarded by a lodge-keeper who, on hearing the rattle of our wheels, emerged from an adjoining cottage and, having examined our credentials, allowed us to enter.

Ahead of us stretched a gravelled drive with gardens on either side, consisting mostly of open lawn with an occasional tree. A few disconsolate figures, patients I assumed, were wandering about or sitting on wooden benches of the type found in public parks. Despite the bright sunshine of that July morning, the place had a bleak, institutional air about it, an impression which was confirmed by our first sight of Ivy House itself.

It was a large, ugly building with squat towers at either end, its grey façade almost entirely covered with that dark-leaved climbing plant from which it had no doubt derived its name. From the dense mass of this gloomy foliage, the windows seemed to glower out at us, as if suspicious of our arrival.

The fly drew up before the porch and we both alighted, Holmes immediately assuming the identity of a man suffering from melancholia. As I have remarked before,[9] he is a master of disguise although, on this occasion, there was no need for him to have recourse to a wig or false moustaches. With his chin sunk low upon his breast and his features drawn down into an expression of deepest misery, he shuffled his way slowly up the steps, the very picture of the most acute depression.

I rang at the doorbell and we were admitted by a maid who conducted us across the hall, panelled in dark oak, to a ground-floor study, overlooking the front gardens.

Here we were greeted by Dr Ross Coombes, who rose from his desk to shake hands with us.

He was an elderly, white-haired gentleman with distinguished, fine-drawn features but possessing a nervous manner which I found surprising in a man of such a high professional reputation.

Without question, however, the room was dominated by its other occupant, a lady in her mid-forties, whom Dr Ross Coombes introduced as Mrs Hermione Rawley, the matron of the clinic.

As a younger woman, she must have been strikingly beautiful. Even in her middle years, she was still handsome, her abundant black hair, only lightly touched with grey, drawn back into a chignon. As we entered, her large, brilliant black eyes regarded us with an expression

---

[9] Dr John H. Watson comments that, in adopting a disguise, Mr Sherlock Holmes' 'expression, his manner, his very soul seemed to vary with every fresh part that he assumed.' *Vide*: 'A Scandal in Bohemia'. Dr John F. Watson.

of keen alertness, as if reading our very thoughts, a most unnerving experience.

Just as disconcerting was an aura of power and authority which surrounded her, compared to which all of us seemed strangely diminished.

I was uncomfortably aware of her presence and, as I went through 'Mr James Escott's' case history which Holmes and I had prepared together and handed over my medical notes to Dr Ross Coombes, I found myself stumbling once or twice over its recitation.

By the time it was concluded, however, I had sufficiently collected my wits to make my final statement without hesitation.

'I must insist', I concluded firmly, 'on seeing my patient whenever I feel it is necessary. There may be urgent family business which I shall need to discuss with him.'

It was Holmes who had suggested this device in the event that he was refused all visitors, as had happened in the case of Colonel Warburton.

I saw Dr Ross Coombes look across at Mrs Rawley who inclined her head.

'That will be allowed, Dr Watson,' said he, passing on the permission.

Nothing remained to be done except to pay a week's fees in advance, an exorbitant sum of twenty-five guineas, which I handed to Dr Ross Coombes who, in turn, gave it to Mrs Rawley. Rising from her chair, she unlocked a door on the far side of the study with one of the keys which hung at her waist on a long chain, and withdrew into an adjoining room.

I had but a brief glimpse of its interior before the door closed behind her. It seemed to serve as both an office and bedchamber, for I saw a large bureau standing against the opposite wall as well as the footboard of a bed.

Within a few moments, she had returned with a receipt which Dr Ross Coombes signed before giving it to me.

The business completed, I made my farewells, the last with Holmes who, raising his gaze from the carpet which he had been mournfully studying throughout the interview, offered me a limp hand to shake, at the same time giving me a look of such piteous dejection that, as I took my departure, I was genuinely distressed at leaving him in such a sorry plight.

It was only when I was in the fly, on my way back to Guildford station, that it occurred to me my concern was wasted. Holmes' affliction was entirely fictitious, at which thought, to the great surprise of the driver, I burst out laughing at my old friend's skill at deception.

As Holmes had suggested, I waited for three days before returning to Long Melchett. On this occasion, I asked the fly to wait some distance short of the main entrance to Ivy House and I walked on towards the iron side gate. There I halted and, having made sure no one was observing my actions, I bent down and retrieved the piece of paper, folded up small, which Holmes had left for me in the crevice of the brickwork.

The message read: 'Matters are progressing satisfactorily. I suggest you make arrangements with Dr Ross Coombes to visit me tomorrow (Tuesday) and that you book a room for yourself for that night at the local inn. Please make sure you bring my bunch of picklocks with you to Ivy House; also equip yourself with a dark lantern and a length of stout rope for your own use later. My very best regards, S. H.'

I was puzzled by this last item, for, although I could understand why Holmes might have need of the picklocks, I could not see to what use he proposed I should put the rope, unless it was to effect the rescue of Colonel Warburton.

Its purpose was made clear to me the following day when, having carried out Holmes' instructions, I returned to Ivy House.

We were walking about the gardens of the nursing-home, taking care to distance ourselves from its windows although, as a precaution, Holmes maintained 'James Escott's' shuffling gait and lowered gaze.

'You have the picklocks, Watson?' he enquired.

'Yes, Holmes.'

'Then slip them as unobtrusively as you can into my pocket.'

As I did so, I remarked, 'I have also brought the rope and the dark lantern.'

'Not with you?' he demanded, raising his head momentarily to glance at me sharply from under drawn brows.

'No, Holmes,' I hastened to assure him. 'They are in my valise at the inn. But what is the rope for? Is it to assist in Warburton's escape?'

'No, my dear Watson. Such an attempt would be futile. He is kept in one of the upper rooms with the barred windows, reserved for those whose behaviour can at times be violent.'

'Then he is truly mad?' I asked, saddened to think that my old army friend might indeed be subject to fits of insanity.

Holmes shrugged his shoulders.

'As I have not seen him, I cannot say. He is confined to his room most of the time and is allowed out only if accompanied by two attendants. But, mad or not, there is no point in rescuing him until we have discovered the evidence which will explain why he was incarcerated in this manner in the first place. And be a good fellow and refrain from asking me what the evidence consists of. Until I have examined it myself, I have no notion of its contents. I only know that it must exist and that it is kept under lock and key. Hence my request for the picklocks. As for the rope, that is needed not to arrange your friend Warburton's exit but to gain your entry.'

'My entry, Holmes? Entry to where?'

'To the grounds of Ivy House. Now please pay particular attention to my instructions, for I may not have time to repeat them. Visits are strictly limited and at any moment Dr Ross Coombes or the matron may send one of the male attendants to escort me back to the house.'

For the next few minutes I listened with a sense of rising excitement as Holmes rattled off the details of his plan.

He concluded by saying, 'And pray remember, Watson,

that, in raising the alarm, you give two peals upon the bell, not one. That is most important.'

'Why, Holmes?'

'I shall explain later when there is more opportunity. You realise, of course, Watson, that in carrying out our enterprise we shall be breaking the law? Does that cause you any concern?'

'Not if it assists Warburton's case,' I assured him.

'Stout fellow! Then, my old friend,' said he, shaking hands, 'I shall expect to see you here again at two o'clock tomorrow morning.'

III

That night, I dozed fully clothed in the armchair in my room at the local inn, the Cricketers, for it hardly seemed worth the trouble of undressing and going to bed.

Holmes had estimated that I should need an hour to carry out my part in his plan. Consequently at one o'clock, I rose and with the rope coiled over my shoulder and the dark lantern in my pocket, I crept quietly down the stairs in my stockinged feet. Unbolting the kitchen door, I let myself out into the yard.

Then, having put on my boots, I set off for Ivy House, my heart beating high at the adventure to come.

It was a warm, still night and, although there was no moon, the stars, which hung huge and brilliant in the clear sky, were bright enough to light the way and I had no difficulty in finding the path which led along the side of a field to the back of the nursing-home.

Although Holmes had been a patient there for a mere three days, he had used the time to spy out the land most effectively for, as I turned the corner of the high brick wall which enclosed the gardens and followed it along its rear extension, I could see ahead of me an apple tree exactly as he had described it, one thick branch hanging low over the brickwork and its palisade of broken glass.

It took me only a few moments to throw one end of the rope over this branch and, securing it with a slip knot, to haul myself up into the tree, bracing my feet against the wall. Once at the top, I saw the roof of a potting-shed below me, again just as Holmes had described, and after lowering myself on to it, I dropped from there to the ground.

Here I waited for two or three moments in order to recover my breath and get my bearings.

Ahead of me and a little to the left, I could see the dark bulk of Ivy House looming against the night sky, its squat turrets giving it the grim outline of a mediaeval fortress.

Not a light showed in its façade and not a sound broke the silence.

Nevertheless, I made my way cautiously to the stable block behind the main building, its position marked by a square clock tower. As I entered the yard, I saw in the starlight that the gilded hands showed a few minutes before two o'clock. According to Holmes' schedule, I was a little late, but his plan was almost accomplished and there was not much more left for me to do.

The rope for the alarm hung below this clock tower, running up through a series of iron staples fixed to the wall into the belfry where it was connected to a separate bell. As Holmes had instructed me, I tugged vigorously on this rope twice before waiting a few seconds and then repeating the signal three more times.

Above me in the darkness, the sonorous double peals rang out, shattering the silence with their clamour. Then, without waiting to see their effect, I hastened out of the yard and along the side of the building to the front garden, where I concealed myself behind a tree which Holmes had pointed out to me the previous day as a convenient hiding-place. From this vantage point, I was able to keep the front of the nursing-home under observation.

Lights had already sprung up in some of the windows and I thought I heard the far-off sound of voices calling out, although this may have been mere fancy on my part.

But there was no mistaking the sound of a sash being softly raised and, abandoning my place of concealment, I sprinted towards the house where Holmes was standing at one of the ground-floor windows, waiting to help me over the sill into the room beyond.

'Well done, Watson!' he whispered, his voice jubilant. 'And now the lantern!'

I handed it to him and there was the sudden flare of a match in the darkness before the flame faded to a steady cone of yellow light. Its glow illuminated the tall, thin figure of Holmes, clad in dressing-gown and slippers, moving purposefully towards the bureau which I had glimpsed through the open doorway of Mrs Rawley's room on my initial visit to the nursing-home, the bunch of picklocks ready in his hand.

While I held the lantern, Holmes first opened the bureau, the lock of which yielded easily, but the large black cash-box which he extracted from an inner compartment proved more stubborn and I heard him give a low exclamation of impatience as he probed delicately at the keyhole with one of the thin metal rods.

Meanwhile, I could hear the sound of footsteps hurrying past in the hall and the voice of Dr Ross Coombes calling for the lamps to be lit.

Holmes, however, is an expert[10] and eventually the lock of the cash-box gave way under his skilful fingers. Raising the lid, he took out a bundle of papers which he thrust quickly into his dressing-gown pocket before relocking the box and replacing it in the bureau, which he also secured.

'It is time we left, Watson,' said he, extinguishing the light and leading the way towards the open window. As I climbed out, he added, 'I am relying on you to put the last part of our plan into action later this morning, as we have agreed. Now go at once, my dear fellow. Good night and good luck to you.'

The next instant, the sash was lowered, the catch fastened

---

[10] Mr Sherlock Holmes possessed a 'first-class, up-to-date burgling kit' equipped with a 'nickel-plated jemmy, a diamond-tipped glass cutter, adaptable keys and every modern improvement.' *Vide*: 'The Adventure of Charles Augustus Milverton'. Dr John F. Watson.

and the curtain drawn across the window. But a small gap remained and I must confess that, instead of leaving immediately, I could not resist watching with one eye to this gap for Holmes to make his own escape from the room, my mouth dry with apprehension lest, at this last moment, he should be discovered.

He behaved with characteristic coolness, walking casually to the door which he opened a few inches, revealing the lighted hall beyond. Then, having listened intently for a few seconds, his whole body alert, he slipped silently from the room and the door closed behind him.

As soon as he had gone, I took my own departure, returning to the inn by the same route which I had followed earlier. Once I had gained the safety of my room, I undressed and lay down upon the bed. But, though tired from the night's adventure, I could not sleep and my thoughts turned again and again to those events which were still to come and which, I fervently hoped, would bring about the conclusion to the case and the solution to the mystery of Hal Warburton's madness.

IV

Compared to the activities of the night before, my instructions for the following morning were relatively simple to carry out.

As soon as I had breakfasted, I hired the landlord's gig and set out for Guildford to call on Inspector Davidson of the Surrey County Constabulary.

Holmes had spoken of him as an intelligent and energetic officer, a description which was accurate as I discovered when I was shown into his office and noticed for myself his alert expression and firm handshake.

However, although he was expecting me, Holmes having taken the precaution of calling on him during his initial enquiries into Ivy House and its occupants, he seemed as much in the dark as I over the precise nature of the investigation.

'All I know is the case could involve the most serious allegations,' Davidson told me. 'If it wasn't for the fact that Mr Holmes himself came to see me about it, I would hesitate to take it on. But, being a keen admirer of his methods, I am prepared to go along with his request and accompany you to Ivy House, although I would feel a good deal easier in my mind if I knew exactly what evidence Mr Holmes has discovered and what charges it relates to.'

'I am afraid I cannot help you there, Inspector,' I replied a little awkwardly. 'Mr Holmes has not seen fit to confide in me the full details of the case, except to stress its urgency.'

'Then we had better set off at once,' Davidson announced, much to my relief, for I had thought he was about to change his mind and withdraw his consent.

Even so, he questioned me closely during the drive to Ivy House and I was hard put to it to conceal the unlawful actions Holmes and I had carried out.

His catechism was cut short by our arrival at Ivy House where we found Holmes, still maintaining his role as 'James Escott', walking dispiritedly up and down the terrace.

However, as soon as our gig had halted, he abandoned this disguise and, throwing back his shoulders, strode forward to meet us.

'Now, Mr Holmes, about this evidence . . .' Inspector Davidson began.

But there was no time for him to complete his sentence. Holmes had taken charge of the situation. Sweeping us before him, like an eager sheepdog rounding up a reluctant flock, he hurried us up the steps and into the house, brushing aside a startled maid as we crossed the hall to Dr Ross Coombes' study, the door of which he flung unceremoniously open.

Dr Ross Coombes, who was seated at his desk, rose to his feet at our precipitate arrival, his worn features expressing consternation and, I thought, relief as well, strange though such a response might seem under the circumstances.

However, it was Mrs Rawley who addressed us.

She had been standing beside Dr Ross Coombes' desk, bending down to show him an account book which lay open before them. As we burst into the room, she drew herself up to her full height, fixing us with a basilisk-like stare from those brilliant, black eyes of hers.

'What is the meaning of the unwarranted intrusion?' she demanded.

Beside me, I felt Inspector Davidson shrink down inside his uniform at her indomitable presence and even I, who had encountered it before, began to wonder if Holmes was acting wisely in forcing this confrontation.

Surely it would have been better to have gone about the whole affair more circumspectly?

Holmes, however, seemed untouched by any such considerations. With a flourish, he drew from his pocket the bundle of papers which, a few hours earlier, he had removed from the bureau.

'I believe these belong to you, Mrs Rawley?' he announced.

'Or would you prefer to be addressed by another of your marital titles, such as Mrs Edward Sinclair or Mrs Harold Warburton?'

My shock on hearing this last name was nothing compared with the effect Holmes' remarks had upon the lady in question.

She sprang forward like a tigress, claws extended, and would have raked Holmes' face with her fingernails had he not seized her by the wrists and thrust her down into a chair where she sat glaring up at him, eyes glittering and teeth bared, every vestige of womanly decency and refinement stripped from her once-handsome features.

In the struggle, her hair had become unpinned from its neat chignon and hung about her face in wild coils, putting me in mind of an illustration in a school textbook on Greek mythology of Medusa, whose head had been wreathed with snakes and whose mere glance could turn the most courageous man to stone.

Seeing her seated there, I felt that same cold clutch of fear at my heart which, as a child, I had experienced when, turning the page, I had first come across that terrifying visage.

As for the others, Dr Ross Coombes had sunk back into his chair and, with a groan, had covered his face with his hands, while Inspector Davidson had taken several steps backwards as if to distance himself from the dreadful transformation of the comely matron into this savage creature, twisting this way and that under Holmes' grasp and screaming out at him that he was a thief and a liar.

Only Holmes seemed unaffected. Still gripping her by the wrists and bending down his long frame so that his face was on a level with hers, he remarked in a low, civil tone, 'Pray compose yourself, madam, or I shall be obliged to ask the inspector to put you into handcuffs and escort you from the room. I am sure you would not wish to make so undignified an exit in front of the servants.'

Whether or not it was this threat or Holmes' courteous manner which finally calmed her, I cannot tell. But by degrees, her hysterical outcries diminished until at last she fell silent and lay back in the chair, her eyes closed, an exhausted and broken woman.

'And now,' said Holmes, turning to Inspector Davidson and handing him the packet of papers, 'I shall leave these documents with you to peruse at your leisure. In them, you will find evidence to charge Mrs Rawley with several counts of bigamy as well as blackmail and extortion. As for Dr Ross Coombes' part in this sorry affair, it will be a matter for the official police to decide the extent of his guilt. On my own reading of the evidence, however, I should conclude that he was as much a victim of the conspiracy as one of its instigators.'

At the sound of his own name, Dr Ross Coombes raised his head and, speaking for the first time, addressed my old friend in a voice which grew stronger and more authoritative with each word he uttered.

'I do not know who you are, sir, except you are clearly not Mr James Escott who is suffering from melancholia. But whatever your true identity, I am grateful to you for destroying this monstrous web which for so long has held so many men and women in its thrall.

'For my part, I shall plead guilty to any charges which are brought against me and I shall do my utmost to persuade Mrs Rawley to do the same.'

Here, he broke off to look across at her, his glance full of a curious mixture of pity and contempt, before, withdrawing his gaze, he continued, 'I am also willing to furnish the authorities with any additional information which might be necessary before the case comes to court. If in the meantime you require any immediate assistance, you have only to ask.'

'Thank you, Dr Coombes,' Holmes said gravely, giving a small bow of acknowledgement. 'I should like my client, Colonel Warburton, to be sent for so that he may be removed from your clinic without any further delay. My name, by the way, is Sherlock Holmes, and it is on the Colonel's behalf that I have undertaken these enquiries.'

I perceived from the doctor's expression that Holmes' name was not unknown to him, but he refrained from commenting on it and instead, rising to his feet, crossed to the fireplace and rang the bell to summon the maid.

On her arrival, he gave her instructions discreetly through the half-open doorway before he returned to his desk, where he closed the ledger which he and Mrs Rawley had been consulting on our arrival and which he handed to Inspector Davidson.

'You will no doubt wish to examine the financial records of the clinic,' said he. 'They are all there, including the legitimate as well as the illegal payments made by such so-called patients as Colonel Warburton, among others, for whose forced admission into my clinic I accept part responsibility.'

I could restrain myself no longer. The excitement of the night's activities, combined with lack of sleep and the rapid turn of events that morning, the full significance of which I had still not properly grasped, had left me utterly bewildered.

'But why, Dr Coombes?' I burst out. 'Until your retirement, you were one of the most eminent neurologists in the whole country! How is it possible you were drawn into this monstrous scheme?'

'You should ask the lady seated over there,' he replied, quietly. 'She can give you a full explanation.'

But Mrs Rawley remained silent, her face averted and a pocket handkerchief pressed to her lips.

'Then,' said Dr Ross Coombes, after a long moment's pause, 'I see I am obliged to make a statement on my own account. It is a shameful story, gentlemen, and I take no pleasure in the telling of it. However, the facts are perfectly straightforward.

'While I was still in practice in Harley Street, I took Mrs Rawley into my employ as housekeeper. She was efficient and seemed a discreet and utterly trustworthy person, a necessary quality as, shortly after Mrs Rawley's arrival, I began an unwise relationship with one of my patients, a married lady, which, had it been made public, would have ruined us both.

'I hasten to add that the association consisted of nothing more than an exchange of letters and very occasional private meetings in my consulting-room in out-of-business hours at which she confided in me her personal problems. She was unhappily married to a brute of a husband who nevertheless held a high position in society. I was a widower of many years' standing. It was this mutual loneliness which brought us together, combined with a shared affection and regard. Nothing more.

'However, our behaviour was extremely foolhardy, for it was open to misinterpretation. She could have faced the ignominy of divorce court proceedings, with the almost certain loss of her children, I the risk of being struck off the medical register for unprofessional conduct.

'I thought I could trust Mrs Rawley implicitly. It was only when I spoke of selling up my practice and retiring to the country that she revealed herself in her true colours. She then threatened that, unless I agreed to her plans, she would expose my past relationship with my patient which, I should add, had long since been severed when the lady and her family had moved out of London. She had, Mrs Rawley informed me, taken copies of the letters the lady had written to me and which, most imprudently, I had kept in my desk as mementoes of our affectionate regard. She had, moreover, noted down a detailed record of our clandestine meetings and our conversations on which, it appeared, Mrs Rawley had eavesdropped at the door of the adjoining room. Unless I agreed to her proposals, she would send all this information to the lady's husband.'

'But you had nothing to fear once you had retired from medical practice,' Holmes pointed out.

'No, Mr Holmes, but there was still the lady's reputation to consider as well as my own good name.'

'And what were these proposals? I assume they were connected with your decision to open the clinic?'

'Exactly so. Mrs Rawley said she had no intention of continuing in her subservient role as my housekeeper. I was to put the capital I would receive from the sale of the Harley Street practice into buying these premises and taking in private patients. As she had had some experience of nursing, she would act as matron on the basis of an equal partnership and would, moreover, assume responsibility for the finances and the day-to-day running of the clinic.'

'So, in effect, she had virtual control?' Holmes enquired.

Dr Ross Coombes said nothing, merely bowing his head in agreement.

'At what point did Mrs Rawley suggest that such patients as Colonel Warburton should be admitted into the clinic?' Holmes asked. 'I assume the idea was hers, not yours?'

'Yes, Mr Holmes, although to my undying shame I confess I failed to protest vigorously enough when she first mooted it. All I can say in my own defence is that, at the time, I was not fully aware of all the implications. The suggestion was made a few months after the clinic was opened when there were some unfilled vacancies. Mrs Rawley said that she knew of a former patient of hers, with whom she was still corresponding, who would benefit from a few weeks of treatment at Ivy House. I will not identify him, although you will find his name in the ledger and also no doubt among Mrs Rawley's private papers. After he arrived, it soon became apparent to me that he was here under duress and, far from suffering ill-health, was a victim of extortion and blackmail. The fees were substantially raised for him and for the others like him, both men and women, who, over the next two years, were admitted to the clinic.'

'Oh, I do not think Mrs Rawley's motives were entirely mercenary,' Holmes said softly, casting a glance at the lady who sat stony-faced, staring straight in front of her. 'Have you never seen a cat playing with a mouse, Dr Coombes? Then you will have observed the pleasure the cat takes in tormenting its prey, first allowing it to run a little way off before drawing it back with its claws and tossing it up into the air. The money was important but it was the game which was paramount. To watch your victims suffer, sir! There lies the ultimate delight, the most exquisite gratification!'

At this juncture, the door opened and Colonel Warburton entered the room. If we had wished for living proof of the dreadful misery inflicted by Mrs Rawley on her victims then Hal Warburton exemplified them all.

Never have I seen an individual more altered. From a tall, upright, vigorous man he was reduced to a pitiful, stooped wreck of his former self as he stood hesitating on the threshold, clutching his valise in his hand and peering about him uncertainly.

'My dear fellow!' I exclaimed, hurrying forward to greet him and trying to conceal my shock at his changed condition.

As we shook hands, I was relieved to see a smile break upon his haggard countenance.

'Watson!' cried he. 'What a pleasure to see you again after all these years!' And then his expression changed and he gripped me fiercely by the arm. 'In God's name, do not tell me that you, too, are in this vile woman's clutches!'

'No, no,' I hastened to assure him. 'Quite the contrary. I am here to take you away. Mrs Rawley's evil scheme has been exposed and you, my old friend, are a free man.'

Under the circumstances, a lengthy explanation seemed inappropriate and I confined myself to introducing Warburton to Holmes and Inspector Davidson before giving him a brief account of the events which had led to our presence in Ivy House.

Holmes and I departed soon afterwards for Guildford station, taking Hal Warburton with us and leaving the inspector to charge Mrs Rawley and Dr Ross Coombes with the various offences of which they had been accused and to some of which the doctor had already admitted his own guilt as well as Mrs Rawley's.

It was only when we were safely installed in the privacy of a first-class carriage on our way back to London that Hal Warburton was able to tell us how he himself had fallen victim to Mrs Rawley's blackmail.

As a medical practitioner as well as his friend, I was reassured to see that he had by then recovered a little from his dreadful ordeal at her hands and had regained some of his former assurance.

He had first met her, he explained, when he was a young subaltern, stationed at Aldershot.[11] As his father was dangerously ill at the time with pneumonia, he was given special leave to visit him on compassionate grounds. It was on this occasion that he first met Mrs Rawley, who had been called in by the family physician to nurse his father and who was then practising under the name of Miss Harding.

'I must confess,' Warburton admitted with a rueful glance in our direction, 'that I immediately fell under her influence, as I believe she intended. In my own defence, I should perhaps add that concern over my father, as well as my own youth and inexperience in affairs of the heart, made me particularly vulnerable to Miss Harding's charms. She was an exceedingly beautiful woman, older than I, and seemed of a warm and sympathetic nature. During the seven days I spent at my father's house, a passionate relationship developed between us which continued through an exchange of letters after I returned to Aldershot. A few weeks later, my father died and I was again given leave to attend his funeral and to arrange his financial affairs. In the meantime, my ardour

---

[11] Aldershot, in Hampshire, contains the largest military camp in the British Isles. It was at Aldershot that Mr Sherlock Holmes investigated the supposed murder of Colonel Barclay of the Royal Mallows. *Vide*: 'The Adventure of the Crooked Man'. Dr John F. Watson.

had somewhat cooled and I decided to break off my relationship with Miss Harding as being unsuitable.

'However, when I spoke to her on the subject, she became extremely angry. I had compromised her good name, she told me, and unless I agreed to marry her immediately, she would be forced to write to my commanding officer and ask for an interview at which she would disclose the letters I had written to her.

'As the scandal would have ruined my army career, I had no choice but to agree and we were married shortly afterwards at a quiet ceremony in London, attended by no one except two of the vicar's elderly parishioners who acted as witnesses.

'By mutual consent, we agreed to keep the marriage a secret and we parted immediately after the ceremony, I to return to my regiment, she to lodgings in Streatham where, as agreed between us, I sent her a monthly sum of money for her upkeep. I never saw her again. Less than a year later, I received a letter on her behalf from a solicitor, requesting that in future I paid her the allowance through him.'

'Which no doubt increased over the years and which you continued to forward even after you were posted to India?' Holmes enquired. 'It was a clever scheme on her part, Colonel Warburton. By acting through a solicitor, Miss Harding, your so-called wife, was able to conceal from you her own whereabouts, should you have made enquiries, but to keep herself informed of yours.'

'"So-called wife"!' Hal Warburton exclaimed, starting up in his seat.

'Indeed, yes,' Holmes replied coolly, taking from his pocket a small notebook and turning the pages. 'When I examined the documents which I extracted from Mrs Rawley's bureau, I jotted down the dates of the various marriage certificates I found among them. Your wedding took place, I believe, on 25th November 1867? On that day, Mrs Rawley had already been married twice, once legally to a Mr Randolph Fairbrother, the second time bigamously to a Mr James Thirkettle, both of whom were paying her maintenance money through different solicitors and, like you, had no doubt good reasons for keeping their marriages secret. There were other subsequent husbands, five in all, whose names are not at this moment relevant.'

'Then I am indeed a free man!' Warburton gasped.

'And legally married to your present wife,' Holmes pointed out, at which my old army friend seized us both silently by the hand in turn, too overcome by emotion to express his feelings out loud.

V

'To give the lady her due, she showed great intelligence in her choice of prey,' Holmes remarked, a note not unlike grudging admiration in his voice although his lean features bore an expression of extreme distaste.

It was after our return to London when, on arriving at Waterloo, we had taken a hansom to our lodgings, having seen Hal Warburton into another cab to return to Hampstead and to a joyous reunion with his wife.

'Quite reprehensible, of course,' my old friend continued. 'Blackmail is one of the vilest crimes[12] which inflicts the most exquisite mental suffering upon

[12] In speaking of another blackmailer, Charles Augustus Milverton, Mr Sherlock Holmes remarks that not even the worst murderer gave him such a feeling of revulsion. *Vide*: 'The Adventure of Charles Augustus Milverton'. Dr John F. Watson.

its victims, the equivalent to death by a thousand cuts. From the moment you brought the case of Warburton's alleged madness to me, it was quite apparent he was being blackmailed.'

'Was it, Holmes? I must confess that such a thought never entered my head.'

'My dear fellow, the signs were obvious in his insistence that his marriage in India should be kept secret and in his reluctance to return to this country. His lack of capital to set up home after he had resigned his commission also suggested the payment of extortion money. As a bachelor and a high-ranking officer, he should have had enough put aside from his army pay to guarantee himself a comfortable retirement, especially as his style of living, as you described it, was far from extravagant.

'My suspicions were further aroused when I made enquiries into Ivy House. You yourself posed the question most succinctly, I thought. Why should Dr Ross Coombes, an elderly and famous neurologist, decide to open a clinic when, like Warburton, he should have been able to afford to retire in comfort? Why, indeed? It seemed highly likely that he, too, was a victim of blackmail.

'As soon as I saw Mrs Rawley, I was convinced that she was the extortionist. Her manner towards Dr Ross Coombes, together with the fact that she appeared to have charge of the finances as well as making the decisions, all pointed in that direction.

'You will recall that, when you paid over "Mr Escott's" fees, she carried the money into an adjoining room, which apparently served both as her bed-chamber and her office. That, too, I found suspicious. There were plenty of rooms upstairs. Why, therefore, should she choose to sleep on the ground floor, unless it was to keep guard both day and night over something important, such as evidence which might prove her guilt? The most likely place of concealment seemed to be the bureau which I had observed in her room.

'During my three days' incarceration in Ivy House, I kept watch on Mrs Rawley's movements and noted that her chamber was always kept locked. No one was allowed to enter it apart from the housemaid to clean it and even she was strictly supervised by Mrs Rawley.

'My suspicions were now confirmed. But the dilemma remained of how to contrive Mrs Rawley's absence from her room for long enough to allow me to remove the evidence. Hence my little stratagem of smuggling you into the grounds of Ivy House and raising the alarm by ringing the bell.'

'But why twice, Holmes?' I interjected. 'You were most insistent on that although, in the urgency of the occasion, there was not time for you to explain its importance.'

'Because, my dear Watson, a single peal signified fire and I did not wish Mrs Rawley to believe the house was ablaze. Had she thought so, her first action would have been to save the documents from the conflagration, in a similar fashion to another lady of our acquaintance.[13] That was not my intention at all. A double peal, however, signalled any other emergency, apart from fire, of sufficient gravity to rouse the household. The alarm instructions, by the way, were posted up in the hall for all to study, including myself. In the meantime, I had left my room by the back stairs and concealed myself in the lobby. As soon as Mrs Rawley, together with Dr Ross Coombes and other members of the staff, had vacated the premises to discover the cause of the alarm, I picked the lock of Mrs Rawley's door, which she had taken the precaution of securing behind her, and let you in through the window.'

'But were they not suspicious when they discovered there was no emergency?'

'At first; especially Mrs Rawley. But when, on her return, she found that both her room and her bureau were still locked and that nothing had been disturbed, it was assumed that one of the village youths had rung the bell as a prank. By great good fortune, Mrs Rawley had no reason to open the cash-box this morning, otherwise she would have found it empty.

'To continue with my account. After your departure, I returned to my room by the same route and spent the

[13] Mr Sherlock Holmes is almost certainly referring to Miss Irene Adler, who revealed the hiding-place of the King of Bohemia's photograph when he tricked her into thinking the house was on fire. As he remarks, when faced with such an emergency, a woman's 'instinct is at once to rush to the thing which she values most'. *Vide*: 'A Scandal in Bohemia'. Dr John F. Watson.

next few hours until daylight examining Mrs Rawley's documents and making notes upon their contents which established her guilt as a blackmailer as well as a bigamist, a career which had extended over many years. As a nurse, she gained access to many wealthy households and was therefore in a privileged position to discover those guilty secrets which the families preferred not to be made public. She then used that knowledge to extort money from her victims. In addition, she was, when younger, an extremely beautiful woman, an advantage she used to ensnare any suitable gentlemen into marriage, often the sons or other male relatives of the patients she was called upon to nurse, such as your friend Warburton, who were then forced to pay her maintenance.

'As her charms faded, she turned to other methods, using Dr Ross Coombes as a means to extract further payments from those unfortunate individuals who were already at her mercy. Whenever she felt the need for money or, more to her purpose, the desire to gloat over their suffering, they were forced to admit themselves to the clinic, for which doubtful pleasure they were charged an exorbitant sum in the way of fees. In this manner, both her mercenary as well as her crueller inclinations were satisfied. It was a brilliantly wicked scheme for, on the face of it, it appeared perfectly legitimate, especially as the clinic was ostensibly owned by such a well-known specialist as Dr Ross Coombes.

'I have estimated that, over the years Mrs Rawley was active as a blackmailer, she must have amassed a fortune of over £50,000. No doubt the full facts will come to light when the case is brought to court.'

A few months later, during the trial at Guildford Assizes, Holmes was proved to be correct to within a few hundred pounds.

At this hearing, Dr Ross Coombes was true to his word and pleaded guilty. Mrs Rawley also entered the same plea. Faced with his decision and the weight of evidence against her, she had no other choice.

Holmes and I were not called upon to attend. Because of the guilty pleas, our part in the affair was not made public and we were not asked to give evidence.

Nor, to my immense relief, were Colonel Warburton and Mrs Rawley's other victims, who were merely referred to at the trial by letters of the alphabet.

Both Mrs Rawley and Dr Ross Coombes were sentenced to terms of imprisonment, she to ten years, as the more guilty of the two. In view of his lesser part in the affair, Dr Ross Coombes received a shorter sentence.

As far as I have been able to ascertain, he retired to a small house in Kent on his release from prison, where he died a few years later in decent obscurity.

As for Hal Warburton, I kept up my friendship with him, my wife and I often dining at their house and they at ours.

There remained only one minor mystery which, in the excitement of following up the complexities of the case, I had entirely forgotten.

It was finally solved one evening during the time when the trial was still being held at Guildford.

I had called on Holmes to avail myself of his copies of the more sensational newspapers which I would not allow into my house for the sake of my wife and the servants.

'Holmes,' said I, the thought suddenly occurring to me, 'what was the significance of the sprig of myrtle?'

Much amused, he looked up from his own edition of the penny press.

'My dear fellow, the answer is there in front of you if you care to read carefully through the reports of the various pseudonyms Mrs Rawley used when marrying her husbands. Miss Rose Bannister. Miss Lily Fletcher. Need I go on, apart from pointing out that a violet and a daisy were also pressed into service? In summoning her spouses to the nursing-home, Mrs Rawley enclosed with the official letter a floral emblem of the name by which each of them would have known her, in case there was any question of her identity. Under the circumstances, the apparent interpretation of myrtle as a symbol of maidenly love has a peculiarly ironic ring to it, does it not?

'The language of flowers, Watson! To her victims, it must have seemed more like a communication from hell itself! I am inclined to agree with Falstaff, that wise old reprobate, when he referred to women as "devils incarnate",[14] for when they turn to crime, no mere man is capable of matching the subtlety of their wickedness.'

---

[14] In Shakespeare's *Henry V,* Act II, Scene 3, Sir John Falstaff said that 'the devil himself would have about him women' for they themselves were 'devils incarnate'. Dr John F. Watson.

THE CASE OF THE ADDLETON TRAGEDY

I

As I acknowledged in 'The Adventure of the Golden Pince-Nez', so many cases were undertaken by my old friend Sherlock Holmes in the year 1894 that, when I looked through the three large volumes containing my notes, I was hard put to it to decide which of them deserved publication. Choosing between the merits of one particular inquiry compared to another is never easy. However, it was with considerable reluctance that I have decided, at Holmes' specific request, not to publish the following account of the Addleton tragedy.

Naturally, I am disappointed, for it possesses some singular features, most particularly in the light it sheds on the darker side of human nature. However, I feel obliged to bow to Holmes' opinion and I shall therefore lay this narrative to one side among my other unpublished papers.

It was, I recall, one early afternoon in mid-November[1] when our client, Miss Rose Addleton, was shown into our sitting-room in Baker Street.

She was a pretty, slightly built young lady, not more than one and twenty, charmingly dressed in blue and carrying a serviceable leather hand-grip which seemed out of keeping with the daintiness of the rest of her attire.

'I trust you will forgive me, Mr Holmes, for my unexpected arrival without an appointment or a preliminary letter,' she said with admirable directness, after she had introduced herself. 'But the matter is so urgent, as we are in London for only a short time, that I have come in the hope you will grant me an immediate consultation.'

'"We"?' Holmes enquired, inviting her most cordially to sit down. He seemed as touched as I by her youthful dignity.

'My parents and I. It is at my mother's request that I am here. She is most anxious, as I am, too, about my father, Professor Henry Addleton.'

'Not Professor Addleton of Christchurch College, Oxford?'

'Yes, the very same. You know him?'

'I read his treatise *Ancient British Monuments and Burial Sites* when it was published in 1882. It is a most erudite and scholarly work. I take it, from your earlier

---

[1] This adventure must have occurred shortly before the case involving the death of Willoughby Smith at Yoxley Old Place, Kent, which took place towards the end of November 1894. *Vide*: 'The Adventure of the Golden Pince-Nez'. Dr John F. Watson.

remarks, that you have come without your father's knowledge?'

'Yes, Mr Holmes. Indeed, I am sure he would be very angry if he knew I was discussing his affairs in this manner. I should explain that we came down from Oxford only this morning and shall stay overnight at Bentley's Hotel.[2] At present, my parents are visiting the British Museum. On the pretext of a headache, I stayed behind so that I might have the opportunity of consulting you in their absence. Tomorrow morning, my mother and I will leave to stay with relatives in Kent while my father will set off to spend a week in Cornwall. It is on account of his visit there that I have come to see you.'

'I think,' said Holmes, leaning back in his chair and regarding her with the keenest attention, 'that you had better give me a full account.'

'I am not sure myself of the whole story; neither is my mother,' Miss Addleton replied. 'However, these are the facts, as far as I know them.

'About ten days ago, my father received a letter from a Mr Montagu Webb of Tintagel in the county of Cornwall. In his letter, which my father read aloud for my mother's and my benefit, Mr Webb explained that he was an amateur archaeologist whose hobby is to study

---

[2] The Bentley Hotel was situated near the Strand. It was at this hotel that the Cambridge University rugby team stayed before playing their match against Oxford University and from where Godfrey Staunton disappeared. *Vide*: 'The Case of the Missing Three-Quarter'. Dr John F. Watson.

the prehistoric sites on Bodmin Moor. It is his intention to write a monograph on the subject for the local historical society.

'In the course of his explorations, he had discovered a hitherto unknown ancient British barrow, close to a disused mine known as Wheal Agnes. There had evidently been heavy rain for several days which had washed away part of the mound, revealing a corner of a cist grave.[3] Telling no one of his discovery, Mr Webb returned to the site the following day and, by digging away the remainder of the earth, was able to expose the burial chamber fully. When he removed the slabs of stone covering it, he discovered traces of human remains together with pottery and other objects which had been buried with the body.

'My father was extremely excited by Mr Webb's letter. As you know, Mr Holmes, he specialises in ancient British history and the discovery of a previously unknown barrow with its contents still intact is a rare event indeed.[4]

'He immediately entered into correspondence with Mr Webb, instructing him to say nothing about the find and to cover up the burial chamber temporarily until he himself could examine it. He also asked Mr Montagu

---

[3] A cist grave is a prehistoric coffin or burial chamber formed from slabs of stone. Dr John F. Watson.

[4] A similar discovery was made on Bodmin Moor fifty-seven years earlier in 1837 when the famous Rillaton Cup of ribbed gold, dated to about 1500 BC, was recovered from a cist grave in the Rillaton Barrow, not far from the village of Minions. The cup, only 3½ inches high, is on display at the British Museum. Dr John F. Watson.

Webb to make arrangements for him to visit Cornwall as soon as possible, so eager was he to begin his own excavations.

'A few days later, my father received another letter from Mr Webb informing him that he had carried out his instructions and suggesting that my father catch the 10.55 from Paddington to Bodmin on Friday; that is tomorrow. Mr Webb would meet him at Bodmin station and would book rooms for them both at the Blue Boar for the week. They would then have seven whole days in which to uncover the barrow and study the grave and its contents at their leisure.

'With the letter, Mr Webb sent a small package containing three sample pieces of some of the broken pottery he had found in the cist chamber. It was on receiving them that my father began behaving in a most strange manner.'

'I assume he was angry that the pottery had been removed from the site?'

'Oh, yes, Mr Holmes; very angry indeed. He is strongly of the opinion that all excavations should be carried out under strict scientific methods and that nothing should be moved until it has been properly recorded *in situ*. He accused Mr Webb of unprofessional conduct, although I understand that his action in forwarding the pottery shards was well meant. It was to give my father the opportunity of examining them in detail before undertaking the journey to Cornwall. But there was something else which had a more profound effect on him than the mere receipt of the pottery.'

'What was that, pray?'

'The pottery itself. It was after he had examined it that his behaviour showed such a marked change.'

'How precisely?'

'He became extremely morose, cancelled all his lectures and tutorials and remained in his study for most of the day, emerging only for meals. At night, my mother and I could hear him pacing up and down until the early hours of the morning. It is unusual for him, although I can remember him behaving in a similar manner in the past.'

'When was this?'

'The first time was twelve years ago when I was only nine.'

'So there have been other occasions?'

'Oh, yes, Mr Holmes. As I grew older, I noticed they occurred every spring.'

'Can you be more exact?'

'It was invariably towards the beginning of March. He would become increasingly withdrawn and silent, hardly exchanging a word with either my mother or myself. Then, after about ten days, his agitation would reach a climax. This always happened in the morning, when the first post was due to be delivered. Instead of waiting for the maid to bring it in, he would take it himself from the postman, as if he were expecting a certain letter to arrive. He would then shut himself up in his study and the same pattern would repeat itself. He would refuse to leave the house and we would hear him walking restlessly about late at night. After a fortnight, his conduct would gradually return to normal.'

'How long did this continue?'

'For five years and then quite suddenly it stopped. I have reason to recall the date with absolute certainty. It was 21st February, my father's birthday. It was his habit to retire to his study after breakfast with *The Times* before leaving for college. He was already beginning to show those signs of unease which always occurred in the early spring. But on that particular morning, he came hurrying out of his study, a changed man. By nature, he is not normally jovial, nor does he find it easy to express his emotions. But I remarked how cheerful he looked. He was smiling broadly, like someone relieved of a dreadful burden. After that, he never again showed the same deterioration in his conduct until a few days ago, when he received the pottery samples from Mr Montagu Webb.'

'Was your mother able to offer any explanation for these changes in his manner?'

'No, Mr Holmes; although I asked her the first time he became so taciturn, assuming it was I who had unwittingly displeased him by some childish misdemeanour. But she assured me that he was suffering from overwork. However, a child can often perceive the truth more clearly than an adult and I remember thinking that he seemed more frightened than tired.'

'Frightened? Of what, pray?'

'I wish I knew, Mr Holmes! Since this recent recurrence of his strange conduct, my mother has taken me into her confidence and expressed her concern more openly, particularly as I myself am so much older. Indeed, it was on her urging I have come to consult you. But even she is uncertain of the precise nature of the problem, except that it seems to be connected with some incident in my father's past, exactly what she does not know as he has refused to discuss the matter with her. Whatever it is, she is convinced his life is threatened in some way. I have heard her pleading with him on several occasions not to go to Cornwall. However, he seems determined to undertake the journey. I think he himself is aware that some danger awaits him there which, for some unknown reason, he cannot, indeed must not, avoid.'

'And it would appear that he was warned of that danger when he examined the ancient British pottery, sent to him by Mr Montagu Webb?' Holmes enquired.

'So it would seem,' Miss Addleton replied. Opening the leather hand-grip, she took out a box about six inches square which she handed to Holmes. 'I have the shards here, Mr Holmes. I took the opportunity of removing them from my father's valise so that you might examine them.'

'Excellent!' Holmes exclaimed. Rising eagerly from his chair, he carried the box over to his desk where, having taken off the lid and unwrapped the pieces of pottery from their protective wadding, he subjected each in turn to a minute scrutiny with the aid of his powerful magnifying glass.

During this examination, Miss Addleton and I watched in silence, the young lady with some trepidation, I agog with curiosity to know what, if any, evidence Holmes might discover. It was impossible to tell from his expression. His lean profile was as inscrutable as a Red Indian's when at last, laying down the lens, he turned to us.

'Interesting!' was all he vouchsafed to remark, before adding, 'Would you care to look at them, Watson?'

I accepted the invitation with alacrity, crossing to the desk and, as Holmes had done, studying all three shards separately, first with the naked eye, then under the glass.

Each of them was not much larger than a half-crown and was composed of coarse, gritty clay which, when magnified, showed unmistakable signs of having been hand-worked. Two bore an elaborate zigzag pattern, deeply incised, while the third, evidently part of a rim, was decorated with small indentations to resemble the twists in a piece of rope.

'Well, Watson?' Holmes enquired when I had finished my examination. 'What are your conclusions?'

'I am no expert,' I protested. 'However, they seem perfectly genuine to me.'

'Oh, my dear fellow, there is no question of that. They are perfect examples of ancient British pottery of the Bronze Age period.[5] Have you no other comments you wish to make?'

---

[5] The classification of the prehistoric period into the Stone, the Bronze and the Iron Age, known as the Three Age System, was first devised by the Danish archaeologist, Christian Jurgensen Thomsen, in the early nineteenth century. It was adopted by the British Museum in 1866. Dr John F. Watson.

'Only that they seem remarkably clean.'

Holmes smiled at my ignorance. 'Not surprising, Watson. Mr Montagu Webb would hardly have sent them to Professor Addleton with the earth of the barrow still clinging to them. And now, Miss Addleton, since my colleague appears to have completed his examination, I shall return the samples to your safe keeping. No doubt, you will wish to replace them before your father discovers they are missing.' Quickly rewrapping the shards in the wadding, he packed them in their box which he handed to her with a slight bow. 'Dr Watson will escort you downstairs and call a cab to take you back to your hotel.'

Miss Addleton received the box with evident reluctance. She seemed as bewildered as I by Holmes' dismissive manner and the haste with which he had concluded the interview.

'Then you have decided you cannot help, Mr Holmes?' she asked.

Holmes raised his eyebrows.

'Whatever gave you that impression, Miss Addleton? I have every intention of accepting the case. It has some most interesting features. You and your mother may rest assured that Dr Watson and myself will investigate the evidence with the greatest assiduity.'

'What evidence, Holmes?' I enquired when, having seen Miss Addleton into a hansom, I returned to our sitting-room.

'The pottery, of course,' he replied.

In my absence, he had lit his pipe and was seated in the

armchair by the fire, his legs stretched out to the blaze and his head wreathed in smoke.

'But you said it was genuine!' I exclaimed, greatly astonished.

'So it is, my dear fellow. However, it is not entirely what it seems. In whatever ancient barrow it may have been discovered, it was not found recently as Mr Montagu Webb asserted in his letter.'

'What makes you so sure?'

'Because of certain marks I found on the shards. Although, as you rightly pointed out, the pottery had been washed free of dirt, it was something else remaining behind which was significant.'

'I do not follow you. To what are you referring?'

'To a small, round, sticky patch on the back of each piece. I can see from your expression, Watson, that you not only failed to observe them but you still have not grasped their significance for our inquiry. Then permit me to explain. The patches indicate that the shards have been labelled at some point. As the gum was discoloured by age, it further suggests that this was not done recently. Therefore, one can only assume that the pottery was part of a collection, presumably Mr Montagu Webb's, and that, having removed some identifying labels, possibly catalogue numbers, he then posted them to Professor Addleton, claiming he had discovered them only a short time before in a previously unexcavated barrow on Bodmin Moor.

'Two questions arise from this conjecture. Firstly, what

was Mr Montagu Webb's motive in doing so? We may not discover the answer to that until the case has been solved. My second question is this. Was Professor Addleton aware of Mr Montagu Webb's deception? I think we may safely deduce from his conduct after he examined the pottery that he not only knew of it but the discovery frightened him.

'During the interview with Miss Addleton, we further learnt that her father's behaviour had undergone similar changes in the past, the first occasion being twelve years ago. I find that highly pertinent.'

'Do you, Holmes? To what?'

'My dear Watson,' Holmes replied, 'you were present during the interview with the young lady and therefore should be as familiar as I with the relevant data. If you care to think back over what was said, you should be capable of making the connection for yourself. It is simply a matter of dates although, you may take my word for it, the successful outcome of the case may depend upon it.

'To continue my explanation. Miss Addleton was of the opinion that the answer lay in some secret in her father's past, so carefully hidden that even her mother was not aware of its exact nature except she feared it presented a threat to her husband's life.'

At this point, Holmes broke off to put a question directly to me. 'Have you any dark secrets which you yourself would have hesitated to confide in your own wife?'[6]

---

[6] In 1894, Dr John H. Watson was a widower, his wife having died between 1891 and the spring of 1894. The exact date and cause of death are unknown. Dr John F. Watson.

I was quite taken aback.

'No, Holmes,' I replied, at last. 'I can think of nothing.'

'I can well believe it, my dear fellow. There is an honest transparency about you which I find altogether refreshing. But let us suppose there was some event in your past which you would prefer remained hidden. What might it consist of?'

'Something I was deeply ashamed of,' I suggested tentatively.

Holmes seized on my remark. 'Watson, you may have supplied the answer! Shame can be as strong an emotion as love or hate, anger or greed. It may explain why Professor Addleton, despite his obvious fear of the consequences, is determined to travel down to Bodmin tomorrow. It is possible that, having lived with that shame and the fear for so long, he feels he must face them both in order finally to expiate them. However, all this is mere speculation. It is facts we must seek out. They are the very bricks on which any successful investigation is founded, otherwise one is building with straw. I therefore propose making a few preliminary enquiries into the case without further delay. In the meantime, Watson, you can assist me by looking up the time of the trains to Bodmin for tomorrow morning. As Professor Addleton is catching the 10.55, I suggest we travel by an earlier one.'

'So you intend going down to Cornwall?' I asked, reaching for the timetable from the bookcase.

Holmes raised his eyebrows.

'Of course, my dear fellow. There is a limit to the

amount of data I can uncover in London. It is on Bodmin Moor that the mystery of the ancient British barrow will be solved.'

'There is the 9.05 from Paddington,' I informed him.

'Then we shall take that,' Holmes remarked, rising to his feet and crossing to the door where he paused to add, 'While I am gone, you may care to undertake a little research of your own, my dear fellow. If you look on the bottom shelf of the bookcase, you will find a copy of Professor Addleton's treatise, which may prove illuminating, particularly with regard to the crucial matter of the date. May I recommend that you read with care the first few pages?'

With that closing comment, he bustled out of the room and moments later I heard him whistling below in the street for a hansom.[7]

He was gone for several hours, not returning until it was almost time for dinner.

In his absence, I took his advice and, having found the volume, settled down by the fire to examine it. It was a large book, handsomely bound in red and lavishly illustrated with drawings of artefacts discovered at various prehistoric sites, including pottery of the type Montagu Webb had sent to Professor Addleton. But I confess I could make nothing of the date, although I noted it had been published by Snelling and Broadbent in 1882.

---

[7] It was customary to summon a cab by giving one whistle for a four-wheeler, two for a hansom. Dr John F. Watson.

Nor were the front pages any more revealing. They consisted merely of a frontispiece on which the title and the name of the author were set out, followed by a second page devoted to the dedications. The first and longer was to the professor's wife, Elizabeth Mary Addleton, in which, in a charmingly worded paragraph, he expressed his gratitude for her unfailing support and encouragement during the many years it had taken him to compile the volume.

Below was another much shorter dedication which I glanced at only briefly. It was addressed to some assistant or other who had helped Addleton in classifying and analysing the research material.

The next two pages were taken up entirely with a list of contents under chapter headings.

I spent a desultory half-hour or so dipping into the book but found it too academic for my taste with its long lists of implements and detailed descriptions of flanged axes and barbed arrowheads, and I soon turned my attention to the evening newspaper.

However, on Holmes' return, I was diverted from even this less taxing reading matter.

He came hurrying into the room, flourishing in one hand a large-scale Ordnance map of Bodmin Moor which he had bought at Stanford's[8] and which he spread open

---

[8] The map-maker's and retailer's, Stanford's Geographical Establishment, had the sole agency for the sale of Ordnance Survey maps. In *The Hound of the Baskervilles*, the firm is erroneously referred to as 'Stamford's'. Dr John F. Watson.

upon the hearthrug, inviting my assistance in finding Wheal Agnes, the abandoned mine near to which the ancient British barrow was situated.

After much searching, we discovered it at last, about fifteen miles from Bodmin and four from the nearest village of Minions.

'It seems an isolated place,' I said doubtfully. 'How do you propose reaching it, Holmes? On foot?'

'Certainly not, Watson.'

'Then how?'

'By some form of conveyance.' He looked up briefly from his study of the map and I saw his eyes had a far-away look in them, as if his mind was concentrated on those distant Cornish locations. 'While I was out, I took the precaution of sending a telegram to the Blue Boar at Bodmin, booking rooms for us and also requesting that a fast, light vehicle be placed at our disposal.'

He sounded abstracted and, not wishing to disturb his train of thought, I refrained from enquiring into the research he had undertaken that afternoon or from referring to the matter of the dates to which he attached such importance.

His preoccupied mood continued throughout the rest of the evening and it was only when I rose from my chair to wish him goodnight, adding some remark about the need to pack a valise for our visit to Cornwall, that he seemed aware of my presence.

He was sitting by the fire, plunged deep in reverie, his

eyes on the flames, although I doubt if he were conscious of those either.

'A valise?' he enquired and then, with an obvious effort, he brought his mind back to the present. 'Of course! And, Watson, please make sure you include your army revolver.'

He said no more, his gaze returning to the fire, and I went quietly from the room, leaving him to his silent deliberations.

II

When we set off for Cornwall the following morning, Holmes was in a more cheerful frame of mind, although he was still preoccupied and seemed disinclined to discuss the case, preferring to spend the journey reading the newspapers and idly commenting on their contents.

It was an overcast day and, by the time we reached Bodmin station and took the fly to the inn, a fine drizzle was falling from low, grey skies, casting a gloomy aspect over the small Cornish town with its steep, narrow streets and huddled houses of stone and slate.

Having arrived at the Blue Boar and deposited our luggage, we made our way downstairs to the bar parlour, from where we had a clear view of the front door of the hostelry. While we waited for the arrival of Professor Addleton and Mr Montagu Webb, Holmes took the opportunity to make a final study of the map, verifying the route we would take across the moor.

For my part, I must confess that the time passed exceedingly slowly. I was eager not only for my first glimpse of the two participants in our investigation but also for the events themselves to unfold. The mysterious circumstances surrounding the case and the threat of some unknown peril attached to it had whetted my appetite for adventure. I could feel the weight of my revolver in my topcoat pocket and from time to time I surreptitiously ran my fingers over its butt, wondering if I would need to use it and, if so, against whom.

Holmes showed no such impatience. He was sitting forward in his chair, his long, thin frame bent over the map which he held open upon his knees, totally absorbed in his task.

At last, the long wait was over. There was the sound of wheels drawing to a halt outside the inn and soon afterwards two men entered. The first, whom I took to be Montagu Webb from the manner in which he ushered his companion through the door, was a gangling, loose-limbed man in his late sixties but possessing the awkward self-consciousness of a schoolboy. Flapping an arm, he led the way towards the clerk's desk, talking all the time in a high-pitched voice.

'This way, my dear Professor. I am sure you will find the amenities here, though simple, are perfectly adequate. I suggest that we set off for the moor as soon as possible. I am eager to show you my little discovery before the light fades.'

'Yes, yes,' Professor Addleton said testily. He seemed exasperated by Montagu Webb's over-zealous attentions.

He was a tall, trim figure, dressed in well-cut tweeds; of countenance austerely dignified, of bearing confident and erect. A small grey moustache, neatly clipped, gave him a military rather than a scholarly appearance. But for all his self-assurance, there was an air of unease about him, evident in the set of his shoulders and the manner in which he glanced suspiciously about him.

Before his gaze had encountered ours, Holmes quietly folded up his map and, slipping it into the pocket of his ulster, rose to his feet.

'Come, Watson,' said he. 'It is time to go.'

We left by a rear door which led directly out into the inn-yard where the dog-cart, which Holmes had taken the precaution of hiring the previous day, was waiting for us, the horse already between the shafts.

As Holmes took up the reins, he remarked, 'I estimate we have at least a quarter of an hour's start on them.'

'A quarter of an hour, Holmes?'

'Time for Professor Addleton to leave his luggage in his room and change his boots. Did you not notice them? They were of expensive, highly polished leather, not the type of footwear for tramping about on Bodmin Moor. I have no doubt he will replace them with a more serviceable pair.

'In the meantime, we must make sure that we arrive with enough time in hand to explore the lie of the land and find a suitable hiding-place not only for ourselves but for our conveyance. On such open terrain, a dog-cart will look as conspicuous as a London omnibus.'

We set off at a brisk pace, taking the route which led northwest out of Bodmin across the moor to Launceston. It was a narrow but hard-surfaced road and we made good progress. However, before reaching the village of Bolventor, we turned off to the right down a stony track into a wild and barren landscape. Its atmosphere of brooding desolation was made even more melancholy by the slate-coloured sky which hung so low that the clouds themselves seemed to have descended to the horizon where they had dissolved into a grey mist. It clung about the summits of the tors which I could dimly discern in the distance thrusting up from the plain like the crude forms of prehistoric beasts, crouching there and keeping watch over that vast wilderness.

Everything, the rock outcrops, the coarse grass, the occasional wind-bent tree, was coated with a thin rime of moisture. There was no sign of life apart from a few rough-haired wild ponies grazing by the track until, startled by the sound of our wheels over the stones, they threw up their heads and galloped away.

About a mile further on, we came to the ruined engine-house of Wheal Agnes, its roof long since decayed and fallen in, but its walls and chimney, built of stout granite blocks, still standing.

'Ah!' cried Holmes, his eyes lighting up as he reined in the horse. 'We must thank whatever ancient gods who rule over this domain, Watson, for they are kind to us.

Here is the perfect place to conceal the dog-cart. Now, be quick, my dear fellow. We have not a moment to lose.'

We both jumped down and Holmes, taking the horse by the bridle, led it into the engine-house where he tethered it to one of the fallen roof timbers which littered the interior.

That done, we emerged from the building to take stock of our surroundings.

Behind the engine-house, the moor rose by degrees to ascend finally in a steep escarpment of granite slabs, their deep fissures filled with stunted bushes or low vegetation. The track swung round the base of this rocky outcrop to disappear from sight in the direction of the village of Minions.

To our left and at a distance of about a hundred yards stood a ring of standing stones which, Holmes had informed me, was known locally as the Coven. Centuries ago, or so the legend tells, twelve witches were surprised one night as they celebrated their ungodly sabbath by a holy man who, horrified by their wickedness, had turned them all to stone, including the warlock who was conducting the ceremony. His was the thirteenth and largest stone which stood in the centre of the circle.

In that lowering light, the huge weatherworn block might indeed be taken for a human figure standing there, larger than life-size, its head sunk between its shoulders and the two long cracks which ran down over the surface marking the position of the arms.

But it was the area immediately behind the engine-house which engaged Holmes' attention. It was covered with spoil-tips, great heaps of waste stone and earth which had been dug from the mine when it was in operation and dumped there upon the surface. Now overgrown with grass and brambles, they resembled to my imagination the graves of some long-extinct race of giants.

As a fancy, it was not far from the truth.

Beckoning me to follow him, Holmes set off up the slope towards the furthest of these heaps where his keen eyesight had observed a patch of freshly turned, blackish soil, roughly covered with grass and debris.

'I believe we have found our ancient British barrow, Watson,' said he.

At first sight, the mound was no different from the others which lay all about us, except part of it had collapsed forward, the soil and stones of which it was composed having been partially washed away by rain-water draining down from the escarpment which towered above it.

Hardly had we reached it and were bending down in order to examine the exposed section, when Holmes lifted his head and listened intently.

'Someone is coming!' he said in a low, urgent voice.

'The professor and his companion?' I asked, turning to look back along the track in the direction from which we had come.

But the road was empty and there was no sign of life save for two ravens which had risen with startled cries and a clatter of their great, black wings from the granite cliff above us and were circling above our heads.

‘No; from the other side of the escarpment. Come, Watson! We must hide at once.’

He set off at a run down the slope, leaping like a stag from mound to mound, making not for the engine-house as I had supposed but for the Coven and in particular for the large standing stone in its centre.

As I dropped down beside him on the wet grass, I could see the purpose behind his choice. As a hiding-place it was ideal, for it was not only broad enough to conceal us both but it also afforded us a clear view of the track leading to Wheal Agnes as well as the crag and the ancient British barrow which lay at its foot.

‘And now we wait, my dear fellow,’ Holmes murmured in my ear. ‘I fear, however, that some devilish business is afoot.’

With that, he took his revolver from the pocket of his ulster, at the same time laying one finger against his lips to indicate silence. I followed his example, taking out my own army pistol which I held ready in my hand.

Although the vigil lasted only a few minutes, rarely have I known time pass so slowly. The utter desolation of the landscape stretching out for mile after empty mile in every direction, combined with the proximity of those ancient stones crowding close upon us, gave me the unnerving sensation that some primordial and terrifying force was gathering up its power in readiness to unleash itself in one great cataclysmic outburst.

It seemed to fill the very air, curdling the light and turning it more dense and opaque, as if charged with some unspecified danger. I felt the skin on the back of my neck stiffen and an involuntary shudder of both fear and excitement ran through my frame.

Glancing sideways at Holmes, I saw that he, too, was tense with nervous strain, his jaw rigid and his eyes hooded over with their lids, giving him the watchful profile of a hawk poised to strike.

At last the silence was broken by the rattle of wheels over stones and a light gig containing two men came into view along the track. As it drew nearer, I perceived they were Professor Addleton and Mr Montagu Webb, the latter holding a whip which he was flourishing in the direction of the abandoned mine.

Even before the gig drew to a halt, I could hear his high, foolish voice carrying clearly through the still air.

'Here we are, Professor Addleton. The barrow is a mere few minutes' walk away.'

The two men climbed down, Mr Montagu Webb tethering the horse to a stunted bush which grew at the side of the track where he left it to browse along the verge. They then set off up the slope, picking their way through the spoil-heaps, Mr Webb still talking in his eager, excitable manner, his companion silent. From time to time, however, the professor halted momentarily to survey his surroundings with the same distrust I had observed on his arrival at the inn. In turn, the ruined engine-house, the escarpment, even the circle of menhirs where Holmes and I were concealed, came under his scrutiny. To my relief, the huge warlock stone appeared to offer us ample protection, for his gaze passed over it.

In the meantime, his companion urged him on. 'Just a few more yards, Professor! There! Now you may see the barrow straight ahead of you. As you will observe, I have obeyed your instructions and have covered up my own small attempts at excavating the site.'

'Not very adequately, in my opinion,' Professor Addleton replied curtly. 'There are still signs that the soil has been disturbed.'

Nevertheless, despite his obvious displeasure at Webb's amateurish methods, he leant forward over the barrow, studying its surface with great attention, his earlier suspicion quite forgotten.

Montagu Webb gave a loud, neighing laugh. 'My dear sir, no one ever comes near the place. Look about you! It is utterly deserted! It was only by the greatest good fortune that I myself discovered the barrow. Now, Professor, is it your intention to begin your own excavations immediately? Or would you prefer to wait until tomorrow? The light will be gone in less than an hour.'

Hardly had he finished speaking than a piercing cry rang out, so inhuman in its pitch and intensity that it might have been the shriek of some savage creature of the moors.

'Vengeance!' it screamed.

It was impossible to tell from whence the voice came for it seemed to resound from every direction, from the walls of the ruined engine-house to the distant, mist-shrouded tors.

I felt it reverberate even amongst the standing-stones which encircled us so that, for one confused moment, I fancied that it was those ancient monoliths which had cried out and my blood ran chill at the very thought.

The sound frightened Montagu Webb's horse which reared up, its terrified neighs echoed by our own pony.

As for the two men, they had stopped dead in their tracks and, like me, were glancing fearfully all about them.

Holmes clutched at my sleeve.

'There, Watson!' he whispered urgently, pointing to the escarpment.

A figure had suddenly appeared on its summit as if conjured out of the misty air. Even now, I find it difficult to describe that apparition and the effect it had upon me.

It wore a long black cloak and seemed taller and thinner than any mortal man. For a few seconds, it stood there immobile, silhouetted against the lowering sky, the very embodiment, or so it seemed to me, of the malignant power which earlier I had felt ruled over that desolate landscape.

The next instant, it lifted its right arm and I saw the dull gleam of something metallic in its hand.

Beside me, I was aware that Holmes had grasped his revolver and had raised his own hand, one finger tight upon the trigger, the barrel pointing at that figure looming against the skyline.

But before I could aim my own weapon, events came crowding upon us so rapidly that I could make no sense of their sequence.

There was a double report, the one following so close upon the other that I took it at first to be a single explosion. I saw a spurt of flame burst out from the crest of the ridge. Almost simultaneously, Professor Addleton spun about and then collapsed forward, spreadeagled across the ancient British barrow which, only a few moments before, he had been examining with such eager attention.

As he fell, there came the second flash from the escarpment and the sinister figure gave a scream, as blood-curdling as its first awful cry, before toppling headlong, its arms outstretched, its cloak billowing about it so that it resembled some huge bird of prey, swooping down from its granite eyrie to crash on to the rocks below.

Before I had time to collect my wits, Holmes was on his feet and was sprinting across the grass to the scene of that double tragedy.

I ran after him, making first for Professor Addleton who was sprawled face upwards across the burial mound, thrusting aside Montagu Webb, to join Holmes who was already kneeling beside the inert body.

As I felt for the carotid artery in the neck, I was aware of the dreadful wound in the professor's abdomen which I could do nothing to relieve and which would need immediate surgery if his life were to be saved.

Behind me, I could hear Montagu Webb's voice, shrill with shock and horror, repeating over and over again, 'He told me it was a hoax! Nothing more than a hoax!'

'Is he dead?' Holmes asked me.

He had risen to his feet and was standing over Professor

Addleton's recumbent form, his arms folded and an expression of such sombre melancholy on his face that I quickly averted my own gaze, feeling I was intruding on his private wretchedness.

'Just alive,' I told him. 'But I dare not move him, Holmes. He is bleeding internally. It would be the finish of him.'

There was a short silence and then Holmes burst out with sudden vehemence, 'I blame myself entirely, Watson! I should have acted more swiftly!'

Without another word, he took off his ulster and laid it across the professor with such gentle solicitude that I felt my throat thicken at the sight of this unwonted tenderness on the part of my old friend.

'Stay with him while I examine the other victim,' I said gruffly, struggling to maintain a detached and professional manner.

It took only a glance to convince me that the man was beyond human aid, even if he had survived the bullet which he had fired into his own heart. He lay horribly twisted at the foot of the crag, the back of his head shattered where it had struck repeatedly against the rocks.

By some quirk of fate, his face remained untouched and I found myself gazing down on the features, not of some fiendish villain as I had half expected, but on those of a man in his late thirties, fine-drawn and intelligent, yet bearing in their lineaments the unmistakable marks of some long-suffered torment which were etched deep into the flesh.

I covered him as best I could with his own cloak, drawing the edge of it over his face, and then returned to where Holmes was still standing beside the professor, like a sentinel on guard, his eyes fixed with the same look of brooding melancholy on the distant tors.

It may have been his stern and aloof bearing which had persuaded Montagu Webb to withdraw. But, for whatever reason, I found to my relief that he had retreated to a boulder a few yards away, where he sat wringing his hands, silent apart from an occasional low moan.

'It is no use,' I said to Holmes as I approached. 'The man is dead.'

'I feared as much,' Holmes said grimly. 'Then see what you can do for the living.'

As I knelt beside Addleton's prostrate form and prepared to loosen his collar, I saw his eyelids quiver.

'Holmes, he is regaining consciousness!' I cried.

In an instant, Holmes was transformed from his former state of utter dejection.

Whirling about, he shouted to Montagu Webb, 'Take the gig and go straight to Bodmin! Inform the police and make sure they return immediately with some more comfortable conveyance. And drive like the very devil, for, by God, the blood of these two men is on your head!

'And on mine, too,' he added in a lower tone as Webb bolted off to carry out Holmes' orders.

'Yours!' I protested as the gig went rattling away at great speed along the track. 'But what could you have done to avert this ghastly tragedy?'

'I had Haydon Cowper within my sights and yet I hesitated to pull the trigger. Had I done so, Professor Addleton's life would have been spared.'

'Haydon Cowper?'

'The man who lies dead yonder,' Holmes said, pointing to the foot of the escarpment. 'Did you not read the dedication in Professor Addleton's book? "Also to Haydon Cowper for his invaluable assistance in classifying and analysing the research material." It was a trivial point which might not have had any significance had it not been for Miss Addleton's evidence. If you recall, Watson, she told us that her father first began to show signs of deep anxiety twelve years ago, when she was a child of nine; in other words, in 1882. When I pressed her for a more specific date for this unexpected change in his behaviour, she said it was in the spring of that year. Yesterday, I enquired at the publisher's, Snelling and Broadbent's, and discovered that the precise date of publication of *Ancient British Monuments and Burial Sites* was the tenth of March of that year.

'Miss Addleton also informed us that her father's symptoms reappeared regularly over the next five years, always in early March, and that he was particularly agitated on certain mornings, at the time when the first post was due to be delivered. It required only the simplest reasoning to deduce that his distress was associated with a letter that he expected. Miss Addleton herself drew that conclusion. However, she failed to make a vital connection – that the receipt of the letters was timed to correspond with a very special anniversary which I suggest was the publication date of her father's book.

'Anniversaries, in fact, proved to be highly significant, for we come now to her father's birthday on 21st February 1887, a date which Miss Addleton had particular cause to remember, for it was on that day that her father's behaviour showed a sudden and marked change for the better. It occurred quite dramatically after he had retired to his study after breakfast with that morning's copy of *The Times*.

'Yesterday, I also took the opportunity to call at that newspaper's offices and to read through their back copy for that particular day. In it, I discovered a small but interesting item in the obituary column, announcing the death of Mr Haydon Cowper after a short illness.'

'False, of course,' I interjected.

'Without a doubt, my dear fellow. However, there is nothing to prevent anyone from sending a notice of death, even their own, providing they pay for the insertion. The date was, I believe, deliberately chosen not only as an ironic gesture but also with the intention of lulling Addleton into a false sense of security. It was Haydon Cowper's birthday gift to his former professor and mentor.'

'Haydon Cowper was one of Addleton's students!' I cried. 'How did you discover that, Holmes?'

'From an old acquaintance of mine, Dr Harbinger, a former Oxford don whom I had occasion to consult in 1891 when I was gathering evidence about the Moriarty gang, among whom, as you know, was Colonel Sebastian

Moran, the late Professor Moriarty's chief of staff.[9] The Colonel was an Oxford man and it was from Dr Harbinger that I learnt several important facts about him, including his obsession as an undergraduate with airguns.[10]

'Dr Harbinger is now an elderly gentleman, long since retired from the university to live with a married daughter in Chelsea. However, he has remained in touch with his former colleagues and still takes a lively interest in Varsity affairs. I called on him yesterday and it was from him that I learnt some, at least, of the story concerning Haydon Cowper.

'He was a graduate in Professor Addleton's department of Ancient History, a highly gifted man with a brilliant academic future in front of him whom Professor Addleton picked out from among his other students to assist him with compiling and classifying his notes for his book.

---

[9] Colonel Moran, born in London in 1840, was the son of Sir Augustus Moran, CB, a former British Minister to Persia. Educated at Eton and Oxford, he later served in India with the 1st Bangalore Pioneers. After some unspecified scandal, he retired from the Indian Army and came to London, where he was recruited by Professor Moriarty to carry out certain high-class criminal activities on his behalf. Mr Sherlock Holmes suspected him of being involved in the death of Mrs Stewart of Lauder in 1887. *Vide*: 'The Adventure of the Empty House'. Dr John F. Watson.

[10] Colonel Moran used an expanding bullet fired from a powerful airgun, made by von Herder, the blind German mechanic, to kill the Hon. Ronald Adair. On Mr Sherlock Holmes' return to England in 1894, he was able to arrange for the arrest of Colonel Moran, the best heavy game shot in India, for Adair's murder by Inspector Lestrade. *Vide*: 'The Adventure of the Empty House'. Dr John F. Watson.

Unfortunately, Haydon Cowper also possessed certain unstable qualities of character and at times behaved in a most erratic manner. Several incidents occurred, mostly threats of a quite absurd nature made to fellow students which eventually came to the attention of the college authorities. It appeared the young man had a tendency to respond quite violently at times to even the most trivial slight, whether real or imaginary. There was a particular outburst of such behaviour in March 1882. Note that date, Watson, as it, too, is significant for it was shortly before the publication of Professor Addleton's book and was, I believe, associated with it.

'Dr Harbinger could not give me precise details, as the affair was hushed up at the time, but I understand that Haydon Cowper was also heard to utter threats against Professor Addleton and on one occasion was discovered banging on the door of the professor's room, demanding admission. As he was led away, Haydon Cowper made a strange remark to the effect that gratitude came cheap and that he himself intended dedicating a great deal more than mere thanks as soon as he had the opportunity.

'From this remark, I think we may safely assume that he was referring to Professor Addleton's dedication to him in the Introduction of *Ancient British Monuments and Burial Sites*, which had aroused his anger, although the reason remains obscure . . .'

At this point, there came a faint groan from the recumbent figure lying beside us, at which my old friend abruptly broke off his account.

Professor Addleton was now fully conscious, his eyes wide open and fixed with a look of staring intensity on Holmes' face. Painfully, his lips began to move, struggling to frame two words which were barely audible.

'Joint authorship,' Addleton whispered.

'Joint authorship? But that, of course, was absurd, was it not, Professor? You had spent many years excavating and studying the ancient sites while Haydon Cowper was merely your assistant. My name, by the way, is Sherlock Holmes and it is on your behalf that Dr Watson and myself are here. No, I beg you, do not attempt to answer, my dear sir. You are gravely wounded and the least exertion could be highly injurious. It is far better that I continue with my account and that you indicate by some small sign whether or not I have stated the facts correctly. A mere blink of the eyelids will be sufficient, one for yes, two for no. Do I have your agreement?'

The professor's lids closed once over his eyes and Holmes immediately resumed his narrative, this time addressing Addleton directly.

'These latest outbursts on Haydon Cowper's part were, according to Dr Harbinger, the final straw as far as the college authorities were concerned. A meeting was held at which it was decided that the young man should be sent down. He was ordered to leave that very same day. Dr Harbinger could not tell me who was present at that meeting but I assume that you, Professor Addleton, were one of its members. Am I correct, sir? I see you give no sign.'

Both Holmes and I were watching the professor's

face intently but the eyes remained fixed and there was no movement of the lids, not even the faintest quiver to indicate that he had heard or understood Holmes' remarks. However, his mouth trembled and an expression of acute suffering passed over his face, suggesting not so much physical pain as a deep agony of mind.

After a silence, Holmes resumed his account, inclining his head lower so that Addleton could hear his remarks quite distinctly.

'It is not my intention to cause you any more distress, my dear Professor, and therefore I shall pass on to a brief outline of the subsequent events which led up to your tragic meeting here on Bodmin Moor with Haydon Cowper, your former student.

'Cowper was a proud and arrogant man who felt his dismissal from Oxford keenly. His promising career was finished, his reputation ruined and, rightly or not, he blamed his disgrace on you, Professor Addleton. Apart from the fact that he had expected, quite unjustifiably, that he would be acknowledged as joint author of your book, he no doubt also looked to you to speak up for him when it was decided he should be sent down. Consequently, his sole thought was for revenge and, to this end, he sent you threatening letters on the anniversary of the book's publication over the next five years.

'At least, I assume they were threatening from the description of your conduct given to me by your daughter who came to see me yesterday and asked me to look into the case.

'The letters had the desired effect of making you fear for your life but, as time passed, I suggest that Haydon Cowper's bitterness increased, for what reason we may never know. Perhaps he suffered other set-backs or, over the years, his personality became more disordered. We can only speculate. However, one thing is certain. Merely to threaten your life was no longer sufficient. Haydon Cowper made up his mind to take the ultimate step of murder.

'We may date this decision, I believe, to 21st February 1887, your birthday, when you read an obituary notice announcing Haydon Cowper's death. No doubt you were suspicious at first? Yes, I see you have indicated that I am correct in this assumption. But as no more letters arrived, you began to believe that Cowper was indeed dead and that you were no longer in danger.'

Once more, Professor Addleton's eyelids closed briefly in assent.

'Meanwhile,' Holmes continued, 'Haydon Cowper was awaiting an opportunity for his final act of revenge. We shall no doubt eventually discover from Mr Montagu Webb how he was drawn into the plot; innocently, it would appear, from his protestations that he thought the affair was merely a hoax. He is a foolish and gullible man who therefore, as far as Haydon Cowper was concerned, made an ideal cat's-paw.

'He persuaded Webb to write to you, informing you that he had discovered an ancient British barrow on Bodmin Moor which had never been excavated. As a further lure, he may have suggested that Webb send you some pieces of pottery, ostensibly from the burial chamber. However, Webb made the mistake of failing to remove some sticky patches on the backs of the shards which indicated that they had at some time been labelled as part of a collection. As those marks were apparent as soon as I examined the samples, I assume that you, too, had observed them?'

Again, there came the single flicker of the eyelids.

'And so you immediately suspected a trap, designed by Haydon Cowper?' Holmes suggested. 'I am correct, am I not, sir? Ah, I thought so! Then why, Professor Addleton, did you agree to come to Cornwall, knowing that your life could be in danger? Was it in the hope that Montagu Webb had indeed discovered a previously unknown barrow with its contents still intact? Was it this that overrode all fears for your personal safety? Or was it . . . ?'

Before Holmes had time to complete his question, a shudder passed over Professor Addleton's features like a sharp breeze disturbing the surface of a pool. Once more, the lids were lowered but this time the eyes remained shut and there was no answering movement.

Scrambling to my feet, I bent down and felt for a pulse in his neck but that, too, was motionless.

'I am afraid he is gone, Holmes,' I said gravely.

Holmes joined me and we stood together in silence for a few moments, gazing down at the lifeless figure. Then he drew up his ulster to cover the dead man's face, remarking as he did so, 'A fitting last resting-place, wouldn't you agree, Watson? Had he been given the choice, who knows that Professor Addleton might not have chosen to end his days here on this ancient burial mound, a sacrifice to the old gods.'

It was said lightly but I could see that, under his whimsical manner, my old friend felt Addleton's death keenly. His lips tightly compressed, he turned away and walked to the edge of the track to await the arrival of the party from Bodmin.

I left him alone for ten minutes before joining him, by which time he had regained his composure, although his manner was still muted.

'Holmes,' I began tentatively, 'what was the question you were about to ask Professor Addleton just before he died?'

'Oh, that,' he replied, shrugging his shoulders. 'It was whether or not shame had played a part in his decision to come to Bodmin Moor, despite the obvious danger.'

'Shame? I do not follow you.'

'Then you have clearly forgotten our conversation of yesterday afternoon. Do you not recall I asked you for what reason you would hesitate to confide in your wife some incident from your past? Your reply was illuminating and not just of your own character, my dear fellow. You said it would be some action of which you were ashamed. I was interested to know if Professor Addleton was driven by the same motive. Haydon Cowper was a brilliant student who had contributed to the success of Addleton's book and, while we do not know for certain, I am convinced in my own mind that Addleton was a member of that committee which decided Haydon Cowper should be sent down from Oxford. As the vote was unanimous, no one spoke up in his defence, not even his own professor. If that is so, it would explain Haydon Cowper's desire for revenge. It might also explain Addleton's own actions in coming to Cornwall. It is possible that he wished to meet his former student face to face and, by offering him an apology, make his peace with him at last. If that was his intention it was tragically too late. It is also too late for us to discover the answer. However, this is mere theory, Watson, and I should not wish it to be put forward at the inquest. It is better that it should be buried with the victims.'

A wagonette from Bodmin arrived soon afterwards, containing two police officers from the local constabulary. With their assistance, we placed the bodies of Professor Addleton and Haydon Cowper side by side in the back of it and covered them with blankets.

As Holmes remarked at the time, it was ironic that death should have united them at last and brought about a form of reconciliation.

It was a sombre procession which set out from Wheal Agnes through the gathering dusk, preceded by the wagonette. I followed behind, driving the hired dog-cart, while Holmes brought up the rear in Haydon Cowper's gig which we discovered he had left some distance from the escarpment on the track leading to Minions. This explained why we had not heard his approach. It was only the sudden flight of the ravens which had alerted Holmes to his presence.

The light was fading and, in the gathering dusk, the landscape had taken on a gentler and more elegiac quality, the contours softened and the wind-bent trees no longer sinister but melancholy, like the mute, bowed figures of mourners.

At the inquest, held later at Bodmin, at which Holmes and I gave evidence and which was attended by Addleton's daughter, but not his widow, we learnt of Montagu Webb's part in the whole tragic affair as well as a few facts concerning Haydon Cowper's subsequent career after his departure from Oxford.

It seemed that over the years he had been dismissed from various posts as a private tutor for that same instability of character he had shown at Oxford, the last a household at Launceston. This had occurred only shortly before the tragic events on Bodmin Moor.

As for the ancient British barrow on Bodmin Moor, it had been discovered not by Montagu Webb but by Haydon Cowper who, while at Launceston, had explored the moor. It was he, also, who had excavated the site and later persuaded Montagu Webb, a member of the local historical society, to write to Professor Addleton, claiming the discovery of the barrow as his own and inviting him to come to Bodmin. The deception was intended as part of an innocent practical joke, he told Webb. On his arrival, Addleton would be both delighted and amazed to find his former student, Haydon Cowper, waiting for him. There would be a joyful reunion in which Montagu Webb would have played a significant part.

It was Montagu Webb in fact who, in his eagerness to persuade Professor Addleton of the authenticity of the discovery, had taken it upon himself to send some broken pieces of pottery from his own collection to the professor, alleging they had come from the burial cist.

In his summing up, the coroner confessed that he had difficulty in understanding Haydon Cowper's motives. He could only assume that he had borne his victim some deep-seated grudge, the exact nature of which was not clear. However, having heard all the evidence regarding Haydon Cowper's irrational behaviour, he had no hesitation in returning a verdict that Haydon Cowper had first murdered Professor Addleton and then taken his own life, the balance of his mind being disturbed.

And so, as Holmes had wished, the secret of Professor Addleton's shame, if such it was, went with him to the grave.

There was no opportunity to speak to Miss Addleton after the inquest. She was accompanied by a solicitor and, as soon as the court rose, they left immediately by cab for the station.

I believe Holmes wrote to her later, expressing his regret for not having prevented her father's death. It was not in his nature to confide in me such personal details. I only know that for several days afterwards he was in low spirits and spent his time either confined to his room, playing his violin, or lying on the sofa in our sitting-room, staring moodily up at the ceiling. It was not until Inspector Lestrade arrived one evening, requesting his assistance in the singular affair of the forged Holbeins, that he recovered his former good humour.

It was over breakfast about a month later that he at last referred directly to the Addleton case.

Passing the copy of *The Times* to me, he remarked, 'There is an item at the bottom of page three, Watson, which you may find interesting.'

It was a short report which, after giving a brief summary of the circumstances surrounding Haydon Cowper's death, went on to state:

'Among his effects were discovered the contents of an ancient British barrow which he had evidently excavated shortly before his demise. They included some rare examples of prehistoric pottery and a beautifully worked stone axe which, according to the experts who have examined them, are among the finest objects of that period to be discovered in recent years.

'In the absence of any heirs, the entire collection has been handed over to the museum in Truro where it will be put on public display.'

'A final irony, is it not, Watson?' Holmes added as I laid down the newspaper.

'In what way, Holmes?' I asked, not quite sure what he meant.

'Why, such a discovery would not only have been the crowning glory to Professor Addleton's career as an archaeologist but would have gone far in restoring Haydon Cowper's reputation as well. Too late, though, my dear fellow! Too late!' Picking up the newspaper and shaking out its pages, he continued, 'By the way, Watson, I should be grateful if you refrained from publishing an account of the affair. As a great admirer of Professor Addleton's work, I should not wish his reputation to be besmirched in any way. Nor mine, come to that.'

'Yours, Holmes!' I exclaimed.

For a moment, he looked at me directly, his expression sombre.

Then he said abruptly, 'Failure can be as keen a shame as any other human frailty. In this particular instance, I should prefer mine not to be made public.'

I gave him my word and, apart from a passing reference to the case,[11] I shall withhold this account from my readers, placing it among my private papers.

As for Holmes, he never again spoke of the Addleton tragedy nor of that moment of indecision when, with Haydon Cowper in his sights at the top of the granite ridge, his resolution wavered and he hesitated to pull the trigger.

---

[11] Dr John H. Watson merely refers briefly to 'the Addleton tragedy and the singular contents of the ancient British barrow' in a list of other cases which occurred in 1894. *Vide*: 'The Adventure of the Golden Pince-Nez'. Dr John F. Watson.

THE CASE OF THE SHOPKEEPER'S TERROR

'Helloa! Now there's a strange state of affairs!' my old friend Sherlock Holmes exclaimed, coming to a sudden halt on the pavement and pointing with his stick.

It had rained heavily all day but, the weather having cleared by five o'clock, Holmes had suggested a walk to stretch our legs. Our ramble had taken us east into the tangle of side-streets which lay behind Tottenham Court Road and had led us eventually into Coleville Court.

It was a narrow turning of mean little houses, the monotony of their brick façades broken here and there by shabby premises, mostly those of pawnbrokers and dealers in second-hand articles.

As far as I could see, the shop he was indicating was no more remarkable than its neighbours. A board above its shuttered window bore the name 'I. Abrahams' and the words 'Curios Bought and Sold', while the blind was pulled down over the glass panel in the door.

'It is closed, Holmes,' said I, wondering what had drawn his attention to it.

'Exactly, Watson! Now, why should old Abrahams wish to shut his shop at this time of the day? He is generally open for business until late in the evening. I propose making enquiries.'

'You know him?' I asked, as we crossed the road.

'I have bought the occasional item from him in the past[1] and, if I happen to be in the neighbourhood, I make a point of calling on him,' Holmes replied. 'He is an honest fellow with a reputation for fair dealing.'

He had reached the door and, after rapping several times on it and receiving no reply, he put his eye to the crack between the shutters.

'Perhaps he is not at home,' I suggested.

'No, he is in. There is a light at the back.'

'Then could he be ill?'

'We shall soon find out,' Holmes said. Bending down, he called through the letterbox, 'Mr Abrahams! Are you there? This is Sherlock Holmes.'

There were several moments of silence before the blind over the glass was lifted cautiously aside a little as some unseen person inspected us round the gap. Then, with a

---

[1] Mr Sherlock Holmes purchased his Stradivarius violin, worth at least five hundred guineas, from a 'Jew broker's' in Tottenham Court Road for fifty-five shillings. It is possible he was referring to Mr Abraham's shop although this is not certain. Dr John F. Watson.

rattle as a chain was lifted and bolts were drawn, the door was opened just wide enough for us to enter.

'Quick, come in, Mr Holmes!' a voice whispered urgently.

Hardly had we done so than the door was slammed shut behind us, the bolts and chain refastened, and the bent figure of an old man, all that I could see of him in the gloom, shuffled ahead of us into a room at the rear of the shop.

It was an extraordinary chamber, hot and bright in the gas light, and so stuffed full of objects that at first I felt quite overwhelmed by their sheer numbers. Whole platoons of ornaments, knick-knacks and vases, all in need of cleaning, crowded every horizontal surface. Piles of books rose in tottering pillars from the floor or lay scattered about the threadbare carpet while the walls were so covered with pictures, rusty sabres and tarnished looking-glasses that it was almost impossible to discern the pattern of the paper behind them.

In the middle of this dusty confusion stood a little, old, bent man in his seventies, so thin as to be emaciated. He was wearing a pair of dress trousers and a red velvet smoking jacket, both very shabby and evidently intended for someone much stouter than he, for they hung upon his wasted frame like a scarecrow's garments. A pair of steel-framed spectacles, one lens of which was cracked, and a tasselled cap of black satin perched upon his sparse white hair completed his eccentric outfit.

My chief impression of him, however, was one of terror.

Old Abrahams was clearly very frightened. It was evident in his trembling hands and in his voice as, clutching my old friend by the arm, he asked in quavering tones, 'You were not followed here, Mr Holmes?'

'Not that I was aware of,' Holmes replied in surprise. 'Who would wish to follow me?'

'A bearded man with a limp and such a scowl on his face! Never in all my born days have I seen a more fierce-looking scoundrel. He has been watching this place ever since that young man, the one who has since been murdered, came into my shop. It's the box, Mr Holmes! You mark my words. That is what the villain is after. I fear he means to murder me, too, in order to get his hands on it.'

Letting go of Holmes' sleeve, the old man hobbled across the room as fast as his frail legs would carry him and, unlocking an old-fashioned safe, took out a small ebony casket which he thrust into my companion's hands.

'There it is! Take it, Mr Holmes! I want nothing more to do with it.'

Holmes set the box down upon the table and turned it round several times, examining it on every side with the keenest attention while I looked over his shoulder.

It was six inches square, its surface deeply carved in an Oriental style with a curious and intricate pattern of dragons, their scaly tails intertwined and their eyeballs bulging from their sockets like round, black beads. In places, though, the wood was so badly chipped that I doubted if it was worth more than a few pence.

It was locked, as Holmes discovered when he tried to raise the lid. However, a small key protruded from the brass escutcheon and the box contained something for, when he shook it, we could hear objects rattling about inside.

At the same time that Holmes made this examination, he asked questions of old Abrahams in a soothing manner in an attempt to calm him and to gain a more coherent account of how the box had come into his possession.

'You say a young man brought it into your shop. When was this?'

'Early yesterday morning, soon after I had opened for business.'

'Had you seen him before?'

'No, never.'

'What did he look like?'

'He was fair-haired and clean-shaven, wearing a cap and muffler, and with a tattoo of a butterfly on the back of his right hand. He came rushing in here as if the devil himself were at his heels, pushed that box at me and asked me to look after it. He said he would come back later to fix a price, if I wanted to buy it. That was the last I saw of him. Then this morning, my next-door neighbour, Mr Stein, called to see me, much excited. Had I heard about the terrible murder? A young fellow, with a butterfly tattooed on his hand, had been found stabbed to death in the yard behind the Crown public house in Charlotte Street. Oh, Mr Holmes, it must be the same man who called at my shop yesterday! What am I to do? I am sure the scoundrel with the black beard and the limp killed him. If ever I saw murder written on a man's face, it was on his!'

'Pray compose yourself, my dear sir,' said Holmes, 'and try to give me exact particulars of this bearded man. When did you first see him?'

'Yesterday, at the very same time the young man brought the box to me. He was lurking about outside on the pavement. When the man left, the ruffian came up to my window, peered in and then set off after him.'

'Have you see him since?'

'Several times, Mr Holmes, prowling up and down in front of my shop as if keeping a watch on it. And late last night, as I was locking up and drawing down the blind, there was his face pressed up against the glass! I know he means to break in, kill me in my bed and then make off with that box. Since I heard about the murder, I have not dared to open the door or step outside into the street.'

'So you have not yet informed the police of what you know?'

'I am too frightened. Suppose I inform against him and the villain comes looking for me out of revenge? It is more than my life is worth! Besides, what is in the box? As it is not mine, I have not liked to open it. It could contain stolen property. If the police find it, they will charge me with receiving. I am an old man, Mr Holmes, and have always tried to deal honestly. If I go to prison, my business will be ruined!'

At this thought, poor Mr Abrahams sank down on a

worn armchair by the fire and, putting his hands over his ears, rocked to and fro in an agony of despair.

Over the top of his bent head, Holmes gave me a glance of mingled amusement and compassion.

'Come, Mr Abrahams,' said he. 'You must not always look on the dark side. Shall I open the box for you and at least set your mind at rest on the question of its contents?'

The old man looked up fearfully. 'But I told you, it is not mine. Do you want me to be accused of tampering with someone else's property?'

'As its apparent owner is dead, I think there is small chance of that,' Holmes remarked drily.

It was meant kindly but did little to cheer old Abrahams. Reminded of the murder, he covered his ears once more and resumed his rocking motion, groaning aloud to its rhythm.

'You are too scrupulous,' Holmes told him. 'For my part, I confess curiosity far outweighs such finer considerations. You have my word I shall accept full responsibility.'

As he spoke, he turned the key and lifted up the lid before, giving a low exclamation of surprise, he tipped the contents out upon the table.

A most extraordinary collection of objects came tumbling out, consisting of an ivory buttonhook, a little cut-glass scent bottle, and a string of coral beads such as a child might wear.

'None of it seems worth the trouble of stealing,' I remarked.

'Quite so,' Holmes murmured in an abstracted tone.

He stood in silence for a moment, gazing down at the receptacle and its scattered contents, and then, briskly scooping up the latter, he replaced them in the box which in turn he stowed away in the pocket of his ulster.

'Put your coat on, Mr Abrahams,' said he. 'You are coming with us.'

'Where to?' the old man quavered.

'To your daughter's. I believe she lives nearby, does she not? Then we shall take you there. My colleague, Dr Watson, will call a cab while I help you pack a bag and arrange for your neighbour, Mr Stein, to take charge of the premises in your absence.'

'But what of the bearded man? And the murder?'

'You may leave all of that in my hands, Mr Abrahams,' Holmes assured him. 'You have presented me with a most curious little mystery which it will give me the greatest pleasure to enquire into.'

Poor Mr Abrahams seemed little comforted by Holmes' promise to look into the matter. He still feared the bearded man might follow him to his new address or ransack the shop in his absence. However, after much persuasion, he finally agreed to accompany us to his daughter's house, where we left him in her care.

I had assumed that Holmes had agreed to take on the enquiry simply to put the old man's mind at rest. But I was proved wrong, for no sooner had we returned to our Baker Street lodgings than he took the casket from his pocket and, handing it to me with a flourish, said, 'Now, Watson, use your powers of observation and tell me what you make of it.'

'I have already done so, Holmes. I cannot see why anyone should wish to acquire either the box or its contents. A buttonhook and a coral necklace! They are worth next to nothing.'

'And yet, according to old Abrahams, the young man who left the casket with him was murdered because of it.'

'I find that quite absurd.'

'So do I, my dear fellow, which is why the case is so interesting.'

'Then you intend following it up?'

'Of course.'

'Would it not be better to leave it to the police who no doubt are already investigating the young man's murder?'

'I shall certainly consult them. However, before handing the box over to them, I wish to examine it more closely myself, which is why I brought it with me. Does nothing about it strike you as curious?'

'Not really, Holmes.'

'Look at its dimensions, my dear fellow!'

'I can see nothing strange about them,' said I, turning the casket over in my hands.

Without a word, Holmes stalked over to his desk, returning with a ruler with which he measured the exterior of the base of the box.

'As you see, it is exactly five inches high; six if one includes the lid,' he announced. 'And now for the interior.'

Opening the box and emptying out the contents, he placed the ruler upright against the inner side.

'But that is only three inches deep!' I cried.

'Exactly, Watson! I noticed the discrepancy when I saw the box at old Abrahams' shop. The conclusion is obvious. There must be a secret drawer or compartment, two inches high, concealed in the bottom of the box. That being so, we may also safely assume that hidden somewhere about the receptacle is a catch which, when pressed, will reveal it.'

With his long, sensitive fingers, he began to probe gently at each heavily embossed panel in turn, working his way round the sides until he had reached the back. Like the rest of the casket, it was carved with the figures of two dragons, facing one another, their mouths spouting flames and their tails intertwined. It was behind one of the bulging eyes of the creature on the left that the catch was hidden for, as Holmes pressed it, there was a sharp click and the bottom of the box flew upwards, revealing a lower section, empty apart from a small packet of yellowing tissue paper.

Taking it out, Holmes carefully folded back the wrappings and there, nestling in the centre, lay a ring.

'Now that is indeed worth stealing!' Holmes said softly.

As he lifted it towards the light, I saw the dull gleam of a gold band and the brighter sparkle from the large red stone with which it was set.

'Is it valuable?' I asked.

To my eyes, it was heavy and old-fashioned, the band too broad, the square-cut stone too large to grace a lady's finger, although I confess that the fiery gleam which burned in the heart of it had a certain barbaric beauty of its own.

'My dear Watson, if I am not mistaken, what you are looking at is a ruby which, from its size and magnificence, must be worth a fortune. The question is: to whom does it belong? Not, I should imagine, to the young man in the cap and muffler who left the box at old Abrahams' shop. Then is it the property of the bearded man with the limp? I doubt that also. The owner of such a ring does not skulk about on pavements or peer in at windows and yet the bearded man is clearly intent on recovering the box and presumably the ring with it. There is also the young man's murder to consider. Where does that fit in? It is a pretty little puzzle, is it not? Have you any thoughts on the mystery?'

'Well, I assume the ruffian with the beard murdered the young man in order to get his hands on the box.'

'No, no!' Holmes cried. 'That will not do at all! We must keep to the facts, Watson. Old Abrahams stated quite clearly that when the young man left the box with him yesterday morning, he was observed to do so by the bearded man who was watching from the street outside. Therefore, he knew the box was in old Abrahams' possession, as his subsequent behaviour in keeping the curio shop under surveillance confirms. Knowing that the young man no longer had the box, why should he wish to stab him that same evening?

'Although murder is frequently illogical, there is a perversity about this particular crime which defies all rational explanation. By killing the young man, the bearded ruffian, if it were indeed he who committed the crime, has not only gained nothing but has lost a great deal by bringing down on his own head the full weight of an official police investigation.'

'Perhaps it was no more than a falling out among thieves,' I suggested.

Holmes seized on my remark with more enthusiasm than I had intended.

'You think the two of them may have stolen the ring and then quarrelled over its ownership? A possibility, Watson. A distinct possibility! However, I know of no major robbery which has been committed recently. Surely the theft of such a valuable jewel would have been reported in the newspapers.'

'Its rightful owner may have preferred it was not made public.'

'Ah, its rightful owner! But, my old friend, is that person also the owner of the box and the curious collection of objects inside it? And was it that same person who concealed the ring in the secret compartment? You follow my logic? If it were merely a case of simple theft and murder, I should leave it to the official police. I am sure Inspector Lestrade and his colleagues at the Yard are quite capable of solving such a mundane crime. It is these more obscure aspects of the case which I am so eager to follow up.'

'Then you intend informing the police of what we know?'

'Of course, my dear fellow. I shall call at Scotland Yard this evening, where I shall hand over the box and give a full account of what we have so far discovered. In the meantime, while Lestrade is making his investigation, you and I shall pursue our own researches. You are game, are you not, Watson?'

'Indeed I am, Holmes,' I said warmly.

However, as events were to prove, I was not present during these enquiries.

The following afternoon, while I was out, Holmes received a visitor at our Baker Street lodgings who introduced him to another case, that of the disappearance of Lady Frances Carfax.[2] As he was reluctant to leave London while old Abrahams was still in such mortal terror of his life, Holmes asked me to travel to Lausanne in order to enquire into her ladyship's whereabouts on his behalf.

On my return to London, having failed to trace her, I found myself so caught up in the Carfax case, which proved exceedingly complex, that I quite forgot to ask Holmes how the other investigation had proceeded in my absence.

---

[2] For a full account of this case, readers are referred to 'The Disappearance of Lady Frances Carfax'. Dr John H. Watson was taking a Turkish bath when Lady Frances Carfax's former governess, Miss Dobney, called on Mr Sherlock Holmes to report her disappearance. Both this case and that of old Mr Abrahams are undated but evidently took place when Dr John H. Watson was in residence at Baker Street, either before his marriage in the late 1880s or after the spring of 1894 when, on Mr Sherlock Holmes' return to England, he moved back to his old lodgings. Dr John F. Watson.

It was not until after our dramatic rescue of Lady Frances some two weeks later that I recalled the Abrahams affair.

It was a remark made by Holmes when we were discussing the Carfax inquiry over breakfast one morning which brought it to mind.

'It was, of course, fortunate,' said he, 'that we found her silver pendant in that pawnbroker's in Westminster Road. Had we not done so, she would have been buried alive by her abductors with no one the wiser about her fate.'

'Speaking of jewellery,' said I, 'were you able to discover the owner of the ruby ring?'

'Indeed I was, and a most strange story it proved to be.'

'Tell me about it,' I urged. 'Who was the bearded man? Was it he who murdered the young man in the cap and muffler? And why . . . ?'

'My dear Watson,' Holmes cried, laughing and holding up his hands in protest. 'So many questions!'

'I am eager to know the outcome of the case.'

'Your curiosity is quite understandable and I give you my word it will be satisfied. You intend calling at your club tomorrow afternoon, do you not?'

'I have promised Thurston a game of billiards.'[3]

'Then,' said he, rising from the table, 'if you care to stroll in the direction of Coleville Court after your game and

---

[3] Thurston, Christian name unknown, was the only person with whom Dr John H. Watson played billiards. *Vide*: 'The Adventure of the Dancing Men'. Dr John F. Watson.

pay old Abrahams a visit, you will receive a full account of the case in the very same setting in which the mystery was solved. Does not that strike you as appropriate? Until that moment, I refuse to answer any further questions. And now, my dear fellow,' he added, his eyes sparkling mischievously, 'you must excuse me. I have two important telegrams I must send.'

However, it was not his final word on the subject. After lunch the following day, when I was about to leave for my engagement with Thurston, Holmes looked up from the *Telegraph* to add in an offhand manner, 'By the way, Watson, when you call at the curio shop this afternoon, do pay particular attention to the window display. You will find it most interesting. In the meantime, enjoy your billiards, my dear fellow!'

Despite this injunction, I found very little pleasure in the game. My thoughts were so occupied with the coming appointment with Holmes that I missed several easy shots, much to my chagrin and to the delight of Thurston, who won easily. He proposed a second match which I declined, pleading urgent business. Taking my leave of him, I hurried out of the club, hailed a passing hansom and directed its driver to take me to Coleville Court.

On this occasion, I found that the shutters were down and the blind up at Old Abrahams' shop. It was evidently open for business. Indeed, as I alighted from the cab, I could see the bent, white-haired figure of old Abrahams himself, spectacles on nose, seated behind the counter.

However, remembering Holmes' advice to take note

of the window, I lingered outside for a few moments to survey its contents.

To my astonishment, I saw placed in its very centre the same small ebony casket in which Holmes had discovered the ruby ring. Its lid was closed and a handwritten ticket, placed on top of it, bore the inscription, 'Bargain. 9d.'

'Mr Abrahams!' I cried, pushing open the door and approaching the old shopkeeper in some haste. 'What is the box doing in your window? I thought it had been returned to its rightful owner.'

I broke off, my surprise turning to utter confusion, for I saw confronting me not one but two Mr Abrahams, the second appearing like the aged twin of the first through the door leading into the rear room.

As I stared quite dumbfounded from one to the other, the first elderly gentleman who was seated behind the counter rose to his feet and, laughing heartily, removed the spectacles and tasselled cap, together with its surrounding fringe of white hair, and, straightening his shoulders, stood revealed as my old friend Sherlock Holmes.

'I am sorry to startle you, Watson,' said he, 'but I could not resist re-enacting for your benefit a little scene from the drama which took place here in the shop while you were absent in France on the Carfax inquiry. The disguise was evidently successful, for it quite clearly deceived you.'

'Indeed it did, Holmes,' I admitted ruefully. 'But what was its purpose?'

'To lure a certain gentleman with a black beard and a limp into the open,' Holmes began.

He was interrupted by the real Mr Abrahams who, until that moment, had stood watching my discomfiture with evident delight, cackling with laughter and rubbing his frail hands together.

Suddenly his smile faded and his features assumed that expression of terror I had perceived on my first meeting with him. With a cry, he lifted a trembling finger and pointed towards the door.

Turning in that direction, I was horrified to see, pressed close against the glass panel, a man's bearded face, glaring in at us and scowling most dreadfully.

It was a terrible countenance, dark and threatening, the brows knotted fiercely together, the eyes glittering with menace.

'Holmes!' I cried in warning, for my old friend seemed oblivious of the man's alarming presence.

He glanced casually towards him but remained remarkably cool.

Strolling over to the door, he flung it open and announced in a pleasant manner, 'Ah, Hunniford, my dear fellow, you are exactly on cue. Do come in. Mr Abrahams, of course, you know. But you have not yet met my colleague, Dr Watson. Watson, allow me to introduce George Hunniford, a former inspector at Scotland Yard, at present working, like myself, as a private consulting detective.'

'You flatter me, Mr Holmes,' said the man, limping forward to shake me vigorously by the hand. 'I wish I had a quarter of your skill and reputation. It is a matter of following far behind in your footsteps.' Seeing my expression, he grinned broadly. 'I am sorry, Dr Watson, if I alarmed you. It was Mr Holmes' idea to set up this little scene for your benefit. I sincerely trust you won't take it amiss.'

'Of course not,' I replied a little stiffly; for I was secretly annoyed at being made the butt of their amusement.

However, it was impossible to remain angry when the occasion had afforded the rest of them such obvious enjoyment, especially Holmes who, still laughing, clapped me on the shoulder, declaring as he did so, 'You must forgive me, my dear old friend! The temptation was irresistible. But what you have seen here this afternoon is a true re-enactment of the events which occurred when you were otherwise engaged in Lausanne. Allow me to explain.

'After I had reported what I knew to Inspector Lestrade and handed over to him the box and the ruby ring, I devised with his co-operation a little scheme to entrap the man with the beard. At the time, he was, of course, suspected of the murder of the young man in the cap and muffler who had left the box at Mr Abrahams' shop. Consequently, once the ring was removed from the secret compartment and placed in safe keeping at Scotland Yard until its rightful owner could be found, Lestrade returned the box to me. Disguising myself as Mr Abrahams, I then placed it in a prominent position in the window, just as you saw it this afternoon. Accompanied by a police sergeant who concealed himself in the rear room, I then kept watch inside the shop for our suspect to return.

'I saw him several times during the day, walking up and down the street and lurking about in a most suspicious manner, if you will pardon my criticism of your methods, Mr Hunniford. A private consulting detective should never *lurk*. It always draws attention to himself. When undertaking a surveillance, one should always behave in as inconspicuous a manner as possible so that one blends with one's surroundings. Now, had you disguised yourself as an ordinary citizen going about his normal business, you would not have aroused Mr Abrahams' fears. And please, my dear man, do remove that absurd beard. It is so patently false that it deceives no one.'

'It was the best I could find at short notice,' Hunniford replied apologetically, stripping away his heavy black whiskers and revealing a pleasant, clean-shaven countenance of an open and cheerful expression.

'Ah, that is a great improvement!' Holmes declared. 'To continue my account. At lunchtime on that Thursday, my patience was rewarded. The bearded man entered the shop and, taking ninepence from his pocket, asked to buy the box. As he did so, the sergeant came bursting out of the back room and promptly arrested him on suspicion of robbery and murder.

'Unfortunately, I was not able to arrange a re-enactment of that particular episode in the drama, Watson. Inspect Lestrade, who does not share your sense of humour, refused to lend me a police officer on the grounds that it would be detrimental to the dignity of the force. You must therefore imagine the scene.

'The bearded man protested his innocence most strenuously but to no avail. He was handcuffed, bundled into a cab and taken to Scotland Yard where, once I had divested myself of my disguise and handed over the care of the shop to the real Mr Abrahams, I joined them. It was there that I heard a most remarkable account from the suspect who had by then revealed his true identity.

'As it is your story, Mr Hunniford, I suggest that you take over the telling of it.'

'Willingly, Mr Holmes,' said he. 'First, however, I ought to explain that I left the police force two years ago, after falling off the wall of a warehouse yard while I was chasing after a notorious villain, a very clever cat-burglar named Bert Morrison. But more of him in a moment.

'I broke my leg badly in two places and wasn't able to continue active duty, so I was retired early on a pension. As the wife had relatives in Somerset, we decided to move down there and open a small boarding-house in Yeovil. That was all very well for a time but I soon found myself missing the excitement of life in the force and the challenge of pitting my wits against London's criminal fraternity. So, thinking to put my experience to good use, I placed an advertisement in the local newspaper, offering my services as a private consulting detective. I must confess that it was Mr Holmes' success in that particular field which put the idea into my mind in the first place.

'To cut a long story short, I had a few commissions,

mostly cases of poaching or petty pilfering from the shopkeepers of the town. And then, about three weeks ago, a Mr Horace Morpeth wrote to me. He was, he explained in his letter, the butler to Lady Farthingdale, the owner of Witchett Manor. Would I call at the house at my earliest convenience to investigate a burglary which had taken place there a couple of nights before? The police had been called in but had so far made no progress in their enquiries and her ladyship was anxious to recover her property.

'Now there was a case more to my liking than a shop assistant helping himself to the odd shilling or two from the till or a poacher making off with a brace of pheasants. So I hired a trap and drove over to Witchett Manor that very same afternoon. And what a weird place I found it, Dr Watson!

'It was a large Tudor house, all old beams and crumbling plaster, set in an isolated position well off the road and surrounded by gardens which had long since gone wild. The interior was no better. I do not think the place had seen a broom or a cleaning rag for years, for there were cobwebs everywhere and dust that thick you could write your name in it.

'The butler, an elderly man, met me at the door and, before taking me to see her ladyship, invited me into his own little private cubby-hole where he told me about the background of the case. Lady Farthingdale was, it seemed, very old and eccentric, the widow of the former Ambassador to the kingdom of Nepal. After her husband's death, she had become more and more of a recluse, seldom venturing out of the house. Although exceedingly wealthy, she had convinced herself that she was on the brink of poverty and would end her days in the workhouse. Consequently, she was extremely miserly. As the servants died or retired, she refused to replace them until the household had been reduced to Morpeth, the butler, and one old woman servant. To save on coal, they lived in just a few rooms, the rest of the house being closed off.

'Her ladyship was also in mortal fear of burglars and was in the habit of concealing money and valuables in the strangest of places. Morpeth himself had once found a diamond brooch in the tea-caddy and a bag of sovereigns under a flower-pot.

'Whether or not a former servant had gossiped or the isolated position of the house had attracted the attention of a burglar, Morpeth could not say. But two nights earlier, Lady Farthingdale's worst fears were realised and the house was broken into. Because so many of the valuables had been hidden in places where even the most enterprising thief would not think of looking, the haul was not very great. All that was taken was a few pieces of household silver, a pair of gilded vases and a little wooden box, carved all over with dragons, which as far a Morpeth was aware contained nothing more than a few paltry trinkets.

'The local police were informed and had made an investigation but had discovered no clues to the burglar's identity. As the stolen objects were of such little value, they had not considered calling in Scotland Yard. But his mistress being in such a state of distress over the loss of her possessions and the failure of the police to recover them, Morpeth, who had seen my advertisement in the newspaper, suggested that I should be sent for. Lady Farthingday was waiting in the drawing-room and was most anxious to meet me.

'However, my motto has always been first things first. So, at my request, Morpeth took me upstairs to the garret to show me where the villain had entered. It was the only possible place of access for, as Morpeth explained, because of her ladyship's fear of thieves, the rest of the house was like a fortress, with every window shuttered and every door double locked and barred.

'I may still have a lot to learn about disguises and shadowing a suspect but there isn't much anyone can teach me about the methods certain burglars use when breaking into a "drum".[4] As soon as I saw the little window in the slope of the roof and the neat way a hole had been cut in the glass near the catch, I knew it was the work of Bert Morrison.'

'The man you chased over the warehouse wall?' I exclaimed.

'The very same scoundrel,' Hunniford replied. 'There was no question about it. When I climbed on a chair and

[4] A 'drum' is criminal slang for a house or other premises applied to a site of a planned robbery or one where a robbery has already occurred. Dr John F. Watson.

peered out of the window, I could see that the nearest drain-pipe, up which he must have come, was a good thirty feet away with a drop of well over fifty to the ground. No one else could have shinned up there and made his way in the dark across that roof which had a pitch to it like the side of Mount Blank. Agile! Morrison was a veritable monkey and as slippery as an eel into the bargain. While I was at the Yard, I had investigated no less than fifteen burglaries which Morrison had carried out and yet I was never once able to lay him by the heels or prove his guilt.

'His particular liking was for wholesalers' and warehouses where there were rich pickings. But whenever London got too hot for him, he would move his pitch and "turn over", as the underworld terms it, a big country mansion, stealing mostly silver and jewellery which, once melted down or broken up, could not be traced back to him.

'Nothing would have given me greater pleasure than to snap a pair of "darbies" on his wrists and see him hauled off to gaol, for it was on account of him that I had broken my leg and lost my job in the police force. And think what a feather it would be in my cap! Me, a private consulting detective, arresting the most notorious burglar in London! Why, I would have been almost as famous as Mr Holmes!

'With these thoughts in my mind, I went downstairs to meet Lady Farthingdale.

'She was sitting in the drawing-room and a queer-looking old lady she was, too. She was dressed all in black, with a widow's cap on her head and her hands resting like claws on a silver-knobbed cane. But she was still as sharp as a needle. As I crossed the room towards her, I could see she was eyeing me up and down and taking my measure.

'I must have passed muster for, dismissing the butler, she fumbled under the cushion behind her back and, taking out a little wash-leather bag, she dangled it in front of me.

'"There are fifteen guineas in there," said she. "They are yours, in addition to your expenses, if you recover what was stolen from me."

'Fifteen guineas! Why, Dr Watson, it was more than I had earned in three weeks while I was at the Yard.[5] I confess though that, not knowing then about the ruby ring, I couldn't for the life of me understand why she, being such a miser, was willing to part with all that money for what Morpeth had told me was a mere handful of trifles, worth no more than a few pounds.

'"I shall do my best, your ladyship," said I.

'"Then set about it at once," said she with a snap of her lips. "And remember, Hunniford, I want it all back but especially the little wooden box. It contains something I value most highly. If you fail to recover it, you will receive no more than a guinea. Do you accept the terms?"

'It was a hard bargain but, having always been

---

[5] At the turn of the century, a detective inspector of first-class rank earned between £250 and £280 per annum, one of second rank between £180 and £230 per annum, while a uniformed inspector's salary was 56 shillings a week or £145 per annum. Dr John F. Watson.

something of a gambler, I agreed. She then pushed the little money-bag behind the cushion, rang for Morpeth and I was shown out of the house.

'The following morning, I caught the first train to London, a plan already worked out in my mind.

'I knew Morrison frequented the Tottenham Court Road area where there were several public houses he liked to drink in and meet his cronies. As his haul from Witchett Manor was so small, I also reckoned that he would not trouble to take it to his usual "fence", a man down in Isleworth, but would try selling it off for what he could raise on it at the nearby second-hand dealers, some of whom handled stolen property.

'My guess was correct. I tracked Morrison down to a lodging-house in Goodge Street and also managed to trace the silver and the pair of vases, which I bought back on Lady Farthingdale's behalf. But I could not find the little wooden box anywhere. So, assuming Morrison had not yet sold it, I kept watch on his lodgings, disguising myself with the beard in case he recognised me, for I had questioned him a couple of times at the Yard.'

'I assume, from Morrison's subsequent actions, that he saw through the disguise,' Holmes interjected.

Hunniford smiled ruefully. 'I am afraid so, Mr Holmes. It was on the Wednesday morning. I saw him set out from his lodgings so I followed him. But, as you say, he must have recognised me, for he dived into Mr Abrahams' shop, handed the box over and then shot off again like a bullet. I suppose, knowing I was hot on his trail, he was anxious to dispose of it before I could catch up with him.

'I admit I was in something of a dilemma. On the one hand, I was keen to get hold of the box and earn my fifteen guineas. On the other, I did not wish to lose sight of my quarry. So, thinking I could go back later to the shop, I stopped to look quickly in at the window before hurrying after him.

'To be frank, I lost him. I said he was as slippery as an eel and he had the advantage of knowing the area like the back of his hand. By the time I reached the corner of Coleville Court, he had vanished. He also cleared out from his lodgings, as I discovered when I went back there.

'You can imagine my feelings. But, if I had lost Morrison, at least I knew where to find Lady Farthingdale's trinket box. It was safe at Mr Abrahams' shop. Or so I thought. So I kept watch on the premises, hoping I would see it put out for sale. I would then have bought it and that would have been the end of the matter. Instead, I succeeded in frightening poor Mr Abrahams out of his wits, for which I am truly sorry.'

'Arid thereby forcing him to shut his premises,' Holmes pointed out.

'That was a real set-back to my enquiries,' Hunniford admitted. 'However, rather than return to Somerset without it and lose my fifteen guineas, I decided to wait a few more days and see what happened. The rest you know, Dr Watson. Disguised as Mr Abrahams, Mr Holmes put the box in the window where I saw it. Thinking my problems were at an end, I came in to buy it, only to find myself under arrest on suspicion of Morrison's murder about which, at the time, I knew nothing.'

'But if you did not kill him, who did?' I enquired, nonplussed.

It was Holmes who answered.

'A man called Ferrers, with whom Morrison was competing for the affections of the barmaid, Nancy, at the Crown public house,' said he crisply. 'It was a sordid little crime which need not detain us.'

Taking this remark as a cue for his own departure, Hunniford rose to his feet and shook hands all round.

'Neither must I keep you any longer, except to say that Lady Farthingdale received back her ruby ring, I was paid my fifteen guineas and all ended happily as the lady novelists put it, although I should have liked the satisfaction of seeing Morrison behind bars. Still, as they say, there are more ways than one of skinning a cat, or, in his case, a cat-burglar.'

Laughing loudly at his own joke, he picked up the little ebony casket and slipped it into his pocket.

'Well, gentlemen, I must be off,' said he. 'The wife is expecting me on the 5.25 train and I promised Lady Farthingdale I would return the box to her as soon as Mr Holmes had finished with it.'

We took our own leave of Mr Abrahams shortly afterwards, strolling back to our lodgings along Oxford Street.

As we walked, I took the opportunity to ask Holmes

how he had set about devising the little scene which so far he had not explained.

'It was quite simple,' he replied. 'Yesterday morning, I sent two telegrams, one to Lady Farthingdale in which I requested the loan of her trinket box, the other to Hunniford, asking him to collect it from her and bring it to me. Then this afternoon, while you were playing billiards, he and I, with old Abrahams' assistance, arranged the re-enactment which I thought might amuse you. It certainly gave me a great deal of pleasure. But I see that does not entirely satisfy you, my dear fellow. There is something else on your mind.'

I was much taken aback, for there was indeed one other aspect of the case which was troubling me. However, before I could voice the question, Holmes had answered it.

'No, Watson,' said he, 'Morrison did not know that Lady Farthingdale's ruby ring was hidden in the secret compartment of the box, otherwise he would have sold it to the gentleman in Isleworth who generally handled all his stolen booty. How did I know you were about to ask me that? Because you put your right hand up to your collar and cleared your throat, a sure indication that some aspect of the case needed further clarification. I have frequently observed the habit. As it was the only loose thread left dangling, I ventured to tie it up before you asked.

'And, Watson, if you are considering writing up an account of the case, please do me the kindness of refraining. When Lady Farthingdale sent the box by Hunniford, she enclosed with it a message that not one word about the case should be published. She is an avid reader of your accounts of our little adventures together and looks forward eagerly to them appearing in print. However, she prefers not to be featured in one of them.'[6]

[6] No reference is made in the published canon to Lady Farthingdale. However, in 'The Disappearance of Lady Carfax', Mr Sherlock Holmes states that he 'cannot possibly leave London while old Abrahams is in such mortal terror of his life.' Dr John F. Watson.

THE CASE OF THE *FRIESLAND* OUTRAGE

I

It was, I recall, late one stormy evening in November 1894, some months after Sherlock Holmes' miraculous return from death at the hands of his arch-enemy, Professor Moriarty, at the Reichenbach Falls,[1] that the following remarkable events occurred which were so nearly to cost us both our lives.

---

[1] The fateful encounter between Mr Sherlock Holmes and Professor Moriarty took place on 4th May 1891 on a ledge overlooking the Reichenbach Falls, near the village of Meiringen in Switzerland, after Dr John H. Watson had been lured away by a false message. On his return, he found Mr Sherlock Holmes had disappeared, leaving a farewell message. Assuming both men had plunged to their death, Dr Watson, much saddened, returned to London. However, Mr Sherlock Holmes had survived and three years later, in the spring of 1894, reappeared in London to Dr Watson's great joy and relief. *Vide*: 'The Adventure of the Final Problem' and 'The Adventure of the Empty House'. Dr John F. Watson.

Having dined, we had retired to our armchairs on either side of the blazing fire, Holmes deep in a volume on early Elizabethan ciphers, I absorbed in nothing more abstruse than the *Evening Standard,* content that my old friend had no case on hand to force us out of doors in such tempestuous weather.

Hardly had the thought crossed my mind than Holmes lifted his head and, laying aside his book, remarked, 'A cab has just drawn up outside, Watson. I believe we have a visitor. Rather than allow the maid to be disturbed at such an hour, I shall let him in myself.'

'Him?' I enquired.

'Oh, it is undoubtedly a man. Did you not hear the slam of the cab door? No woman would act in quite so positive a manner.'

I had heard nothing above the sound of the wind roaring in the chimney and rattling the windows in their frames, although I was not surprised that Holmes had discerned these distant noises. His hearing is keener than that of any other man I know.

He left the room, returning soon afterwards with a short, powerfully built, bearded man, so broad across the shoulders and so stocky of frame that he appeared quite square in shape. From his pea jacket and peaked cap, I took him to be a seafarer, a supposition which proved correct when Holmes introduced him.

'This is Captain Hans Van Wyk, Watson.' Turning to our visitor, he continued, 'Pray be seated, sir.'

Van Wyk removed his cap, revealing a head of grey hair,

as thick and as grizzled as his beard. His weather-beaten face was deeply creased about the eyes with humorous lines, suggesting a jovial nature, although the gravity of his general demeanour revealed that whatever business had brought him to consult Holmes was of a serious nature.

'Master of the Dutch vessel, the SS *Friesland*,' said he, sinking down into the chair which Holmes had indicated. Although his English was on the whole excellent, he spoke with a guttural accent. 'I apologise for intruding on you so late in the evening, gentlemen. But the lady insisted I came to you, not the official police.'

'I think,' said Holmes, resuming his own seat, 'that you had better begin by telling us who the lady is and why she is in such urgent need of my help.'

'Of course, Mr Holmes. However, I ought first to explain a little of the background to the affair. The SS *Friesland* is a small cargo vessel, plying between the coasts of Germany and Holland and the south-east of England. We also carry passengers; not many, as there is cabin accommodation for only a dozen. Yesterday, we docked at the Free Trade Wharf[2] in the Port of London where we unloaded and took on a fresh cargo, ready for the return voyage to Rotterdam. We are due to sail at

---

[2] The Free Trade Wharf is situated on the north bank of the Thames, a mile and a half downstream from the Tower of London. Known originally as the East India Wharf, it was renamed the Free Trade Wharf in 1858 after tariff reform had lifted former trading restrictions. Dr John F. Watson.

half-past one tomorrow morning on the high tide.

'A few passengers embarked earlier this evening, among them an elderly gentleman, a Mr Barnaby Pennington, and his daughter. I did not see them come on board, although I understand from the steward that they went straight to their cabins.

'Some time later, Miss Pennington went on deck and approached the mate in some distress. It seems that, after she had settled herself into her own cabin, she went to her father's which was opposite hers to make sure that he, too, was comfortable for the night. Having knocked and received no reply, she let herself in, only to find the cabin empty and signs that a struggle had taken place. Her father's luggage had been rifled and a large sum of money, together with some important documents, was missing.

'The mate alerted me and I ordered an immediate search of the whole ship but no trace of Mr Pennington was found. I also questioned the crew. But no one had noticed anything suspicious, although that is understandable. It is a dark, wet night and the men were busy about their own tasks.'

'Miss Pennington had heard nothing?'

'Evidently not, Mr Holmes, apart from some muffled thuds which she took to be coming from the deck. The storm was then at its height.'

'And what of the other passengers. Have you spoken to them?'

'Not personally. I was too occupied with supervising the search and examining the crew. However, the steward questioned them on my instructions. He reported that none of them had heard or seen anything out of the ordinary. There are only four of them on this voyage and the cabins between theirs and Mr Pennington's are unoccupied. I have since taken the precaution of posting a man at the head of the gang-plank in case anyone should try to take Mr Pennington ashore. Of course, it may be a case, as you English say, of bolting the door after the horse has vanished.'

'You mean that someone could have come on board and abducted Mr Pennington without your knowledge?'

Captain Van Wyk spread out his large, gnarled hands.

'On such a night, anything is possible,' he replied.

'You said you spoke to Miss Pennington,' Holmes continued. 'Had she any idea who might be responsible for her father's disappearance?'

'No, none at all, sir; except she seemed to think robbery might be a motive.'

There was a hesitation in the captain's voice which Holmes was quick to perceive.

'You yourself do not believe it?'

'I think there may be more to the case than simple theft, Mr Holmes. When I spoke to the lady, she was strangely reluctant to discuss her father's business affairs. She was also most insistent that I was to come directly to you and no one else. She has written a letter which she asked me to deliver to you personally.'

Feeling in his jacket pocket, Captain Van Wyk produced an envelope which he handed to Holmes who, having opened it and glanced quickly over the sheet of paper it contained, read the message aloud for our visitor's benefit as well as my own.

'"Dear Mr Holmes, Captain Van Wyk will have explained to you the circumstances surrounding my father's disappearance. As I have great fear for his safety, I beg you to make enquiries on my behalf. My father has often spoken of your detective skills in relation to one specific investigation."'

At this point, Holmes broke off to ask Captain Van Wyk, 'Did Miss Pennington happen to mention any particulars of this inquiry?'

'Yes, she did, Mr Holmes!' the captain replied eagerly. 'It was the Blackmore case.'

'Indeed!' my old friend murmured. 'As I remember, it was a most delicate business.' Seeing my look of enquiry, he explained, 'It was an investigation I carried out in '89 when you were in practice in Paddington. I did not call on your services, Watson, as you were laid up at the time with an attack of bronchitis. To continue with the letter. Miss Pennington goes on to add, and the sentence is underlined twice, "On no account must Scotland Yard be informed of this affair." The letter is signed Maud Pennington. Well, Captain Van Wyk,' Holmes concluded, folding up the sheet of paper and placing it in his pocket, 'I shall certainly accept the young lady's request. The case presents some unusual features. You came in a four-wheeler, I believe, which you have retained?'

'It is outside, Mr Holmes,' the captain replied, looking

surprised. 'But how did you know I had asked the driver to wait?'

'It is quite simple. I have not heard the cab drive away,' Holmes said nonchalantly. 'Watson, if you care to accompany Captain Van Wyk downstairs, I shall follow you shortly. I must leave a note for Mrs Hudson in case we are delayed by our enquiries. I should not wish to cause our inestimable landlady any undue concern. You go ahead, my dear fellow, and make sure you wear something suitable against this appalling weather.'

Taking my old friend's advice, I put on a long waterproof and, followed by Captain Van Wyk, led the way out into the street where a four-wheeler was drawn up beside the kerb. While we waited for Holmes, we took shelter inside it from the driving rain.

He joined us several minutes later, limping so heavily that it was with some difficulty he climbed into the cab.

On my enquiring what had happened, he said impatiently, 'In my haste, I sprained my ankle coming down the stairs and had to return in order to strap it up. But it is a mere trifle. Shall we proceed? We have already wasted valuable time through my carelessness.'

Captain Van Wyk gave instructions to the driver and we set off for the docks along deserted streets running with water like so many minor tributaries of the Thames itself, as if that great river had burst its banks and inundated the entire city.

Holmes said nothing during the journey. He sat huddled in his ulster, the flaps of his travelling cap pulled well down about his ears, staring out through the rain-drenched window at the passing scene. From time to time in the light of the street lamps, I caught a glimpse of his profile, looking very austere, his lips compressed and his brows heavily contracted.

I put his silence down to the pain of his ankle but said nothing, not wishing to exasperate him further by referring to his mishap.

Captain Van Wyk and I exchanged a few desultory remarks but we, too, soon fell silent, oppressed by Holmes' taciturn mood and the melancholy drumming of the rain on the roof of the cab.

Eventually, it drew up at the end of a narrow, ill-lit street where we alighted and followed Captain Van Wyk as he led the way on to the Free Trade Wharf.

Here, the full strength of the gale, blowing straight off the river, caught us in its blast. Heads bowed against its onslaught, we struggled forward in the darkness, the captain striding ahead of us, quite at home, it seemed, in this elemental world of wind and water.

I had nothing more than a fleeting impression of my surroundings. Battered by the storm and half blinded by the rain, I was aware only of the tall edifices of warehouses, like the sides of a grimy brick canyon, towering above us on our left and, to the right, the huge hulks of ships at anchor, their masts and rigging pitching to and fro against the night sky and groaning audibly with every squall.

There were no moon or stars to illuminate the scene, only the fitful light of a few lamps, guttering in the wind and casting a tremulous yellow glow over those looming hulks and the river which ran between them as black as oil.

We arrived eventually at the foot of a gang-plank which Captain Van Wyk nimbly mounted, while we followed more slowly behind him, gripping fast to the rail, especially Holmes who had to haul himself up the steep incline.

At the top, a member of the crew in oilskins was standing guard, lantern in hand. Captain Van Wyk conferred with him briefly before, turning to us, he roared out above the storm, 'He says no one has left the ship in my absence, gentlemen! Follow me! I will now show you Mr Pennington's cabin.'

Taking the lantern from the man, Van Wyk set off at a brisk pace towards the stern of the vessel, Holmes and I groping our way as best we could after that bobbing light over the deck which shifted uneasily under our feet on the swelling tide.

At last we saw glimmering out of the darkness aft of the wheel-house a white-painted, flat-roofed structure housing the passengers' accommodation, with a row of port-holes along its side and lifeboats slung above it on davits. Ducking through a low doorway, we found ourselves in a small vestibule which gave access to a passage, lit by hanging lamps, with several doors leading off it on either side.

Captain Van Wyk threw one of these open.

'Mr Pennington's cabin,' he announced.

The interior was small, most of it taken up by a pair of bunks, one of which was strewn with articles of clothing, carelessly flung about. A leather valise, emptied of its contents, lay on its side on the floor.

There were signs, too, that a struggle had taken place inside that confined space. One of the curtains at the port-hole was wrenched from its rings while the basin, which was set below it in a locker, was heavily blood-stained.

Holmes stood just inside the doorway, looking about him, his head lifted like a gun dog scenting game. Then, limping forward, he examined first the basin and the valise, before turning his attention to the port-hole, lifting aside the torn curtain to examine the large brass screw which secured it. But it was tightly fastened down and showed no signs of having been loosened. Even if it had been, the opening was too small to admit even a child, let alone a grown man.

Meanwhile Van Wyk watched these activities with the keenest interest, murmuring to me in an aside, 'It warms up the cockle of my heart to see such an expert at work!' Then, raising his voice, he continued, 'If you have seen enough, Mr Holmes, I suggest we speak to Miss Pennington. I know she is most anxious to meet you.'

Holmes agreed and we followed the captain across the passage to a door opposite, on which Van Wyk tapped several times. Receiving no answer, he finally turned the handle and, opening the door, thrust his head inside.

In the light of the lamp, we saw at once that the cabin

was empty, although there were indications that it had recently been occupied. A lady's mantle hung behind the door and a nightgown, neatly folded, lay upon the pillow.

There were no signs, however, of a violent physical struggle, such as we had seen in the other cabin, and yet there was clear evidence that Miss Pennington had not left of her own volition. Hanging in the air was the unmistakable sweet, sickly reek of chloroform.

It was apparent that the odour was familiar also to the captain, for no sooner had he smelt it than he turned and made for the deck, shouting to us to follow him.

By the time we had joined him, he was already deep in animated conversation in a foreign language which I took to be Dutch with a broad, heavily bearded man who, as I was later to learn, was the mate, Bakker.

From the latter's expression and gestures, I deduced that he was as bewildered as we were by the disappearance of Miss Pennington, following so closely upon her father's.

Captain Van Wyk flung out an arm in an abrupt movement of command and barked out an order to the mate. Then, motioning with his head to us, he led the way up an open companion-way, its iron treads made treacherous by the rain, to his own quarters which were situated below the bridge.

His cabin was more spacious than the passengers' accommodation, although it was similarly equipped with a bunk and a range of lockers including, in this instance, a shelf for logs and a broad table to serve as a desk. Charts were pinned upon the walls and a brass spittoon was screwed to the floor beside the table.

'Well, gentlemen, this is indeed a strange business,' Van Wyk said, when we had divested ourselves of our wet outer garments. 'Two passengers disappeared! Such a thing has never happened before in all the years I have been at sea! I have ordered the mate to make another search of the vessel. He will report to me as soon as it is completed.'

'And if Miss Pennington is not found?' Holmes enquired.

'Then I shall be forced to send for the official police, despite her instructions to the contrary. I cannot see that I have any other choice. The young lady's disappearance has indeed put the cat among the birds. She has not been taken ashore. The man posted at the head of the gang-plank was quite sure no one has left the ship. Have you any explanation to offer for this mysterious affair, Mr Holmes?'

'I confess I am utterly at a loss,' my old friend admitted with a rueful expression. 'Mr Pennington's disappearance might be accounted for. He could have been abducted. But his daughter's! That is a different matter altogether. The only logical conclusion is that she must still be on board.'

'That is my thought exactly. But the search will take at least two hours. There are many places on a vessel where someone could be hidden. If I have to delay the ship's departure, then so be it!' Van Wyk said, shrugging his broad shoulders philosophically. 'In the meantime, you will take a glass of schnapps with me? It will help to keep out the cold.'

I was about to refuse, not having much taste for strong liquor and preferring to keep a clear head for whatever enquiries still lay ahead of us. But when Holmes agreed, I felt it might appear churlish if I declined, so I, too, accepted.

'Then we shall drink to the successful outcome of the case!' our host exclaimed.

Turning away, he opened a locker and took out a squat bottle and three glasses which he filled in turn, handing one each to Holmes and myself and raising his own in salutation.

'Down the hatchway!' cried he, his blue eyes sparkling as, throwing back his head, he swallowed down the brandy in one single draught.

I followed his example, feeling the schnapps burn its way down my throat like liquid fire. As a protection against the cold of that stormy night it was indeed effective. Within seconds, its warmth had begun to circulate through my blood, spreading out to tingle down to the very fingertips.

Meanwhile, Holmes, glass in hand, had wandered across the cabin to examine one of the charts pinned up on the wall above the desk. He seemed abstracted, his mind no doubt still on the mysterious disappearance of Mr Pennington and his daughter. I had seen him in this mood many times before when the problems presented by a case so occupied his mind that he was oblivious of everything else about him.

'You have not yet drunk our toast, Mr Holmes,' Captain Van Wyk reminded him.

'I beg your pardon,' Holmes replied. 'My thoughts were elsewhere. To our success, Captain!'

He was about to raise his glass when he gave a sudden lurch sideways, only saving himself from falling by clutching at the table with his free hand. However, he quickly recovered and, standing upright once more, he threw back his head and swallowed the brandy.

Whether the ship had been struck by a particularly heavy swell or his sprained ankle had caused Holmes that momentary loss of balance, I could not tell, for at that moment I myself was overcome by a violent bout of dizziness. The cabin seemed to be rising and falling in a most extraordinary manner, as if the *Friesland* had already set sail and was tossing about on the high seas.

My last recollection was of Holmes, setting down his empty glass and saying, with a smile of apology, 'I am afraid I am a poor sailor, Captain Van Wyk. I appear not yet to have acquired my sea-legs. But your excellent brandy should soon set that to rights.'

The next instant, the cabin spun about me and I felt myself pitching forward into a black abyss of oblivion.

II

I do not know how long I remained unconscious but, some time later, I was aware of Holmes shaking me urgently by the shoulder. For a moment, I fancied I was in my own bed in our lodgings in Baker Street and that some crisis had occurred for which Holmes required my immediate presence.

However, as I struggled to sit up, I found that I could not move. It was only then I realised that I was lying, facing the wall, on the bunk in Captain Van Wyk's cabin, my hands secured behind my back by a rope which was drawn tightly across my chest, my legs and feet similarly bound. A pad of cotton wadding, placed across my mouth and held in position by a strip of cloth, made breathing difficult and I felt half suffocated for lack of air.

'Lie still and do not make a sound,' Holmes whispered close to my ear as he removed the gag.

I next heard the rasp of something metal cutting into the cords and, as my bonds fell away, I was able to sit upright at last to see Holmes standing beside me, one finger against his lips, his deep-set eyes glittering in the lamplight.

Leaving me seated on the bunk to recover my full senses, he moved with a cat-like speed and silence across the cabin, showing no sign of the limp which had earlier impeded his movements. Kneeling down in front of the door, he inserted into the keyhole a thin metal rod which he began to manipulate to and fro with great care, his head pressed against the panel as he listened for the wards to yield.

While he was thus engaged, I looked about me, still dazed, trying to piece together what had happened in the time I had been unconscious.

From the lengths of rope lying on the far side of the cabin, together with a pad and piece of cloth, I deduced that Holmes, like me, had been trussed up and gagged, although I had no idea how he had managed to release himself.

Nor could I see why Captain Van Wyk had wished to lure us aboard the *Friesland* and to offer us schnapps laced with some strong narcotic drug, for that was what must have happened. There was no other explanation for my sudden loss of consciousness.

I assumed that Holmes, too, had been drugged, although

looking at him as he knelt by the door, every sense alert, his fingers probing delicately at the keyhole, it was difficult to imagine. He appeared to have suffered no ill effects, a recovery I put down to his iron constitution and that seemingly bottomless well of nervous energy on which he was able to draw in times of crisis.

At last, there came a faint click as the lock gave way but instead of opening the door and beckoning to me to follow him on deck as I had expected, he secured the top and bottom bolts before crossing silently back to the bunk on which I was sitting, his finger again pressed to his lips. Seeing my look of interrogation, he mouthed the word, 'Wait.'

But for what? I wondered. For Van Wyk to return and break down the door when he discovered it barred against him? Although the bolts were strong, it would take no more than two men to burst them open.

And then what would happen to us?

I was under no illusions that we were not in mortal danger. The captain had not made us his prisoners only to let us walk free. Indeed, I was surprised that he had not despatched us when he had us drugged and at his mercy.

Such thoughts clamoured in my mind and yet I dared not voice them out loud to Holmes. He had taken the captain's chair at the desk and was leaning back, his eyes closed, as he strained to pick up the faintest sounds beyond the four walls of the cabin.

The storm had abated a little and it was possible to distinguish other noises aboard the *Friesland* besides the relentless roar of the wind and the beating of the rain. I heard footsteps occasionally passing below on deck and the sound of distant voices. Once there came a faint metallic crash, as if a heavy iron door had been slammed shut. As a background to these signs of human activity, there was the constant creak and groan of the vessel itself as it swung restlessly at its moorings.

My tension was exacerbated by Holmes' inactivity. Although we were unarmed, all my instincts told me it would be better to make a dash for it on to the deck where, in the darkness and ensuing confusion, we might have a chance of escape. And even if we failed in our attempt, we would have the satisfaction of going down fighting like men which was infinitely preferable to sitting there, like trapped animals, tamely awaiting our fate.

For the first time in my long association with Sherlock Holmes, I felt that he had failed me and I was bitterly disappointed. I could not believe that this was the same man who had met his arch-enemy, Moriarty, face to face without flinching and, by grappling with him on that narrow ledge above the Reichenbach Falls, had sent him plunging to his death.

With each succeeding minute, my exasperation mounted until I could contain it no longer and prepared myself to make a dash for the door, my intention being to force Holmes into action by taking the initiative. If I moved first, surely he would follow?

As events were to prove, it was fortunate that Holmes forestalled me. Before I could rise from the bunk, he had sprung to his own feet, an expression of intense relief lighting up his keen features.

'There is our signal!' he exclaimed aloud.

'What signal?' I enquired, greatly astonished not only at the sound of his voice after so long a silence but at the remark itself. I had heard nothing apart from the usual sounds on board the *Friesland* and a double blast on a steam whistle from some passing vessel.

'Of Inspector Patterson's arrival. Hurry, Watson! There is no time to lose!'

Suddenly he was in a positive whirl of activity, snatching our coats from the hooks and throwing my waterproof at me before flinging his own ulster about his shoulders. With two rapid movements, he had slid back the bolts and, opening the door, disappeared outside. By the time I had caught up with him, he was already scrambling down the companion-way which led on to the deck.

The sight which met me when I finally descended, close on Holmes' heels, was one of utter confusion. Lanterns were darting to and fro like fireflies in the darkness, their yellow beams illuminating briefly portions of the stern deck, shining black in the rain, and flashing on to a struggling group of men whose mingled shouts and curses, raised to a dreadful pitch, added to the impression that I had stumbled into a scene from a mediaeval inferno.

In the centre of all this wild activity, as if forming its nucleus, I could dimly discern the huge figure of Bakker and the stocky form of Captain Van Wyk, both fighting like mad men.

The next moment, Van Wyk had broken free from the mêlée and, turning rapidly about, came charging forward to where Holmes and I were standing in the lee of the wheel-house.

I doubt if he saw us in the shadows. His goal seemed to be the gang-plank which lay over to our left. Two constables, recognisable by their helmets and their black waterproof capes, were guarding it but their attention was on the main struggle which was taking place further along the deck. Within seconds, all could be lost. Van Wyk would reach the gang-plank and, taking the constables by surprise, might force his way down on to the wharf from where he would easily make his escape among the surrounding labyrinth of alleyways and side-streets.

I must confess that I, who only a short time before had been so eager for action and silently upbraiding Holmes for his lack of it, found it impossible to move. As the powerful figure of the captain came hurtling towards us, his face contorted by rage, I was suddenly overcome by nausea, caused no doubt by the effects of the drug still present in my system.

It was Holmes who responded. As I stood helplessly by, he took a step forward, the muscles of his left arm bunched at the shoulder, his whole body as tense as a coiled spring. Then his fist went flashing past me, the knuckles gleaming white in the lamp-light, and there came a heavy thud as the blow struck the side of Van Wyk's jaw. Like a tree felled by a single stroke of an axe, he went crashing down on to the deck.

Holmes turned to me, his lean features transfigured by an expression of fierce jubilation.

'I think, Watson,' said he, 'that our account with Captain Van Wyk is finally settled.'

Before I had time to reply, a bulky figure, dressed in unofficial tweeds, detached itself from the group of struggling men in the centre of the deck and came striding in our direction: Inspector Patterson of Scotland Yard, I perceived as he drew nearer. I had already made his acquaintance through my association with Holmes and had found him an excellent officer, efficient, co-operative and possessing a wide knowledge of London's criminal fraternity.

'Well, Mr Holmes,' cried he, coming to a halt beside Van Wyk's recumbent body and regarding it with a look of satisfaction, 'I have not seen a better straight left than yours outside the professional ring.[3] And with the captain down and out for the count, thanks to you, we now have all the crew safely rounded up.'

He gestured to where the knot of men was already

---

[3] Mr Sherlock Holmes, who had practised boxing while at university, used his skill at the sport on several occasions, notably against Woodley whom he defeated with a straight left. *Vide*: 'The Adventure of the Solitary Cyclist'. In 'The Adventure of the Yellow Face', Dr John H. Watson refers to him as 'one of the finest boxers of his weight' that he had ever seen. Mr Sherlock Holmes had also fought three rounds with a professional prize-fighter, McMurdo, at the latter's benefit night and was considered by him expert enough to have turned professional. *Vide*: *The Sign of Four.* Dr John F. Watson.

breaking up and was making its way in a more orderly fashion towards the gang-plank, each member of the crew escorted by a police officer, some in uniform, some in plain clothes. Among them, I recognised the mate, Bakker, his hands secured behind his back and his dark, bearded features made even more ill-favoured by a large swelling above his left eye.

On Inspector Patterson's orders, the two constables guarding the gang-plank came forward and, heaving Van Wyk upright, snapped a pair of handcuffs over his wrists. He had recovered a little from the blow Holmes had dealt him, although he was still unsteady on his feet. As he was dragged away, he directed towards us a scowl of such intense hatred that my blood ran cold at the thought that only a short time ago, Holmes and I had lain drugged and bound at the mercy of this unspeakable villain.

With the departure of the crew of the *Friesland,* all of whom with the exception of Captain Van Wyk and the mate were later released as having played no part in our abduction and imprisonment, the night's activities were almost completed. Inspector Patterson left a guard on board the vessel and the four passengers who were found cowering in their cabins, too terrified by the sounds of the violent struggle taking place on deck to emerge, were reassured and escorted ashore.

Holmes and I then left in the company of Inspector Patterson to drive to Scotland Yard where, after we had formally identified Van Wyk and Bakker, they were later charged and taken away into custody.

III

'And now, my good Inspector, you will no doubt wish to hear a more detailed and personal account of last night's extraordinary events than the official statement I have already made,' Holmes said.

It was the following evening when, on my old friend's insistence, Patterson had called at our Baker Street lodgings.

'First, the identity of the villain behind last night's attempted abduction.'

'We already know that!' Patterson interjected. 'It was Van Wyk, the master of the SS *Friesland,* with the assistance of Bakker, the mate.'

'Oh, no, Inspector. He was merely the agent of someone much more powerful and dangerous whose name is familiar to both of you. Can you not guess? Then I shall have to tell you. It is Professor Moriarty.'

'Moriarty!' Patterson and I exclaimed in unison.

'But Holmes,' I protested, as the inspector fell silent in utter astonishment, 'Professor Moriarty met his death at the Reichenbach Falls at your hands. You are surely not suggesting that by some miracle he survived.'

'No, my dear fellow. There is not the smallest likelihood of that. No one, not even he, could have emerged alive from that dreadful abyss. But it is perfectly possible for a man with Moriarty's genius for evil to continue exerting his influence from beyond the grave. He warned me once, here in this very room, that if I brought about his destruction, he would see to it that I, in turn, would be destroyed.[4] On that same occasion, he also informed me that he was the head of a syndicate, the full extent of which even I could not appreciate. In that, he was mistaken. From my enquiries, I had already deduced that Moriarty controlled an international criminal fraternity, responsible for at least forty major crimes, including murder, robbery and forgery.

'I believe I once described him to you, Watson, as a malignant spider. It was an apt simile. His organisation was composed of many threads and extended over a vast

---

[4] For a full account of Mr Sherlock Holmes' interview with Professor Moriarty, readers are referred to 'The Adventure of the Final Problem'. Dr John F. Watson.

area. When, with Inspector Patterson's help,[5] we set about smashing that web by rounding up members of Moriarty's gang, a few managed to elude us, including Van Wyk and his associate Bakker, whose task it was, should Moriarty fail in his attempt on my life at the Reichenbach Falls, to take revenge on their master's behalf.

'The scheme was a simple one and was planned to take place several years after the Reichenbach encounter,[6] by which time Moriarty estimated that I should feel secure and my guard would consequently be lowered. But he omitted to take into account two vital considerations. Firstly, unlike him, I have never underestimated my opponent's capabilities. That man possessed the most phenomenal intellect which I could only admire, much as I detested the criminal ends to which he devoted those remarkable powers. For that reason, I was able to study him objectively as one might a specimen under a microscope. By so doing, I concluded that our minds

---

[5] In his farewell letter left at the Reichenbach Falls, Mr Sherlock Holmes instructs Dr John H. Watson to inform Inspector Patterson that all the papers he needed to convict Professor Moriarty and his criminal associates were in a blue envelope, marked Moriarty, in the *M* pigeonhole of his desk. The Moriarty gang was later brought to trial but two of them, including Colonel Moran, escaped justice. The other presumably was Captain Van Wyk. *Vide*: 'The Adventure of the Final Problem' and 'The Adventure of the Empty House.' Dr John F. Watson.

[6] Over three years had elapsed between Mr Sherlock Holmes' encounter with Professor Moriarty at the Reichenbach Falls in May 1891 and the attempt made on Mr Sherlock Holmes' life on board the SS *Friesland* in November 1894. Dr John F. Watson.

worked on a very similar plane. In short, I could deduce his reasoning and anticipate his every action as if I had entered his mind and shared with him his very thoughts.

'I therefore asked myself the following question. Were I Professor Moriarty, what would I do if, when brought face to face with a protagonist such as myself, I ran the risk of losing my life at his hands?

'The answer was obvious. I should so arrange matters that, at some future date, his life, too, would become forfeit.

'Moriarty's second mistake was in choosing Captain Van Wyk to carry out his plot. Van Wyk is essentially a man of violence, prepared to commit murder and therefore necessary to the scheme but lacking that subtlety of imagination which a swindler or a confidence trickster might have possessed. When he presented himself yesterday evening here at Baker Street with his story of the disappearance of his elderly passenger, Mr Pennington, I was suspicious of it almost at once.'

'Were you, Holmes?' I interjected. 'It sounded perfectly plausible to me. What made you doubt it?'

'The behaviour of Miss Pennington, the alleged passenger's daughter. Once more, it was a question of putting myself in someone else's place. Here was a young lady whose father had apparently disappeared on board ship on a dark and stormy night. Were I in her shoes, my first action would have been to rouse one of my fellow passengers in the nearby cabins. Instead, we were told that she rushed out on deck to seek help from the mate.

'I might, however, have passed over this discrepancy had I not read the letter which Miss Pennington had supposedly written to me. It was undoubtedly in a young lady's handwriting but showed no sign of the agitation that one would have expected from someone in her situation.

'In this letter, she mentioned an unspecified case which I had undertaken and which she claimed to have heard about from her father. I decided to test out my suspicions by asking Van Wyk if he knew to what precise investigation she referred. It was then that Van Wyk demonstrated that lack of imaginative finesse which was to confirm my doubts and bring about his arrest. So eager was he to lure me aboard the *Friesland* that, instead of pleading ignorance, he made the mistake of mentioning the Blackmore affair. I am afraid that I am not at liberty to divulge all the details, nor are they relevant to the present case. Suffice it to say that it was a highly delicate inquiry involving the attempted blackmail of a well-known member of the aristocracy, carried out on Professor Moriarty's orders by one of his agents, a man called Blackmore. By means of a ruse, I was able to arrange for Blackmore's arrest by Inspector Lestrade of Scotland Yard on a quite separate charge of handling stolen property on the understanding that he would receive all the credit, providing I was allowed to remove certain private papers from Blackmore's safe.

'Consequently, although Blackmore's trial was widely publicised in the press, nowhere in those reports was there any mention of my name.

'How, then, had Van Wyk learnt of my connection

with the case unless he were a member of Moriarty's syndicate and had heard it discussed among his associates? I therefore concluded that the Penningtons did not exist and that the story of the father's disappearance was part of a plot against my life, almost certainly arranged by the late professor before his demise.'

'Yet, knowing this, you were prepared to accompany Captain Van Wyk aboard the *Friesland*?' Inspector Patterson enquired in great astonishment. 'Surely you were aware in what grave danger you were placing not only yourself but also Dr Watson?'

'Indeed I was and I can assure you it was not a decision I took lightly.' Turning to me, Holmes continued, 'My only excuse, my dear fellow, is that, throughout our long friendship, I have never known you refuse to assist me in a case, however dangerous it might prove. I acknowledge it was wrong of me to assume you would do so on this occasion and for that I offer you my sincere apologies. I would have suggested that you remained behind on some pretext or other had I not known that you would have objected and, by so doing, might have aroused Van Wyk's suspicions. It was essential to my plan that he believed I had accepted his story unequivocally.'

'Oh, please, Holmes!' I exclaimed, deeply touched. 'There is no need to apologise. Even if I had known the full circumstances, I should have agreed to accompany you.'

'Thank you, Watson. That is what I had expected you would say. Nevertheless, I am deeply grateful. As Cicero so aptly states: "*Adminiculum in amicissimo quoque dulcissimum est.*"'[7]

There was a short silence and then Holmes resumed his account.

'As you will recall, Watson, I sent you and Van Wyk ahead of me to wait in the cab with the excuse that I had to leave a note for Mrs Hudson. Instead, having roused our landlady, I wrote to you, Inspector Patterson, briefly describing the situation and asking for your immediate assistance but not mentioning Professor Moriarty by name for reasons which I shall shortly explain. In the letter, as you know, I suggested that you bring at least a dozen colleagues with you and that you signal your arrival by two blasts on the steam whistle of a police launch. I then handed the letter to Mrs Hudson, with strict instructions that, as soon as our cab had departed, she was to take a hansom to Scotland Yard and deliver the letter into your hands.

'At the same time, I took the precaution of arming myself as best I could. I knew it would be quite useless to take my revolver with me. If my deductions regarding Van Wyk's plans were correct, he would not make an attempt on our lives until the *Friesland* had sailed on the high tide at 1.30 a.m. and was safely out to sea. He would then murder us and fling our bodies overboard. To do so while the vessel was still in port was too dangerous. Had

[7] The quotation is from Cicero's *De Amicitia* and translates as: Man's best support is a very dear friend. Dr John F. Watson.

we put up a struggle, our outcries might have roused the passengers and those members of the crew who were not involved in the plot. Beside, our bodies, even if weighted down, might later have been dredged up by the anchor of another ship. Once out in the Channel, he ran no such risk.

'In the meantime, he would have to keep us secure and silent. The best method of achieving this was, I deduced, first to drug us and then make sure we were safely locked away until after the vessel had set sail. One of the precautions I expected Van Wyk to take was to search our pockets. Had I carried a revolver, it would have been immediately discovered and removed. Those, at least, were my suppositions.

'What occurred after we had boarded the *Friesland* is, of course, known to you, my dear Watson, as you participated in the events. But I am sure you will bear with me while I elaborate on them a little for Inspector Patterson's benefit.

'With the intention of persuading Van Wyk that I accepted his account, I made a pretence of examining Mr Pennington's cabin, incidentally discovering one further mistake which Van Wyk had made in setting up his trap for us. I assume you failed to notice it yourself, Watson, for you made no reference to it, not even by so much as a raised eyebrow.'

'I confess I noticed nothing apart from the obvious signs that a struggle had taken place and that Mr Pennington's luggage had been searched. To what do you refer?'

'To the basin which was liberally splashed with blood and yet there were no other stains elsewhere. Had someone bled so copiously, I should have expected to find evidence of it on the floor or upon the curtains, one of which had been wrenched from its rings during that apparent struggle.

'With the discovery of the alleged disappearance of Miss Pennington, Van Wyk suggested that we retire to his cabin while a second search of the vessel was supposedly made and that, while we waited, we join him in drinking a glass of schnapps. The glasses as well as the bottle were kept in a locker and I noticed that, when he took them out, he was most careful to keep the two glasses intended for our use separate from the one he subsequently drank from himself, causing me to suspect that they already contained a few drops of some powerful opiate, its taste and odour effectively disguised by the brandy.

'I am afraid there was nothing I could do, Watson, to prevent you from responding to Van Wyk's toast. However, you may recall that I carried my own glass to the far side of the cabin where I appeared to lose my balance. Under cover of this, I emptied the contents of my glass into the spittoon which stood beside the captain's desk.'

'But Holmes!' I expostulated. 'I distinctly recall you drank your brandy only a short time later!'

'No, my dear fellow,' said Holmes, laughing heartily. 'What you saw was the pretence of drinking. It is one of the oldest and simplest tricks in the repertoire of any stage magician. An object, a coin say, is placed inside a receptacle such as a box from which it apparently vanishes. The truth is, of course, that the coin has remained concealed in the man's palm and he has merely faked the action of putting it into the container. In much the same way, I kept the empty glass shielded in my cupped hand but went through all the motions of drinking from it, evidently successfully as neither you nor Van Wyk suspected me of legerdemain.

'After you had succumbed to the effects of the drug, I waited for a few moments and then, having observed your symptoms, I proceeded to imitate them, collapsing on the floor beside you. Once we were both apparently unconscious, Van Wyk summoned the mate, Bakker, and the two of them then set to work to search us and truss us up. It was at this point that my knowledge of baritsu[8] proved its usefulness.'

'Baritsu?' Inspector Patterson enquired. 'I have not heard of it.'

'It is a Japanese form of wrestling which I have studied and which I had used before to great effect in my struggle with Professor Moriarty on the path above the Reichenbach Falls. One of its benefits lies in the development of the muscles in the upper arms and torso. When Van Wyk and his accomplice, Bakker, bound the ropes about my

---

[8] Baritsu, or Bartitsu, was a form of self-defence, the name of which was derived from *bujitsu,* the Japanese word for martial arts. Mr Sherlock Holmes used his skill at the sport to escape from Professor Moriarty's grasp and send him plunging to his death at the Reichenbach Falls. *Vide*: 'The Adventure of the Empty House'. Dr John F. Watson.

chest and secured my arms behind my back, I flexed those muscles and, by releasing the tension after they had left, I was able to loosen the ropes sufficiently to allow me to reach the blade of a scalpel I had concealed in the cuff of my coat. After ten minutes' laborious work, I succeeded in cutting through the cord round my wrists and, once my hands were free, the other bonds were soon released. The rest you know. Having roused you, my dear Watson, and untied you, it was simply a matter of waiting for the signal from the steam whistle announcing the arrival of the excellent inspector here and his colleagues.'

'You have forgotten one thing, Holmes,' I pointed out.

'Have I? And what is that, pray?'

'The picklock with which you opened the cabin door.'

'Did I omit to mention it? How remiss of me!' Holmes said carelessly. 'The explanation is quite simple. At the same time as I concealed the scalpel blade, I took the precaution of strapping a small selection of picklocks round my left ankle. It made walking somewhat painful, hence my excuse of having sprained my foot. But it was worth the discomfort. The implements proved indispensable.

'And now, Inspector Patterson – and you, too, Watson, for the consequences will affect you as well – I must offer you an explanation of why I failed to refer to Professor Moriarty by name in the letter I sent by Mrs Hudson. The omission was deliberate.

'You will not have heard, my dear fellow, of the murder in Rotterdam in January '90 of a Hendrik Van den Vondel, although Inspector Patterson was informed of it at the time. Van den Vondel was fatally stabbed one night, apparently in the course of an attempted robbery, near the docks by two men who were seen running away by a passer-by. Unfortunately, the witness was not able to describe them and the two malefactors were never brought to justice. However, there were rumours of a darker and more sinister motive behind Van den Vondel's death.

'Those suspicions were later confirmed by the Dutch authorities who, in the strictest confidence, consulted my brother Mycroft who, as you know, has connections with our own government.[9] They had reason to believe that an international organisation was behind the murder and that it was carried out by two of its Dutch agents whose identities were then unknown.

'It was revealed that Van den Vondel was a plain-clothes inspector of police who was investigating this organisation which, with the aid of forged documents, was engaged in smuggling known criminals from the Continent to this country. They included such notorious villains as Larsson, the Swedish forger, and the Nihilist, Boris Orlov, wanted by the Russian authorities for the bombing of a post office in St Petersburg. Most of these criminals were later rounded up by Inspector Patterson and his colleagues at the Yard.

'This traffic in human cargo was centred on the port

[9] Mr Mycroft Holmes, Mr Sherlock Holmes' elder brother, acted as a confidential adviser to various government departments while ostensibly employed by them as an auditor. *Vide*: 'The Adventure of the Bruce-Partington Plans'. Dr John F. Watson.

of Rotterdam and was apparently carried out with the assistance of certain dock officials who had been bribed to cover up the truth, although the Dutch authorities had no proof either of this or of the identities of those who had organised the illicit trade.

'However, in the light of last night's events aboard the SS *Friesland*, I think we may safely assume that Van Wyk and Bakker were part of the conspiracy and it was they who had murdered the unfortunate Van den Vondel on Professor Moriarty's orders. I suggest therefore, Inspector Patterson, that you make a thorough search of the captain's cabin, for you may well find sufficient evidence among his papers to prove his and Bakker's guilt as well as the names of those port officials who were bribed to keep silent.

'It was because of these international connections that I thought it wiser to make no mention of Professor Moriarty until I had discussed the whole affair with Mycroft, which I did earlier this afternoon. Rather than bring Van Wyk and Bakker to trial in this country, Her Majesty's Government has decided to hand them over to the Dutch authorities, who will no doubt wish to question them closely about the murder as well as the allegations of conspiracy.

'In addition, Inspector Patterson and his men are still hunting for Luigi Bertorelli, an important member of the Sicilian Mafia, and, until he is arrested, not a word of this must be made public.

'For these reasons, Watson, you will not be permitted to publish an account of our adventure on board the

SS *Friesland*. I very much regret this, my dear fellow, but Mycroft's decision is final.'

However, I could not allow the case to pass totally into oblivion, for it illustrates not only the ingenuity and deductive skills of my old friend Sherlock Holmes but also his great personal courage in the face of mortal danger. In addition, it allowed me my sole contact, albeit posthumously, with that arch-villain, Professor Moriarty, whom Holmes once referred to as the Napoleon of crime[10] and whose genius for evil has never to my knowledge been surpassed in this century.

But it is not only for this reason that I have decided to write this confidential account of the outrageous events that took place on board the SS *Friesland*, which I shall deposit among my private papers.[11]

It is also intended as a tribute to the courage of my old friend, Sherlock Holmes, and as a form of apology to him for my doubting, however briefly, his lion-hearted valour.

---

[10] *Vide*: 'The Adventure of the Final Problem'. Dr John F. Watson.

[11] The only reference which Dr John H. Watson makes to the case is in 'The Adventure of the Norwood Builder', in which he states that 'the shocking affair of the Dutch steamship, *Friesland*, which so nearly cost' both him and Mr Sherlock Holmes their lives, occurred in the months following Mr Holmes' return to London in 1894. Dr John F. Watson.

THE CASE OF THE SMITH-MORTIMER SUCCESSION

I

Another singular inquiry which took up much of Sherlock Holmes' time and energy in the year 1894 was the case of the Smith-Mortimer succession although, like the Addleton tragedy, it will not be possible to publish an account of the affair while its participants are still alive. I have particularly in mind Mrs Eugene Mortimer and her small son who have at last, I trust, found happiness after the terrible events which overtook them.

At least, that is my fervent hope.

Holmes and I first made her acquaintance one morning in September of that year when she was shown into our Baker Street sitting-room in the company of her solicitor, Mr Ralph Berkinshaw.

She was a dainty, dark-haired young lady endowed with the most exquisite beauty but who bore on her delicate features an expression of great distress. I recall that, as she was introduced to me and I took her small, black-gloved hand in mine, I felt a sudden surge of protective compassion towards her.

It was an attitude clearly shared by her lawyer. Mr Berkinshaw, who was in his middle thirties, was a tall, self-assured man with pale, rather heavy features, and was distinguished mainly by the elegance of his attire and his Nordic colouring. This was particularly evident in his flaxen hair and moustache, both of which were stylishly trimmed. I observed that he treated his client with great solicitude, personally conducting her to a chair and, throughout the early part of the interview, casting anxious glances in her direction to assure himself that what he was saying was not causing her too much pain.

He began by apologising for having called without an appointment.

'However, the matter is of such urgency,' he continued, 'that there was no time to write an explanatory letter. My client's husband, Mr Eugene Mortimer, disappeared yesterday under unusual circumstances and has not been seen since. Mrs Mortimer, who is naturally most concerned about her husband's whereabouts, wishes you to undertake enquiries on her behalf.'

'Have the police been informed?' Holmes asked.

'Yes, indeed they have. Mrs Mortimer called at my office in the Strand earlier this morning and, as soon as she told me that her husband had not returned home last night, I accompanied her to Scotland Yard where I informed Inspector Lestrade of the situation. I understand a colleague of his, Inspector Gregson,[1] will make enquiries at the London end while Inspector Lestrade intends leaving for Essex this morning to find out if Mr Eugene Mortimer arrived there by train as he should have done yesterday afternoon.'

'Essex? Why Essex?'

'I had an appointment to meet him at Woodside Grange, which is close to the small village of Boxstead, in order to discuss with him the estate of his late uncle. He had agreed to travel down on the 2.10 train from Liverpool Street station. When he failed to appear, I assumed he had been taken ill. However, I understand from Mrs Mortimer that her husband left his house in Hampstead yesterday afternoon, fully intending to catch that train. That is so, is it not, my dear lady?'

'Yes, it is,' the lady replied in a low voice. 'Eugene set off in good time for the station. He told me he would return by the 6.25 when he expected his business with Mr Berkinshaw would be completed. When he had not arrived home by eight o'clock, I assumed he had been delayed. At ten, when he had still not returned, I became seriously concerned about his welfare, assuming in my

[1] Inspector Tobias Gregson, whom Mr Sherlock Holmes refers to as 'the smartest of the Scotland Yarders', investigated several cases in which Mr Holmes was also involved. They are 'The Sign of Four', 'A Study in Scarlet', 'The Adventure of the Greek Interpreter', 'The Adventure of the Red Circle' and 'Wisteria Lodge'. Dr John F. Watson.

turn he had been taken ill or had met with an accident. However, there was nothing I could do. It was too late to send a telegram or to travel down to Essex myself to make enquiries. As I did not know Mr Berkinshaw's home address, I was forced to wait until this morning when I could call at his office to find out if he knew where my husband was or what had happened to him.'

At the memory of that long and lonely vigil, her courage faltered and, with a little sob, she pressed her handkerchief to her lips and turned away her lovely face.

Mr Berkinshaw rose immediately to his feet and held out his hand to her.

'I beg you, Mrs Mortimer, to return home to your little boy. The cab is waiting downstairs to drive you back to Hampstead. It will only cause you further distress to remain here.'

'But will you accept the case, Mr Holmes?' the lady asked, turning to my companion, the tears welling up in her eyes.

'Indeed I shall,' Holmes assured her.

This promise seemed to offer her some consolation, for I heard her murmur, 'Thank God!' under her breath as Mr Berkinshaw, holding her tenderly by the elbow, escorted her from the room.

Holmes and I waited for his return, I still deeply touched by Mrs Mortimer's plight, as well as curious to learn from her solicitor the full story behind her husband's disappearance. Holmes, however, seemed more concerned with the latter consideration for, as soon as the door had closed behind them, he went straight across to the bookcase to refer to his copy of Bradshaw.[2]

'I see,' he murmured half to himself, 'that the 2.10 from Liverpool Street station is a slow train and was due to arrive at Boxstead Halt at 3.55, where I assume Mr Mortimer should have alighted.'

He broke off as Mr Berkinshaw returned. 'A very brave little lady,' the solicitor remarked, resuming his seat. 'Despite her great distress, she insisted on accompanying me here, Mr Holmes. May I also say how much comfort it has given her to know you will enquire into the affair?

'Now, sir,' he continued more briskly, taking out his pocket watch and consulting its dial, 'time is pressing and as we are both busy professional men, I shall give you as concise an account as possible of the circumstances surrounding Mr Mortimer's disappearance and why I had asked him to travel down to Essex in the first place.

'As I said, it concerned the estate of his late uncle, Mr Franklin Mortimer, an exceedingly wealthy bachelor who, on his retirement, bought Woodside Grange where he lived until his death in May. In his will, he left his considerable fortune to be divided equally between his two nephews, Mr Eugene Mortimer, his brother's son, and Mr Johnathen Smith, the son of his sister who had married a Mr Bartholomew Smith, a farmer in Shropshire. I should also explain that, since the death of my own

---

[2] Bradshaw's *Railway Guide*, giving train timetables, was published monthly. Dr John F. Watson.

father three years ago, I have assumed legal responsibility for the late Mr Mortimer's affairs.

'As both nephews were already settled in their own homes, Mr Smith on the family farm in Shropshire and Mr Eugene Mortimer in his house in Hampstead, it was decided that Woodside Grange together with its contents should be sold at auction and the proceeds added to the Mortimer estate. According to the terms of the will, an inventory has been drawn up and a valuation placed on each separate item by an expert from Christie and Manson's[3] prior to the sale, which is due to take place in two days' time. These documents had to be jointly signed by the two heirs in one another's presence. It was for this reason that I had asked them to travel down to Woodside Grange yesterday afternoon in order for them to look over the inventory and the valuations and, once they had agreed to them, to add their signatures.

'As I was busy with other clients in the morning, I could not arrange to meet them at any other time.

'I myself travelled down to Woodside Grange a little earlier to complete work on the documents and to make final arrangements for the forthcoming sale with the late Mr Franklin Mortimer's housekeeper and gardener, Mr and Mrs Deakin, who are still living at the house and acting as caretakers.

---

[3] Christie and Manson's Auction Rooms were situated off St James's Square and were well known for their sales of art treasures. In 'The Adventure of the Illustrious Client', Mr Sherlock Holmes says of a Ming saucer: 'No finer piece ever passed through Christie's.' Dr John F. Watson.

'Mr Eugene Mortimer was, as I said, due to catch the 2.10 train from London.'

'Which, according to Bradshaw, would have arrived at Boxstead Halt at 3.55,' Holmes interjected.

'Exactly so, Mr Holmes. It is the nearest station, being a mere quarter of an hour's walk from the Grange. As it is infrequently used, there is no conveyance available for passengers. Mr Eugene Mortimer, who was aware of this, was prepared to make his way to the house on foot. I expected him at about ten past four.

'As Shropshire is too far away to make consultation easy, Mr Johnathen Smith is staying at a hotel in London until his late uncle's affairs are settled. For reasons which I shall shortly explain, he preferred not to travel down to Essex with his cousin, but caught a different train, the one which left Liverpool Street station at twenty past two. As it is a fast train, it does not stop at Boxstead Halt but continues on to the town of Fordham, three miles away by road. I myself had arrived at Fordham earlier in the afternoon and had driven over to the Grange in a hired dog-cart. I had offered to return to Fordham and meet Mr Smith off his train but he declined, preferring to take the short cut across the fields, the weather being so fine and dry. It is a pleasant walk and would take, I suppose, about half an hour. However, he accepted my invitation to accompany me in the dog-cart back to Fordham after our business was completed. We had agreed to journey back to London together on the 6.12 train.

'I come now to the reason why the two cousins preferred

to travel separately. There was a long-standing quarrel between them caused by rivalry over the same young lady whom you have just met.'

'You are referring to Mrs Eugene Mortimer?' Holmes enquired.

'Indeed I am,' Mr Berkinshaw replied, inclining his flaxen head. 'Before her marriage, she was Miss Constance Hunt, the only daughter of a close friend of the late Mr Franklin Mortimer. On Mr Hunt's death several years ago, Mr Franklin Mortimer took a paternal interest in her welfare, in the course of which he introduced her to his nephews.

'As you and Dr Watson have seen for yourselves, she is a charming young lady and it was perhaps inevitable that both the cousins should fall in love with her. However, her choice fell on Mr Eugene Mortimer and she subsequently accepted his proposal of marriage. I understand that Mr Johnathen Smith was exceedingly jealous to the extent that on the evening the engagement was announced, he struck his cousin Eugene and knocked him to the ground. They have not met since and, whenever they called on their late uncle, always made sure their visits never coincided. Indeed, so strong was their mutual antipathy that I was forced to arrange separate appointments with them in my office.

'It is possible you may make Mr Smith's acquaintance during the course of your enquiries, Mr Holmes, and while I do not wish to prejudice you against him in any way, I think you will agree with me that he is an impulsive and hot-headed young man, quite capable of violent action.

'I come now to the events of yesterday afternoon. As I have already explained, I expected Mr Eugene Mortimer to arrive at the Grange at ten past four and Mr Johnathen Smith about five minutes later.

'To be frank, Mr Holmes, I was not looking forward to the occasion. It was the first time the cousins had met face to face since their quarrel six years earlier and, had it not been necessary for them both to be present when the inventory and valuations were inspected and signed, I should have preferred to see them separately.

'As subsequent events were to prove, the meeting had to be abandoned for, although Mr Smith duly arrived, his cousin failed to keep the appointment. We waited for over an hour, expecting him on a later train but at length, with Mr Smith's agreement, I cancelled the meeting and we left together for Fordham to catch the next train back to town.

'It was not until this morning when Mrs Mortimer called at my office, most anxious about her husband's whereabouts, that I realised he had disappeared.

'I now feel able to voice certain misgivings which I could not have expressed in her presence. They concern Mr Johnathen Smith's conduct yesterday afternoon.

'When he arrived at the Grange, I noticed he was highly agitated, a state of mind I put down to his reluctance to come face to face with his cousin. In addition, he was somewhat dishevelled in appearance.

'At the time, I thought little of it. However, when

Mrs Mortimer informed me of her husband's disappearance, I recalled these facts which I feel it is my duty to pass on to you, Mr Holmes, now that you have agreed to take on the case. They may, of course, have no bearing on your own enquiries. I sincerely trust that they do not.'

'You think that Mr Smith may have been involved in his cousin's disappearance?' Holmes asked abruptly.

Mr Berkinshaw seemed taken aback by his directness.

'It is not my place to draw conclusions. I leave that to you and the official police. However, as I have agreed to act as Mrs Mortimer's legal adviser in this affair, I have to bear her interests in mind and those of her small son. In her husband's absence, she has no one else to turn to. I have already passed the same information regarding Mr Smith to Inspector Lestrade. It seemed only right that you should also be apprised of those facts.

'I intend going down later today to Boxstead in case Inspector Lestrade should require my assistance. I have already sent a telegram to Mrs Deakin, the housekeeper, warning her to expect me. I assume that you, too, will prefer to begin your own enquiries in Essex, rather than in London?'

'In view of what you have told me, it seems the logical place to start,' Holmes agreed.

'Then perhaps we may travel together?' Mr Berkinshaw suggested pleasantly, rising and holding out his hand. 'I propose catching the 2.10 from Liverpool Street station, the one which Mr Eugene Mortimer should have caught yesterday.'

'Dr Watson and I shall be on it,' Holmes assured him, accompanying him to the door.

On his return, he held up a warning hand.

'No, Watson,' said he, 'not a word about the case. I refuse to discuss it until we have found if Mr Eugene Mortimer did indeed arrive at Boxstead Halt yesterday afternoon. Until that simple fact is established, we shall be indulging in mere speculation. Even Inspector Lestrade is aware of its importance to the investigation, for he is apparently travelling down to Essex with that same question in mind. And now, my dear fellow, if you care to pass over those papers lying beside you on the table, I shall continue my study of the Saltmarsh affair, a curious business but one at least in which the main evidence is beyond doubt.'

There was no further discussion of the Smith-Mortimer case, not even later on the train down to Essex in company with Mr Berkinshaw, Holmes making it clear that he preferred a more general conversation.

It ranged over a series of topics until the train drew into Boxstead Halt, a small rural station, where we alighted and where Holmes immediately sought out a railway official. The only one he found on duty was a rubicund, middle-aged man who appeared to combine the functions of station-master and porter as well as ticket-clerk and collector.

On Holmes' enquiring if a gentleman had alighted from the 3.55 train the previous afternoon, he answered at once in a strong local accent.

'Yes, 'ee did, sur. I punched 'is ticket for 'un meself. A return it was, from Lunnon. You're the second gen'leman to be asking after 'im. T'other one was a lean, ferrety-faced fellow in a tweed suit; said 'e was from Scotland Yard.'

'Inspector Lestrade,' Holmes said, suppressing a smile at this unflattering description.

''Ee didn't give 'is name. 'Ee just asked about the passenger off the train. Well, I'll tell 'ee the same as I told 'im. The gen'leman set off up the road in the direction of the Grange. I know, 'cos I watched him as far as the bend by that little wood. After that, I lost sight of 'im be'ind the trees. And that's all I knows.'

'So it would appear then,' remarked Holmes as he thanked the man and we passed through the station barrier, 'that Mr Eugene Mortimer arrived safely. That fact, at least, is now established.'

'But disappeared somewhere along this road before he reached the Grange,' Mr Berkinshaw interjected, his features assuming a most grave expression.

'Which lies where?'

'Over to our left behind that small beech wood which is where the station-master last saw him. You may just catch a glimpse of the chimneys above the tree-tops,' Mr Berkinshaw explained, pointing towards a copse, the foliage of which was already turning russet-coloured with the onset of autumn.

'Then let us follow the same route,' Holmes proposed.

The road was little wider than a lane and meandered along in the desultory fashion of such rural byways between high hedges. There were no footpaths, only wide grassy verges.

After about a five minutes' walk, we reached the copse and the turning where the road swung sharply to the left in the direction of the Grange, which was where Mr Eugene Mortimer had disappeared from view.

It was also here, as we turned the corner, that we caught sight of Inspector Lestrade.

He was standing in the centre of the road, in company with another officer in uniform, a stout, red-faced man, and was directing the activities of half a dozen constables who, like beaters at a pheasant shoot, were making their way slowly along the verges, searching the hedges and peering over gates into adjoining fields.

Several conveyances, including a gig and a wagonette, were drawn up at the roadside.

Inspector Lestrade came forward to meet us, shaking hands cordially with Mr Berkinshaw but greeting Holmes and me more coolly.

'I think it is hardly worth your trouble coming all the way down from London, Mr Holmes,' he remarked. 'But since you are here, let me introduce you to Inspector Jenks of the Essex Constabulary whom I telegraphed this morning to meet me at Boxstead Halt. As soon as we discovered Mr Eugene Mortimer had indeed arrived off the London train, he sent his sergeant to Fordham for extra men to help in the search for the missing gentleman. They arrived only ten minutes ago so we have not yet proceeded very far. I should add,' Lestrade continued with a self-satisfied smile, 'that I have been asked to take charge of the investigation. In the meantime, there is little either you or Dr Watson can do. I suggest you accompany Mr Berkinshaw to Woodside Grange where you will find Mr Johnathen Smith.'

'Mr Smith is here?' Mr Berkinshaw asked in great surprise.

Inspector Lestrade's smile broadened.

'We don't let the grass grow under our feet at Scotland Yard, sir. Soon after you called on me this morning, I went round to see Mr Smith at his hotel on my way to Liverpool Street station in order to inform him of his cousin's disappearance, about which he denies all knowledge. He insisted on coming down here to Boxstead.'

'Then he is not under arrest?' Holmes put in quickly.

'No, Mr Holmes. He is merely helping with enquiries. However, as it is clear Mr Eugene Mortimer disappeared somewhere in this vicinity and Mr Smith was in the neighbourhood at the same time . . .'

He broke off as one of the constables, who was searching the right-hand side of the lane ahead of us, raised an arm and called out urgently, 'Over here, Inspector!'

Lestrade set off along the road at a brisk pace, Holmes and I, together with Mr Berkinshaw and Inspector Jenks, following hard at his heels.

The constable was standing by a gate which gave access to a meadow.

As soon as we reached the place, we could see what had attracted the man's attention. Lying in the field, about three yards from the gateway, was a bowler hat.

'Good man!' Lestrade exclaimed, clapping the constable on the shoulder.

He was about to open the gate and retrieve the hat when Holmes put out a hand to detain him.

'One moment, Inspector,' said he. 'There is something else here which I think you should examine first.'

'And what is that?' Lestrade demanded, reluctantly turning back.

Holmes was pointing to the verge.

'If you look to the right of the gate you will see the grass is flattened as if someone has been standing there. There is also a cigar butt lying nearby; a Dutch cheroot, if I am not mistaken.'

Mr Berkinshaw gave a violent start. 'Are you sure, Mr Holmes?'

'Without a doubt. Its thinness makes it quite distinctive. You seem shocked by the discovery?'

'I have noticed Mr Smith is in the habit of smoking Dutch cheroots,' Mr Berkinshaw replied in a pained voice.

'Is that so?' Lestrade exclaimed. 'Then that could be crucial evidence. I am surprised the constable failed to notice it.'

Stooping down, he picked up the cigar butt, placing it in an envelope which he stowed away carefully in his pocket while the constable, so recently praised, looked on, much abashed.

'And now,' said Lestrade, opening the gate, 'for the bowler hat.'

'Which I have no doubt will prove to be the property of the missing heir,' Holmes murmured to me in an aside.

I looked at him somewhat askance, finding it difficult to judge his mood. There was the familiar air of suppressed excitement about him which was always evident at the beginning of a case. But on this occasion, it was tempered by a touch of wry amusement which I could not account for unless it was caused by Lestrade's criticism of the constable when the inspector himself had failed to observe either the cigar butt or the flattened grass.

But whatever had aroused my old friend's derision, his prediction concerning the ownership of the bowler hat proved correct for, as we caught up with the others who had gone ahead of us, we heard Lestrade give an exclamation of triumph as he turned the hat over to examine the inner band.

'See here, gentlemen!' said he. 'The letters E.M.! I think you will agree it must be Mr Eugene Mortimer's. The question now is – where is its owner?'

Holmes, showing scant interest in Lestrade's discovery, had strolled a few yards further on, hands clasped behind his back, head lowered, apparently following some faint traces in the grass which only he had noticed.

He came to a halt beside a clump of bushes where he remained standing for several moments. Then, taking out his pocket lens, he scrutinised one of those bushes closely before turning and walking back to where we were still clustered about Lestrade.

'Inspector,' said he quietly, 'if you care to walk in that direction, you will find, hidden in the undergrowth, the body of a man which I have no doubt Mr Berkinshaw will identify as that of Mr Eugene Mortimer. Judging by the cord about his neck, he has been strangled.

'However, before you hasten off, may I draw your attention to the two faint parallel tracks in the grass? It was they which led me to the body. They suggest that whoever committed the murder dragged his victim along by the armpits, causing the heels of the dead man's boots to make those tracks. You will, however, find no footprints. The ground is unfortunately too dry.

'Caught on a bramble close by the body, you will also find a coat button to which a few light brown threads are still attached.'

I saw Lestrade exchange a significant glance with Inspector Jenks at this last piece of information and then the two of them, accompanied by Mr Berkinshaw, hurried off towards the clump of bushes, taking care not to tread on the tracks which Holmes had indicated.

'You are not coming, Holmes?' I enquired when he showed no sign of following after them.

'No, Watson. I have seen enough. But do not let me prevent you from making your own examination of the body. As a medical man, you will be able to advise Lestrade as to an approximate time of death.'

The corpse, that of a young man in his early thirties,

lay in a dry, shallow ditch and was almost completely concealed by a thick undergrowth of brambles. It was turned on its side so that most of the features were mercifully hidden from view, apart from one cheek, livid with suffused blood, and the back of the neck where the cord used to strangle him had bitten deep into the flesh.

He had been dead for at least twenty hours, judging by the rigidity of the muscles,[4] information I passed on to Inspector Lestrade who, as I arrived, was in the act of removing a small brown button which was caught on a nearby bramble.

'You have identified him?' I asked of Mr Berkinshaw, although I already knew from his grave expression as well as those of the two inspectors that the body was indeed that of the missing Eugene Mortimer.

'I am sorry to say I have,' Mr Berkinshaw replied. 'It is a dreadful business, Dr Watson. I do not know how I shall break the news to his widow. She will be inconsolable.'

'And it will not help her to know that the evidence suggests her husband's cousin may have committed the murder,' Lestrade interjected.

Mr Berkinshaw was quick to object to this remark. 'Surely you are jumping to conclusions, Inspector?'

'I think not, Mr Berkinshaw. You yourself have

---

[4] Rigor mortis, which becomes fully established in about twelve hours, lasts for a further twelve before taking the same number of hours to pass off. Dr John F. Watson.

admitted that the cigar butt found by the gate is the same brand as those smoked by Mr Smith. There is also the question of motive. Jealousy. A very powerful emotion is jealousy. It is quite clear Smith harboured a long-standing grudge against his cousin for marrying the woman he himself loved. Then there is this button with the brown threads. You saw Mr Smith yesterday, Mr Berkinshaw. What type of coat was he wearing?'

'A light brown tweed ulster,' Mr Berkinshaw replied unhappily.

'From which I have no doubt you will find a button is missing,' a voice said. While we were talking, Holmes had come up quietly to join us for, when we looked round, he was standing behind us, regarding Lestrade with a smile on his lips. 'You have also forgotten to mention the matter of opportunity.'

'I was coming to that,' Lestrade said. 'I have already made a few quick calculations. Smith's train got in at Fordham at a quarter to four. It is a half-hour's walk across the fields to the Grange. However, if Smith doubled his normal pace, he could have arrived in time to accost Mr Eugene Mortimer on his way from Boxstead Halt. It would have taken him no more than a few minutes to murder his cousin and hide his body in the ditch. He then hurried on to the house, arriving in an agitated and dishevelled state which you yourself remarked on, MrBerkinshaw.

'I therefore propose questioning Mr Smith in the light of the evidence I have uncovered. If it can be proved that the button came from his coat, I shall have no other choice than to arrest him. Inspector Jenks, I shall leave you to arrange for the removal of the body to the mortuary and to send one of the constables up to the Grange with the gig in case it is needed to take Mr Smith into custody. In the meantime, if the rest of you gentlemen care to accompany me to the house, we shall see what our suspect has to say for himself.'

II

Woodside Grange, a large, imposing mansion, lay a little distance away, set back from the road at the end of a long carriage drive.

On the way, we passed the stile which gave access to the footpath leading to Fordham, a mere five minutes' walk from the gateway where it was assumed the murder had taken place, a fact which Lestrade commented on with satisfaction.

'It further proves my point that Smith could have had the opportunity,' he said.

Holmes made no reply. We were approaching the house and he seemed more interested in looking about him, especially at the lawn and shrubbery of the front garden.

Mr Berkinshaw rang the doorbell and we were admitted into a large hall by a plump, grey-haired woman dressed in black whom he introduced as Mrs Deakin, the late Mr Franklin Mortimer's housekeeper.

On his enquiring where Mr Smith was to be found, she replied, 'In the drawing-room, sir,' and turned as if to lead the way when Lestrade called her back.

'One moment, Mrs Deakin,' said he. 'Was Mr Smith wearing an overcoat when he arrived?'

'He was, sir.'

'Where is it?'

'I hung it over there, sir.'

'I should like to see it.'

'Very good, sir,' said the woman.

Going to a large coat stand in a corner of the hall, she returned with a light brown tweed ulster which she handed to the inspector. Then, at a gesture from Mr Berkinshaw, she left us, but not before she had cast an anxious glance in our direction.

Lestrade examined the coat eagerly, turning it over before pointing with an exultant cry to the cuff of the right-hand sleeve, where a button was plainly missing.

'That settles it, gentlemen,' said he. 'I think no further proof is needed of Smith's guilt. The remaining buttons exactly match the one I found near the body.'

Folding the coat over his arm, he hurried ahead of us into the drawing-room.

It was a magnificent room, furnished in the most splendid fashion. But it was not the pictures hanging upon the walls nor the displays of silver and porcelain which drew my attention. It was the tall figure of a man who was pacing restlessly up and down, smoking a thin cheroot which he crushed out into an ashtray as we entered.

Johnathen Smith was over six feet in height, powerfully built and with a rugged handsomeness about his features which were deeply tanned from a life spent in the open air. There was an impatience about his manner, evident in his hot blue eyes, as he confronted Lestrade.

Here was a man, I thought, who, if roused, would be capable of violence.

'Well, Inspector,' said he roughly, ignoring the rest of us. 'I assume your investigation is over and I am cleared of any suspicion of involvement in Eugene's disappearance? It was a ridiculous imputation in the first place.'

'My enquiries are indeed complete,' Lestrade informed him grimly. 'We found your cousin's body a short time ago in a field not far from the house.'

'Eugene dead!' Smith cried, staggering back. 'But how has it happened? Was there an accident?'

'No, Mr Smith. He was strangled. And I have good reason to believe you were responsible for his death. It is therefore my duty to charge you with Mr Eugene Mortimer's murder and to warn you that anything you say may be used in evidence against you.'

As Lestrade intoned the solemn words of the official charge, Holmes glanced at me and motioned with his head towards the door.

We slipped quietly from the room.

'Where are we going, Holmes?' I enquired as he set off

at a fast pace across the hall and down a passage which led to the rear of the house.

'To find Mrs Deakin and make a few enquiries of her,' he replied.

'Enquiries? But surely the investigation is over? Lestrade has arrested Smith and quite rightly so, in my opinion. All the evidence points to his guilt.'

'I agree with you, Watson. The case against Smith looks black indeed. But it has always been my first principle to examine all evidence with a healthy degree of scepticism, especially when it is circumstantial, as it is in this case.[5] It is then most vital to ask the question: Exactly what set of circumstances is one looking at? It is like a child's kaleidoscope. Shake it and the pieces form an entirely different pattern. Ah, I believe this must be the housekeeper's room. I hear voices inside,' Holmes concluded, coming to a halt in the passage and tapping on a door.

A woman called out to us to come in and we entered a small, cosily furnished chamber where we found Mrs Deakin seated at the table in the company of a tall, bearded man; her husband, as we discovered when she introduced him.

Holmes set about the interview briskly, first asking

---

[5] In 'The Boscombe Valley Mystery', Mr Sherlock Holmes refers to circumstantial evidence as 'a very tricky thing' which 'may seem to point straight to one thing, but if you shift your point of view a little, you may find it pointing in an equally uncompromising manner to something entirely different.' Dr John F. Watson.

Mrs Deakin to describe in the fullest detail exactly what had occurred at Woodside Grange the previous day, starting with the arrival of Mr Berkinshaw.

He had driven up to the house, said she, at about half-past two in a hired dog-cart, bringing with him a valise containing documents which concerned the late Mr Franklin Mortimer's estate. As he wished to work on them undisturbed, she had shown him into the study.

Mr Eugene Mortimer was expected at ten past four, his cousin shortly afterwards.

'Who let Mr Smith in?' Holmes enquired.

'Mr Berkinshaw, sir. He told me he would answer the door to both the visitors, Mr Johnathen and Mr Eugene.'

'Where were you?

'In the small pantry, sir. As all the household effects are to be sold, he asked me to clean the table silver and put it away in its boxes.'

'And where is this pantry?'

'At the side of the house, sir.'

'Near the kitchen?'

'No, sir. It is at the far end of the passage,' Mrs Deakin replied, sounding bewildered at this fusillade of questions.

'And you, Mr Deakin, were meanwhile cutting and raking the lawn at the front of the house?' Holmes asked, turning to her husband.

The man looked surprised.

'That I was, sir. Mr Berkinshaw sent me out to tidy up the front garden. A lot of people are expected at the auction and he wanted the place looking its best.'

'And very trim it looks, too, Mr Deakin. I noticed the grass was newly cut as I came up the drive. I suppose you saw Mr Smith arrive?'

'I did, sir.'

'And Mr Berkinshaw admitted him?'

'That's right. He came to the front door himself.'

'Did anyone leave the house between the arrival of Mr Berkinshaw and the departure of the two gentlemen later that afternoon?'

'No, sir.'

'You are quite sure of that?'

'Oh, yes, sir. I was out in the front garden all afternoon and I swear no one came or went. Mr Berkinshaw was sat at the desk in the study window, working away at his papers.'

'You actually saw him writing?' Holmes demanded sharply.

'Why, yes, sir. As I was going up and down the lawn, I could see him quite plain, sitting there in his black coat, his pen scribbling away and that fair head of his bent down over the desk. He didn't move from his chair. And then, after Mr Smith arrived, I could see them both in the drawing-room from time to time, looking out for Mr Eugene. But he never came, sir.'

The man hesitated and, after exchanging a glance with his wife, burst out, 'Has Mr Eugene been found, sir? Me and the wife are so worried about him. We know both the gentlemen well from the visits they used to pay to my late master.'

'I am afraid Mr Eugene Mortimer is dead,' Holmes said gravely, 'and Mr Smith has been arrested for his murder.'

Mrs Deakin cried out in disbelief and, covering her face with her hands, broke into the most bitter sobs.

Deakin regarded us stonily, although I saw his eyes had filled with tears.

'I do not believe Mr Johnathen is guilty,' said he in a tone of quiet assurance. 'Quick-tempered he might be, Mr Holmes, but he'd never harm anybody. I know him and Mr Eugene quarrelled over the young lady and Mr Johnathen knocked his cousin down. But murder him? Never, sir! Mr Johnathen loved Miss Constance too tenderly to cause her any unhappiness or deprive her little son of his father.'

Putting his arm about his wife's shoulders, he led her to a chair.

Holmes touched my arm and we went quietly from the room, leaving the Deakins to their grief.

'Where now, Holmes?' I asked, hurrying to catch up with him as he strode down the passage.

'To the study which must be in the front of the house. Deakin said he could see Mr Berkinshaw through its window.'

We reached the hall and Holmes flung open a door.

It led into a square, sunny room, smaller than the drawing-room and furnished less sumptuously. A plain mahogany desk stood at right angles to a long sash window which overlooked the drive and the lawn. A swivel chair, such as one might find in an office, was placed behind it.

The bookcases lining the walls and a pair of armchairs, covered in buttoned red velvet, which were drawn up in front of the fireplace, gave it the comfortable air of the smoking-room in a gentlemen's club.

Holmes stood for a few moments just inside the door, surveying the room and its contents. Then, moving swiftly forward, he examined first the desk, paying particular attention to the blotting-pad which lay upon it, the top sheet of which he scanned eagerly with his pocket lens. He then inspected the swivel chair, spinning it round to peer at its slatted back.

From the desk, he moved to the fireplace, picking up the brass poker which was propped up against the fender and scrutinising that, too, with the aid of the lens, before passing to the bolster cushions on the two armchairs. These he lifted in turn, subjecting each to the same rapid but scrupulous examination.

It was only when the last cushion had been replaced that Holmes seemed satisfied, although I was greatly puzzled.

'I have seen enough, Watson,' said he. 'I shall now lock this room and leave the key in Mrs Deakin's care with strict instructions that nothing in it is to be disturbed until tomorrow.'

'Tomorrow? You intend returning then? For what purpose, Holmes? Surely Smith's guilt is beyond all doubt? Besides, Mr Berkinshaw has an alibi for the murder.'

Holmes chuckled softly. 'I should not wish to spoil your pleasure by explaining. You shall witness all in good time, my dear fellow, when we shall give the kaleidoscope another shake and see what new pattern emerges. But not a word to Lestrade or anyone else on this matter.'

There was, in fact, no need for concealment. When we returned to the drawing-room, we found that the inspector had already left, taking Smith into custody in Fordham, and only Mr Berkinshaw remained.

The three of us departed shortly afterwards for London, the conversation on the train turning entirely on the iniquity of Smith's crime and the dreadful effect it would have on Mrs Mortimer and her small son, for whom Mr Berkinshaw expressed the utmost compassion.

There was no reference to Holmes' plans for the following day, either then or on our return to Baker Street, and I was left to ponder alone on the significance of his remark concerning the kaleidoscope and the new evidence he expected to discover.

III

Holmes was out all morning on some mysterious errand of his own which I assumed was connected with his enquiries into the Smith-Mortimer case, although he refused to discuss that with me either. Nor would he reveal what was in the small carpet bag he took with him on the journey to Essex.

We caught the 2.10 slow train from Liverpool Street station, the same one we had taken the previous afternoon, alighting at Boxstead Halt.

However, as we were leaving the station, Holmes suddenly announced, 'You go on ahead, Watson. There is a small matter I must attend to first. I shall catch up with you shortly.'

Assuming he wished to make further enquiries of the station-master, I set off alone, passing the gate where

Johnathen Smith had lain in wait for his cousin before strangling him and dragging his body into the ditch.

It was a pleasant September day, the air crisp and dry, the mellow sunshine falling on field and hedgerow, rich with autumn colours.

But to my eyes, the scene was tinged with melancholy as I thought of Mrs Eugene Mortimer, left widowed and her little son fatherless.

Deakin was again raking the lawn at the front of the house as I reached the end of the long drive to Woodside Grange. A dog-cart and a four-wheeled cab also stood before the door, suggesting the presence of several visitors. I was surprised by this as I had imagined that whatever business had brought Holmes and myself back to Boxstead, it would concern only the two of us.

I was even more astonished when, on reaching the porch steps, the front door opened and Holmes appeared on the threshold.

'Holmes!' I cried. 'I left you at the station. How on earth have you managed to arrive before me?'

'Never mind that now, Watson. There are more urgent matters to attend to first. I want you to go to the drawing-room, where you will find Inspector Lestrade and Mr Berkinshaw already waiting. I sent them telegrams this morning, asking them to take the 2.20 train to Fordham. They arrived a short time ago. At my request, Inspector Jenks has accompanied them. I shall join you as soon as my own preparations are complete, which should take no more than a minute or two. And no questions, my dear fellow,' he added, bustling me inside the house.

I found Mr Berkinshaw and the two inspectors as much in the dark as I, for as I entered the drawing-room, all three men jumped to their feet to enquire what plans Holmes had in mind. I had begun to explain that I knew no more than they when Holmes put his head round the door with the suggestion that we take a little stroll together in the garden.

Much mystified, we followed him out of the house and down the porch steps to the lawn where we began to walk slowly across the grass towards a clump of rhododendron bushes on the far side, Holmes remarking as we went on the beauty of our surroundings.

'Now, see here, Mr Holmes,' Lestrade broke in impatiently. 'I have not come all the way down from London to discuss the merits of the ornamental shrubbery over the herbaceous border. In your telegram, you mentioned new evidence. Inspector Jenks and I would like to know what it is.'

'What new evidence?' Mr Berkinshaw demanded before Holmes could reply. 'You said nothing about it in your telegram to me.'

Holmes smiled benevolently.

'Then, gentlemen,' said he, 'since you appear to regard our afternoon walk as a waste of time, shall we return to the house? You will find there all the evidence you need.'

Turning on his heel, he set briskly off, the rest of us, after exchanging bewildered glances, hurrying to catch up with him.

However, we had hardly gone a few paces than he stopped suddenly and, flinging out an arm, pointed dramatically to the front of Woodside Grange.

'Great heavens!' he cried. 'Who is that? But it is impossible!'

For a moment, the four of us stared in silence before breaking out into exclamations of astonishment at what we saw. For seated at the study window was the unmistakable figure of Mr Ralph Berkinshaw in his black coat, his flaxen head bent over the desk, writing with a pen on a document which lay before him.

The effect on Mr Berkinshaw of this double of himself was even more dramatic than Holmes' outflung gesture which had first drawn our attention to it.

With a cry of mingled horror and rage, he began to run towards the house like a man demented. So rapid was his flight that he had reached the study door and was struggling in vain to turn the handle before we caught up with him.

'Stand aside, Mr Berkinshaw,' Holmes told him coolly, taking a key from his pocket. 'The game is over. Now, sir, will you accompany us quietly into the study? Or shall I ask Inspector Jenks to put you in handcuffs and take you out to the waiting cab? The choice is yours. You prefer to come with us? Then,' Holmes continued, as he turned the key in the lock and flung the door open, 'you shall sit over there in that chair and you shall not utter a word until I have finished my account.'

As Mr Berkinshaw, looking much shaken, sat down,

Holmes took up his own position in front of the desk, facing the chair on which was sitting, as we discovered on closer examination, nothing more than a dummy.

It consisted of a bolster from one of the armchairs, propped up against the back of the chair, a black coat draped across it. The brass poker from the fender, wedged between the slats, supported a blond wig, tilted at such an angle that it gave the impression of a head bending down over the desk. On the right-hand side, the jacket sleeve, padded out with paper, was drawn forward across the surface, concealing the base of a metronome but not its rod, which was ticking busily backwards and forwards. As it did so, it gave the most realistic motion to what seemed to be a black pen fastened to the shaft.

'A deception, gentlemen, as you see, but a very ingenious one,' Holmes announced. 'To anyone standing in the garden, Mr Berkinshaw appeared to be seated at his desk, engaged in working on his papers. It certainly convinced Deakin whom Mr Berkinshaw had asked to cut and rake the lawn. By this means, he established an alibi for himself, for Deakin was prepared to swear that, at the time Eugene Mortimer was murdered, Mr Berkinshaw had not left the house but was writing in the study.

'If you care to examine the metronome more carefully, you will see exactly how the illusion of the moving pen was achieved. The upper part of the casing has been removed, leaving the rod exposed. To that, I have attached a strip of black paper with a tiny blob of sealing-wax, to give the appearance of a penholder. I then adjusted the weight on the shaft so that it moved to and fro at a convincing speed.[6] Once fully wound up, the clockwork mechanism would run for at least an hour, which allowed Mr Berkinshaw plenty of time to commit the murder. You wished to say something, Lestrade? I see from your expression that you are not entirely convinced by my explanation.'

'To be frank, Mr Holmes, I cannot see what put you on to this little stratagem in the first place.'

'The evidence, of course,' Holmes replied. 'What else could it be based on? As shall soon become clear, my suspicions of Mr Berkinshaw were already aroused. So yesterday afternoon, I made a point of examining the study and noticed several small but revealing features.

'First, there were fresh scratches on the two middle slats in the back of the chair, suggesting something had been thrust between them. As the handle of the brass poker had similar marks corresponding to those scratches, it was logical to deduce that it was this that had caused them. But to what purpose? This became clearer when I examined the bolsters on the armchairs and discovered that one of them had flaxen hairs clinging to the velvet; not, as might be expected, in the centre of the cushion where a head would normally rest, but on one of its ends. From this evidence, a picture began to emerge of an

---

[6] From the information given here by Mr Sherlock Holmes, I have constructed a similar device using a metronome and a slip of paper and I can assure readers that it works satisfactorily. Dr John F. Watson.

upended bolster, a head of flaxen hair, and a poker thrust through the slats of the chair.

'I had already noticed something unusual about the sheet of blotting-paper on the desk. If you care to examine it, gentlemen, you shall see for yourselves what it was.'

'But it is perfectly clean!' Lestrade protested, bending down to look.

'Exactly!' Holmes exclaimed. 'And yet Mr Berkinshaw apparently sat writing at this desk for at least an hour and a half. Is it not curious that, in all that time, he never once needed to blot his papers? However, you are wrong, Lestrade, in thinking it entirely free of marks. If you examine it more closely you will see four small, round indentations pressed into the blotting-paper, marking out a shape roughly five inches square, which suggests that something fairly heavy, supported on four little feet, stood there for some considerable time. It is quite clearly not a book and yet this description matches no object in the room. It therefore followed that Mr Berkinshaw must have brought it with him, almost certainly in the valise which contained his papers.

'I confess that I could make nothing of it at the time. Nor could I understand how the pen was made to move. It was only late last night, after considering the problem for several hours, that the answer came to me in one of those bursts of imaginative perception such as Newton must have experienced when he observed the apple falling from the tree.

'The object was, of course, a metronome!

'Once I had come to that conclusion, I could then put together the final picture from the scattered pieces of evidence. Mr Berkinshaw had assembled a dummy similar to that which you see before you, using a metronome to create the illusion of the moving pen. All of this was, of course, done when Deakin, who was mowing the lawn, had his back to the window. It would not have taken long. In fact, I accomplished the same task in less than two minutes.

'Then, having wound up the metronome and set it in motion, Mr Berkinshaw left the house by the back door, unobserved by Mrs Deakin whom he had earlier asked to clean the silver and who was fully occupied with that task in a pantry some distance from the kitchen.

'There is a path which cuts across the grounds and comes out on the road at the point where it turns sharply to the left, close by the small grove of beech trees. It is a much shorter route to and from the house, as Dr Watson will verify. This afternoon, I made an excuse to leave him at the station and yet, by taking that same path, I arrived before him. Is that not so, my dear fellow?'

'Indeed it is, Holmes. I wondered how you had managed it. It must take at least a quarter of an hour if one comes by the road.'

'It is precisely thirteen and a half minutes. I timed it myself yesterday. However, if one takes the short cut across the grounds, it is a mere six minutes. I think we may therefore safely assume that Mr Berkinshaw took the same route on Wednesday afternoon and, having emerged on to the road shortly before Mr Eugene Mortimer was due to arrive at Boxstead Halt at 3.55, waited in the gateway for his victim to pass by. As it is a three-minute walk from the station, it was at two minutes to four that he leapt out upon his victim, strangled him and dragged his body into the field where he concealed it in the bushes. If one allows five minutes for the murder to be committed and another six for Berkinshaw to return by the same path to the Grange, we can estimate that he arrived at twelve minutes past four. This gave him time to dismantle the dummy, conceal the wig and the metronome once more inside the valise before, putting on his coat, he went to the door to welcome Mr Johnathen Smith, who arrived shortly afterwards at 4.15 from Fordham.

'Before doing so, Berkinshaw had, of course, first left Mr Eugene Mortimer's bowler hat in the field to draw attention to the place where the body was concealed and had also distributed about the scene of the crime those pieces of evidence which would point to Mr Smith's guilt.

'Indeed, it was these data which confirmed my suspicions.'

'I do not see why,' Lestrade protested. 'You yourself set great store on evidence, Mr Holmes. Well, it was there for all to see in the cigar butt thrown down upon the ground and the button from Mr Smith's coat caught on the bush close by the body.'

Holmes raised his eyebrows.

'Quite so, Lestrade. A cigar butt and a coat button! However, as you clearly failed to notice, the butt was not fresh. The tobacco was old and discoloured. Moreover, its end was compacted as if it had been stubbed out in some container, not merely dropped to the ground to burn away or squashed flat with the sole of a boot.

'As for the button, had you made a careful examination of that, too, you would have observed that the threads attached to it had been snipped off clean, not torn away as one would have expected had it become entangled on the bramble.

'I therefore came to the conclusion that the evidence had been contrived by Mr Berkinshaw, for only he could have had access to Mr Johnathen Smith's coat and one of his cigar butts. Mr Smith had called at Mr Berkinshaw's office for consultations over his late uncle's will. I have no doubt that, during one of those meetings, Mr Smith smoked a cigar, the butt of which he stubbed out in an ashtray on Mr Berkinshaw's desk. I am also convinced that, on some pretext or other, Mr Berkinshaw left his office and cut one of the buttons from Mr Smith's coat which was left hanging in the vestibule.'

During the first part of this account, Mr Berkinshaw had listened in silence, huddled low in his chair, his face still blanched with the horror of that awful moment of guilty recognition when he had seen his double seated at the study window. However, as Holmes continued, the lawyer had regained some of his composure until, as my old friend reached the final part of his narrative, he had quite recovered his self-assurance.

Springing to his feet, he advanced towards us, a smile of triumph lighting up his features.

'Oh, no, Mr Holmes, this will not do! This will not do at all!' he declared loudly. 'I have listened patiently to your explanation and I find it nothing more than a farrago of surmise and speculation. "I have no doubt"! "I am convinced"! That is not proof, sir. As a legal man, allow me to give you a few words of advice. You will have to produce better evidence than that in court if you hope to convince a jury of my guilt.'

'It was written plain enough on your face,' Lestrade said, looking much offended by the man's effrontery.

'My expression, Inspector?' Berkinshaw sneered. 'Are you intending to produce that, too, in court? It was the shock at seeing that dummy of myself, as my defence lawyer will explain. As for the rest of the so-called case against me, it can be as easily demolished as Mr Holmes' ridiculous mannikin!'

Striding over to the chair, Mr Berkinshaw struck at the dummy with his hand, knocking the blond wig to the floor and overturning the bolster.

'So much for that!' cried he. 'And so much, too, Mr Holmes, for the rest of your proof. It is all circumstantial nonsense! Where are your witnesses? And what, pray, was my motive for murdering Mr Eugene Mortimer?'

He seemed about to strike out at the metronome which was still ticking away on the desk when Holmes seized him by the wrist.

'I have witnesses, Mr Berkinshaw,' said he. 'Two to

be precise and both honest citizens. This morning I made enquiries in the Strand where you have your office. Four doors along is a shop selling musical instruments, the proprietor of which is prepared to swear that a fair-haired gentleman, answering your description, purchased a metronome from him on Tuesday morning, the day before the murder. Further enquiries at a theatrical costumier's in nearby King Street established the fact that on the same morning a gentleman of a similar appearance bought a blond wig. It was at these two shops I made my own purchases. You should have gone further afield, Mr Berkinshaw. It was a great mistake on your part to patronise the shops in your immediate neighbourhood.

'I have so far not traced the cord used to strangle Mr Mortimer. The official police may have better luck or you may have already had it in your possession.

'As for motive, I suggest Inspector Lestrade asks an auditor to examine the accounts of the late Mr Franklin Mortimer's estate. I believe he will find certain discrepancies. Ah, I thought so!' he added softly as, with a cry of despair, Mr Berkinshaw broke free of Holmes' grasp and made a rush at the door.

'After him, Jenks!' Lestrade shouted, setting off in pursuit.

By the time Holmes and I had joined them in the hall, the two police officers had cornered Berkinshaw and Inspector Lestrade was in the act of snapping a pair of handcuffs on his wrists.

He made no further attempt at resistance and did not

even look in our direction as, head hanging low, he was escorted out of the house to the waiting four-wheeler.

'Holmes,' said I when the door closed behind them, 'what made you suspect Berkinshaw was taking money from the Mortimer estate? Or was it merely a shot in the dark?'

'My dear fellow,' he replied, 'I never make the mistake of firing entirely at random. One should always have one's target well within one's sights before pulling the trigger. I had Mr Berkinshaw in mine when he called on us at Baker Street.'

'For what reason?'

'His appearance.'

'How, exactly?'

'To be precise, his coat, his shirt, his watch. I wondered then how he could afford to have his morning-suit made in Savile Row, his linen in Jermyn Street,[7] or to purchase so splendid a gold hunter, costing at least twenty-five guineas. In short, his tastes were extravagant. So the first seeds of doubt concerning Mr Berkinshaw were sown in my mind. Therefore, this morning, when carrying out my enquiries in the Strand, I made a point of calling on another solicitor who has an office almost next door to his. There is no one quite like a business rival to gossip

---

[7] Mr Sherlock Holmes may be referring to the exclusive tailoring firm of Henry Poole and Company of 36–39 Savile Row, which had royal warrants from both Queen Victoria and the Prince of Wales. The firm of Skinner and Company, also patronised by Prince Edward, had premises at 57 Jermyn Street. Dr John F. Watson.

about the affairs of a competitor. From him, I learnt that Mr Berkinshaw, who is a bachelor, has a house in Eaton Place and a half-share in a racehorse he keeps at a stable in Newmarket. It was quite clear that he lived in a style more suitable to a gentleman of private means.

'It was also clear from his attentions to Mrs Mortimer that he had designs in that direction. I confess that, being of a sceptical turn of mind, I wondered if it were simply her physical charms which had attracted him or the thought that, if her husband were dead and Johnathen Smith, the other heir, hanged for his murder, she would be the sole successor to the Mortimer fortune. By marrying her, he would not only gain access to that wealth but could cover up the traces of those sums of money he had been secretly extracting from the family estate.'

'Poor Mrs Mortimer! I wonder what will happen to her now?' I mused out loud.

Holmes smiled indulgently.

'I know what you are thinking, Watson. As an incurable romantic you are hoping that Mrs Mortimer and Johnathen Smith will marry and that all will end happily to the merry peal of wedding bells. I am afraid life rarely provides such satisfactory conclusions. And now, my dear fellow, if we step out smartly we should be in time to catch the 5.45 train to London. For my part, I wish for no happier ending than to arrive in Baker Street in time for supper.'

Holmes was correct in both his reading of my thoughts and his prediction regarding Mrs Mortimer's future.

She did marry again but not Johnathen Smith.

About a year later, a notice in *The Times* announced her forthcoming wedding to a Mr Clement Windthrop, about whom I know nothing. I trust she and her small son have found the happiness they so richly deserve after the tragedy which befell them. For that reason, I shall refrain from publishing an account of the case, depositing it instead among my confidential papers.[8]

---

[8] In 'The Adventure of the Golden Pince-Nez', Dr John H. Watson makes only a passing reference to the Smith-Mortimer succession in a list of other cases which took place in 1894 and of which he has kept the notes. Dr John F. Watson.

THE CASE OF THE MAUPERTUIS SCANDAL

I

'What do you know about diamonds, Watson?' my old friend Sherlock Holmes asked abruptly.

It was a cold, blustery afternoon in late March 1887 and Holmes had been sitting in silence for several hours, sunk low in his armchair by the fire in a state of utter exhaustion, a condition which had persisted, much to my secret alarm, for several weeks.

From the number of occasions he had been absent from our Baker Street lodgings, at times for periods lasting several days, I had already deduced that he was engaged in some important and complex investigation which he had not seen fit to confide in me. However, I was ill prepared for the extraordinary revelations which were to follow upon that curt enquiry.

'Very little,' I replied, laying aside the *Morning Post*. His next question was as unexpected.

'Then I assume the name Baron Maupertuis means nothing to you?'

'I have not heard of him. Is he a client?'

Holmes gave a short, bitter laugh.

'Hardly, my dear fellow. He is the most accomplished swindler in the whole of Europe whom I have been given the task of exposing. You may recall that about six weeks ago in February, I received an anonymous visitor. Because the matter was highly confidential, I asked you to be kind enough to absent yourself.'

'I saw him getting out of a cab as I was leaving for my club. He was a tall, middle-aged gentleman, was he not, wearing gold pince-nez and an overcoat with an astrakhan collar? I thought he looked somewhat foreign in appearance.'

Holmes laughed again, this time with genuine amusement.

'Capital, Watson! I see you have acquired some skills of observation. Well, that gentleman was Monsieur Henri Rogissart, the French Minister of Finance, and he was in this country to confer privately with officials in our own Treasury about a situation which is causing considerable disquiet among European financiers and politicians. But without the necessary evidence, there was very little our government could then do except take note of the circumstances and advise Monsieur Rogissart to consult me.

'The story he had to tell was quite remarkable. It concerned a business venture, the Netherland-Sumatra Company, which was set up a year ago by Baron

Maupertuis. The Baron claims that he has discovered a method of manufacturing diamonds which are indistinguishable from real gems.'

'Is that possible, Holmes?'

'It is certainly not beyond the bounds of credibility. Seven years ago, a Scottish chemist, James Hannay, made a similar claim. He placed a mixture of paraffin, lithium and bone-meal inside wrought-iron tubes and subjected it to great heat. In three of his experiments, he found particles which experts pronounced were indeed diamonds.[1]

'It may have been Hannay's apparent success which persuaded the Baron to set up his own laboratory near the Hague, using a similar method with the addition of a secret chemical ingredient which he says is found only in Sumatra and which he has especially imported at great cost. Hence the name, the Netherland-Sumatra Company.

'It is in this laboratory, he alleges, that he manufactures

---

[1] James Ballantyne Hannay (1855–1931), a Glasgow chemist, conducted a series of experiments using 4 mg of lithium and a mixture of 10% rectified bone-meal and 90% paraffin spirit which was placed inside wrought-iron tubes and heated inside a large reverberatory furnace for several hours. Out of eighty such experiments, only three were successful, producing tiny crystals which experts at the time attested were diamonds. In 1943, 1962 and 1975, these crystals, which had been preserved at the British Museum, were retested using more sophisticated techniques which proved the crystals were natural, not synthetic, diamonds. It was assumed that either Hannay or one of his workmen had planted the diamond crystals or, more likely, Hannay's original materials were contaminated by diamond particles. Attempts to manufacture synthetic diamonds were not successful until 1953. Aubrey B. Watson.

not diamond particles but stones weighing approximately a quarter of a carat which, when cut and polished, would produce a gem about half that weight. He further claims that, given the money to expand his laboratory and refine the method, he could produce even bigger diamonds. It was in order to raise the capital for this expansion that he started the company and invited private individuals to invest money in it. The minimum stake is the equivalent of £500.

'Anyone who buys shares is given one of these smaller uncut gems, with the promise of an even larger stone in the future, once the improvements have been made.'

'Are they real diamonds?'

'Oh, assuredly, Watson. There lies the cunning of the scheme. It is a perfectly genuine stone, as any expert will attest. As far as I can ascertain, Baron Maupertuis has by this means persuaded over six hundred shareholders in three different countries, France, Germany and Italy, to invest more than £300,000 in his company, a very large sum indeed. The venture appeals, you see, to two fundamental human weaknesses: greed and a sense of exclusiveness. The company is private; it does not advertise and, in order to become a shareholder, one must be recommended. The Baron, who moves from country to country, always staying at the best hotels, personally interviews each potential investor. Not all are thought worthy. Those who are accepted are given one of the diamonds and invited to inspect the premises where the gem was allegedly made. I understand from those who have made the tour that the laboratory is impressive. They gave the most glowing reports which are, of course, passed on by word of mouth to their wealthy friends. In consequence, the Baron is never short of eager clients clamouring to put their money into his company, from whom he carefully selects those who are the most greedy and gullible. They are less likely to question his business methods.

'In addition, those who were among the first to invest in the scheme are kept content by receiving monthly bulletins describing the continuing success of the Netherland-Sumatra Company and, after six months, an even larger diamond as proof. They therefore have no cause to complain or suspect the Baron of deceit.'[2]

'Just a moment, Holmes!' I broke in. 'If the company is fraudulent, I assume he is not manufacturing diamonds in his laboratory.'

'Certainly not. I thought you had understood that. It is the whole point of the deception.'

'Then how is he acquiring the diamonds which he gives to his shareholders and which you say are genuine?'

'Bravo, Watson! That is, of course, the logical question

---

[2] In 1905, the Frenchman, Henri Lemoine, claimed to have manufactured diamonds in his London laboratory, using a secret method. He persuaded Sir Julius Wernher, the South African financier and governor of De Beers Consolidated Mines, to provide him with financial backing. However, there was so little difference between Lemoine's so-called synthetic diamonds and natural stones that eventually Sir Julius became suspicious. After an investigation, Lemoine was arrested and sentenced to six years' imprisonment for fraud. Aubrey B. Watson.

to ask. The answer is obvious. They are stolen. During the past few weeks, I have paid several visits to the Continent to enquire into that very aspect of the case. It has not been easy. The Baron has covered his tracks most cunningly. However, after a long and exhausting investigation, I discovered that three years ago there was a series of burglaries at diamond merchants' or jewellers' in a number of cities across Europe in which a large quantity of uncut stones were stolen. The robberies, which were carried out by a professional safe-breaker, were confined to countries in the east of the Continent, such as Russia and Poland. At the time, they received little notice in the newspapers of, say, France or Italy and were soon forgotten once the raids had ceased.

'When Baron Maupertuis started his company, who in Cologne or Milan would remember a robbery which had taken place three years before in St Petersburg or Warsaw? Certainly not his shareholders. His merchandise therefore cost him nothing, while the capital raised from the sale of the shares is placed in a numbered Swiss bank account. The interest gained by it is used to meet the Baron's expenses, such as hotel bills and the cost of maintaining his laboratory. There are also his accomplices to pay, who include the two so-called specialists who are supposedly manufacturing the diamonds and the professional burglar who carried out the robberies. So the venture not only finances itself but the capital grows with each new investor. Is it not ingenious, Watson? Much as one deplores the crime, one cannot help admiring the brilliance of the mind which conceived it. Had he chosen to use that financial genius for legitimate ends, he could have been another Rockefeller or a Rothschild.'

'Have you met him?' I asked.

'Once at a reception in Paris. As one might expect, he is a plausible rogue who speaks excellent English and has the most charming manners. He claims to be descended from the cadet branch of the Hapsburgs. As I have not been able to trace him in the *Almanack de Gotha*,[3] I suspect less exalted origins. But whatever his antecedents, he is expected to arrive shortly in London, which was the reason for Monsieur Rogissart's visit.

'Three months ago, the Baron moved his field of activities to France, first to Paris, more recently to Lyons. It was here that he and his company began to attract the attention of a certain Monsieur Chalamont, who owns an engineering firm in the city and who was introduced to the Baron as a potential investor. However, his application was refused.

'In the course of my enquiries on the Continent, I travelled to Lyons and spoke to Monsieur Chalamont. He believes he was rejected because he asked too many searching questions of the Baron into the diamond manufacturing process in which, being an engineer, he was naturally interested. His suspicions aroused and his

---

[3] The *Almanack de Gotha,* a German publication, gave historical and statistical information in both French and German on the countries of the world. It was best known, however, for its detailed genealogies of European royal families. Dr John F. Watson.

amour propre wounded, for no one likes to think his credit is unworthy, Monsieur Chalamont began to make a few discreet enquiries of his own into the Netherland-Sumatra Company. He is fortunate in having several influential friends and, like a stone dropped into a pool, the ripples began to spread until they reached Monsieur Rogissart at the French Ministry of Finance in Paris.

'In turn, Monsieur Rogissart also made enquiries and was much alarmed at what he discovered. In France alone, Baron Maupertuis had succeeded in persuading over a hundred eminently respectable citizens, among them members of the aristocracy and wealthy businessmen, even bankers, some of whom recommended their own clients as potential investors.

'Monsieur Rogissart was placed in a dilemma, the horns of which were exceedingly sharp. On the one hand, there was merely rumour and speculation. No one had openly complained, certainly not the Baron's shareholders, who seemed perfectly satisfied with the arrangements. To authorise an official investigation might cause a scandal. Suppose the Baron's enterprise were legitimate? He himself is a wealthy and prominent individual with many acquaintances in high places. On the other hand, if the Netherland-Sumatra Company is indeed fraudulent, Monsieur Rogissart could hardly ignore the whispers and permit him to continue deceiving the good *citoyens* of France.

'A covert inquiry could take many months and, as I have already explained, the Baron is intending to move his enterprise to England.

'It was at this point that Monsieur Rogissart decided to come to London and lay his suspicions before our own Treasury officials in order to forewarn them of the Baron's arrival and to ask for their assistance in setting up a joint investigation which would prove either the Baron's guilt or his innocence.

'The problem was passed to my brother Mycroft whom you met not long ago in the course of another of my cases.[4] It was he who recommended Monsieur Rogissart to come to me.

'We come now to the nub of the matter, Watson, and the reason why I have confided in you. Baron Maupertuis is expected to arrive in London in four days' time. If he follows his usual *modus operandi,* he will stay here for three to four months before moving on to his next field of conquest, which we have good reason to believe will be the United States of America. Mycroft is strongly of the opinion that, once there, the Baron will gather in what capital he can from his new set of investors and then will quietly disappear, possibly to one of the South American countries where he will assume a new identity. He is highly intelligent and must realise that any fraud can run

---

[4] Dr John H. Watson first met Mycroft Holmes when he introduced his younger brother, Mr Sherlock Holmes, to the case involving Mr Melas, an account of which was later published under the title of 'The Adventure of the Greek Interpreter'. This case, which is undated, has been ascribed by students of the canon to various dates between 1882 and 1890. However, it would appear from this evidence that it must have occurred before April 1887. Dr John F. Watson.

for a limited term only. It is therefore essential that he is brought to justice before that happens.

'I have a plan in mind for unmasking him for which I shall need your assistance.'

'Of course, Holmes,' I said readily. 'I am willing to help in any way I can.'

'I have arranged to meet Mycroft at six o'clock at his club.[5] I should like you to be present. Mycroft will have in his possession a letter of recommendation sent by Monsieur Rogissart in the diplomatic bag from a certain Marquis de Saint Chamond, one of the Baron's most valued investors whom, on my last visit to France, I succeeded in convincing, after much persuasion, of the fraudulent nature of the Netherland-Sumatra Company. With all the enthusiasm of the newly converted, he has agreed to help in its exposure. In his letter, he has recommended to the Baron a wealthy English acquaintance of his, Sir William Manners-Hope, as a potential investor. You, Watson, shall take the part of Sir William.'

'I, Holmes?' I cried, much taken aback at this suggestion.

'Yes, you, my dear fellow. The ruse is quite simple. I would undertake it myself if I had not met the Baron in Paris. He is a remarkably astute man and is quite capable of seeing through the most elaborate disguise.

'When the Baron arrives in London, he will stay at

---

[5] Mycroft Holmes was a founder member of the Diogenes Club in Pall Mall. Dr John F. Watson.

the Hotel Cosmopolitan[6] where he has already engaged a suite of rooms. You will write to him there, on headed paper from your London house, enclosing the letter of recommendation from the Marquis and requesting an interview. I have arranged to have the writing paper specially printed and the Baron's reply intercepted, so that presents no difficulties.

'At the appointed time, you will arrive at the Hotel Cosmopolitan and be shown up to the Baron's suite.'

'But what if he asks about the Marquis?'

'Oh, he undoubtedly will. He quizzes his potential investors most closely but always in the most charming and oblique manner. That is, however, not a problem. Before you meet him, I shall prepare you thoroughly in both the matter of your acquaintance with the Marquis and in your own antecedents as Sir William.

'I am quite sure he will accept you as an investor. The letter from the Marquis will guarantee that. Like all parvenus, the Baron sets great store on his aristocratic clients. You will then hand over a banker's draft for £500 and the Baron in turn will give you your share certificate in the Netherland-Sumatra Company and a diamond which he will claim was recently manufactured at his laboratory in the Hague.

'It is at this point that I must rely on you, my dear fellow. I know from my enquiries on the Continent

---

[6] The Countess of Morcar was staying at the Hotel Cosmopolitan when she was robbed. *Vide*: 'The Adventure of the Blue Carbuncle'. Dr John F. Watson.

that the Baron does not deposit his hoard of stolen diamonds in the hotel safe but keeps it somewhere in his suite, always in another room to the one in which the interview is held. For reasons which I do not propose explaining at this moment, I should like to know exactly where they are kept. That is why you are so essential to my scheme.

'When he leaves the room to collect the diamond, you must use all your powers of observation in an attempt to discover precisely where the stolen gems are hidden.'

'Surely you are asking too much, Holmes!' I protested. 'If he closes the intervening door, I shall have no means of knowing.'

'I admit the task is difficult but it is not impossible. There should be certain clues; for example, the length of time he is gone from the room or whether you hear even the faintest sound of a drawer being opened or a key being turned in a lock. There may also be signs about his person, fibres perhaps upon the knees of his trousers, suggesting he has knelt down upon the carpet, or dust upon his sleeve which would indicate that he has reached into some less accessible corner, overlooked by the chambermaid.'

'And if I fail?' I asked.

'Then so be it,' said he with a shrug. 'When the time comes, I shall have to search for the diamonds myself. That could, however, be a lengthy process which I had hoped to avoid. They are not kept in some obvious place such as a strong box. The Baron never travels with one. But they must be hidden somewhere he regards as secure. He makes no secret of his wealth and is therefore an obvious target for thieves. And now, my dear fellow,' Holmes concluded, 'it is time we called a cab and set off for our meeting with Mycroft. He is punctuality itself and expects the same courtesy in others.'

We found Mycroft Holmes waiting for us in the Strangers' Room, the only part of the Diogenes Club where conversation was permitted.

Unlike his brother, he was a corpulent man, stout of figure and massive of feature, with a somnolent air about him in marked contrast to my old friend's energetic manner. It was only in the sharpness of his expression that I could discern any fraternal likeness.

That expression was evident as we entered and he saw that I had accompanied Sherlock Holmes, although he shook hands cordially enough with me.

'So Dr Watson has agreed to play the part of Sir William,' said he, subsiding into an armchair. 'It is probably a wise decision, my dear Sherlock. If I may say so, Doctor, you give the impression of guileless trust, quite in keeping with a man prepared to throw away his money on a fraudulent enterprise. Now to practicalities. Here is the letter of recommendation from the Marquis de Saint Chamond which arrived at the Foreign Office this morning. With it is a banker's draft for £500 which needs only Sir William's signature. An account in that name has already been opened at the Kensington branch of Silvester's.[7] In addition, Inspector Gregson has already been apprised of those facts which it is necessary for him to know. However, I do not need to point out, I am sure, that he can do nothing without evidence: hard, irrefutable evidence which will stand up to scrutiny in a court of law. That is vital. Baron Maupertuis is an international criminal of the first order who must be caught. If he is not, there will eventually be a scandal which could have political as well as financial repercussions, not only here but in Europe. I do not know how you propose to set about gathering that evidence. I acknowledge it will not be easy.'

'I have given the matter considerable thought,' Holmes began, when he was interrupted by his brother, who held up a warning hand.

'I prefer to remain in ignorance, my dear boy. But do remember, I beg you, that the Baron has many influential clients in high places. If you are contemplating breaking the law, I can offer you only limited protection, should your enterprise fail. I cannot stress that more strongly. I should not wish to see you behind bars.'

With that admonition, he rose to his feet and shook hands with both of us in turn, once more casting in my direction that look of sharp appraisal with which he had greeted me on my arrival.

It was quite evident that he doubted my ability to carry

---

[7] Lady Frances Carfax kept her account at Silvester's, the London banking company. *Vide*: 'The Disappearance of Lady Frances Carfax'. Dr John F. Watson.

out successfully my part in Holmes' scheme to bring the Baron to justice, a reservation which made me all the more determined to prove him wrong.

Therefore, on our return to Baker Street, I threw myself enthusiastically into the preparations for putting that plan into action.

First of all, the letter from Sir William Manners-Hope had to be written on a sheet of headed paper, giving a Grosvenor Square address, which Holmes had had printed for the occasion.

It was an easy task, as Holmes dictated its contents and I merely wrote at his direction. That done, and the letter of recommendation from the Marquis de Saint Chamond enclosed with it, I addressed the envelope to the Baron at the Hotel Cosmopolitan to await his arrival and Holmes summoned the boy in buttons[8] to take it to the post.

The next part was more demanding and took up more time. This was my induction into Sir William's supposed acquaintance with the Marquis for which, with characteristic thoroughness, Holmes had prepared a lengthy treatise, drawn up under headings and covering every aspect of their relationship. Over the next few days, I studied this assiduously, committing to memory

---

[8] Billy, surname unknown, was employed as a pageboy at 221B Baker Street at the end of the '80s. He is described as 'young but very wise and tactful'. *Vide*: *The Valley of Fear*, 'The Adventure of the Mazarin Stone' and 'The Problem of Thor Bridge'. Dr John F. Watson.

so many facts about both gentlemen that, at the end, I felt they were old friends. In this manner, I learnt that the Marquis was a frequent visitor to London, where he had a house in Mayfair, and that I, Sir William, had met him at the Carlton Club, of which we were both members.[9]

Every evening Holmes cross-examined me as closely about my knowledge of these facts as a prosecuting counsel.

In the meantime, the Baron had arrived at the Hotel Cosmopolitan where he received my letter, for three days later his answer was delivered, sent to Sir William at his Grosvenor Square address and intercepted by Inspector Gregson, the Scotland Yard detective appointed to take charge of the official investigation.

In his letter, the Baron suggested that I, as Sir William, should meet him in his hotel suite at 3 p.m. in two days' time.

Holmes greeted this invitation with jubilation.

'The bait is taken, Watson!' cried he, rubbing his hands together with delight. 'In less than a week, we may see the trap close upon him. And now, my dear fellow, let us return to our labours, for by Friday you must be word perfect in your role.'

His catechism continued until shortly before my departure for my appointment with the Baron. Indeed,

---

[9] The Carlton Club was situated in Pall Mall, not far from the Diogenes Club. Sir James Damery was a member of the Carlton. *Vide*: 'The Adventure of the Greek Interpreter'. Dr John F. Watson.

as I was taking up my hat and stick, Holmes shot a last question at me.

'The name of the Marquis's favourite dog, Watson?'

'Justin,' I replied. 'It is a red setter and was given to him by his wife.'

'Well done! All that remains is to wish you good luck, for much depends on your success in this affair.'

II

It was with this exhortation still in my mind that I arrived at the Hotel Cosmopolitan, a large and elegant building, where I was shown upstairs to the Baron's suite on the second floor by a pageboy.

Hardly had I knocked upon the door than it flew open and Baron Maupertuis appeared on the threshold.

'My dear Sir Wiliam! I am delighted to make your acquaintance!' he exclaimed, shaking me warmly by the hand and drawing me into the room.

He was a tall, heavily built man, verging on the portly, with clean-shaven, fleshy features. Yet, despite his large frame, he moved with surprising grace and lightness. In age, I should have put him at a little over fifty and if I had to choose one adjective to describe him, then it would be smooth. His silvery hair, brushed back from his broad, handsome forehead, was smooth. So were his clothes which fitted him like a second skin and which denoted the excellence of his tailor. His hands were small and plump, like a woman's, and had the same softness to the touch. As he greeted me, I noticed that he bore on the little finger of his left hand a large gold signet ring, engraved with his initials.

Holmes had spoken of his charm and this was immediately apparent, although I was aware that, under his agreeably engaging manner, there was a more acute and watchful intelligence. It was particularly noticeable in his eyes, which were a bright, luminous blue, but in the centre of which the darker pupils were as hard and as fixed as flints.

'Pray sit down,' he continued, waving me towards an armchair. 'You will take a glass of champagne?'

I was about to reply that it was a little early in the afternoon when he anticipated my objection, adding with a smile, 'Just a small glass, my dear sir, to celebrate the occasion. It is such a very great pleasure to meet a friend of the Marquis de Saint Chamond. And how is *cher Philippe*? Well, I trust?'

'I believe so,' I replied, seating myself and accepting the proffered glass. 'He was in excellent health the last time I heard from him.'

'You exchange letters?' he enquired.

'Occasionally.'

'And where did you meet him?'

'At the Carlton Club a few years ago,' I replied. 'He was in London on business.'

'Ah, of course! He owns a house in Knightsbridge, I believe.'

'In Mayfair, actually.'

'Really? You must forgive me. Was it not left to him by an English grandmother?'

'You are mistaken, Baron. It was his great-aunt Sophia who married the late Lord Alferton.'

It was indeed fortunate that Holmes had prepared me so thoroughly for this examination, which the Baron conducted with great subtlety and skill, disguising it under the pretence of an exchange of social pleasantries about a mutual acquaintance.

I flatter myself that I passed this test successfully and also the subsequent enquiries into my own antecedents as Sir William. At least, the Baron appeared satisfied with my answers.

Rising to his feet, he said, 'My dear Sir William, I am sure you will forgive my impertinence in asking you so many questions. As no doubt the Marquis de Saint Chamond has explained to you, there are many gentlemen anxious to invest in my company from whom I choose only those I consider the most worthy. I feel I owe it to my other shareholders, among whom are some of the most illustrious names in Europe. I am therefore delighted to invite you to join their distinguished assembly. Congratulations, Sir William!'

Drawing himself upright, he gave me an oddly formal little bow.

I scrambled up from my own seat more awkwardly,

smiling with sheer relief and also with a certain wry amusement at the Baron's effrontery. The man had the infernal impudence to congratulate his victim for having been chosen to invest money in his fraudulent scheme!

'And now,' said the Baron, taking me companionably by the elbow and leading me towards a desk which stood under the window, 'for the formalities, Sir William. If you care to make your payment, I shall take great pleasure in giving you your share certificate.'

As I signed the banker's draft for £500 in Sir William's name, the Baron took from the desk drawer a roll of parchment, elaborately inscribed with the name of the Netherland-Sumatra Company below the emblem of a golden eagle with outstretched wings, to which he added his own signature with a flourish of the pen. We then exchanged documents with as much solemnity as two heads of state handing over to each other copies of some important international treaty.

'You will not regret this, Sir William,' the Baron assured me. 'I can promise that, in a year's time, when I fully expect the laboratory at the Hague to be producing diamonds of one or even two carats, your shares in the Netherland-Sumatra Company will be worth many times their original value. As for the diamonds, you shall now have the privilege of seeing for yourself the excellence of the product in which you have so wisely invested your capital.'

Leaving me at the desk, the Baron crossed the room to

the door which communicated with the bedroom, shutting it softly behind him.

I stood very still, silently counting off the seconds and straining to catch the slightest sound beyond the closed door. But the panels were too thick and I could hear nothing apart from the knocking of my own heart, which sounded to my ears like the beating of a drum.

I recalled Holmes' last words, warning me how much depended upon the successful execution of my part in his plan, and I felt the weight of responsibility lie heavy on my shoulders. If I failed, I should not only let my old friend down but should also confirm Mycroft's unspoken reservation about my ability to carry out the enterprise.

After a minute and a half, the door opened and the Baron re-entered the room.

Trying to hide my curiosity, I watched him as he came towards me but I could discern nothing about his appearance which might suggest the place where the diamonds were hidden; no dust; no fibres; no signs of any kind.

In one hand he was carrying a small wash-leather bag, fastened at the mouth with a drawstring, in the other a little jeweller's box, covered with blue velvet, on the lid of which was stamped in gold the eagle crest of the Netherland-Sumatra Company.

Placing both upon the desk, he drew a handkerchief from his breast pocket which he spread out beside them. Then, opening the wash-leather bag, he spilt its contents on to the square of blue silk. The stones came pouring out to form a little heap, glittering in the bright spring sunshine which came flooding in through the window.

'Exquisite, are they not?' he said softly, touching them almost reverently with one plump, white finger. 'Such colour! Such lustre, even though they are uncut! Imagine them, Sir William, when they are shaped and polished and set into a necklace to adorn the throat of a beautiful woman. They will glitter like a constellation of stars. Now choose, my dear sir. Whichever one you pick shall be yours.'

He pased one hand gently over the mound, spreading out the diamonds so that each separate stone caught the light and flashed it back at me in points of fiery brilliance.

I confess that, despite myself, I was caught up in the thrill of the occasion and the magic with which the Baron managed to invest it, quite forgetting that the whole affair was nothing more than an elaborate fraud.

Very tentatively, I indicated one of the stones which seemed to shine more brilliantly than the others.

'An excellent choice!' the Baron exclaimed approvingly. 'I see you have the most superb taste, Sir William. It is a perfect specimen.'

Picking it up with the pair of tweezers which lay ready to hand, he placed it in the small satin-lined box, which he handed to me with another of his formal bows.

'It has been an honour to meet you, Sir William,' said he, holding out his hand, 'and to welcome you as a shareholder in the Netherland-Sumatra Company.'

It was quite evident that the ceremony was over. In

a few moments, I would be shown to the door and the opportunity to discover the evidence which Holmes so urgently needed would be lost for ever.

I had failed and, with that realisation, my feeling of excitement was replaced by one of utter dejection and it was only with the greatest effort that I managed to maintain my smile.

We shook hands and, as I turned to make my departure, I took a last glance at the scattered diamonds lying on the desk, knowing that, as soon as I had gone, the Baron would gather up the glittering hoard and return it to its secret hiding-place.

It was only then that my attention was drawn to the little wash-leather bag which lay beside the gems and which until that moment I had disregarded. It was an ordinary object, unremarkable in every way except for a small brown stain close to its drawstring mouth.

Hardly had I noticed it than the Baron again took me by the elbow with that amiable intimacy of his and began to escort me towards the door, and there was nothing I could do but accompany him.

III

On my return to Baker Street, I found Holmes pacing up and down the sitting-room in a state of great nervous tension.

'Well, Watson?' he demanded as I entered. 'What have you discovered?'

'Hardly anything Holmes,' I confessed with a heavy heart.

'How long was he gone from the room?'

'About a minute and a half.'

'Then,' said he, brightening a little, 'the hiding-place must be readily accessible. Did you hear anything?'

'Not a sound.'

'Or note anything unusual about his appearance?'

'Nothing, I am afraid.'

He sank down in a chair by the fire, his countenance once more clouded over.

'Except . . .' I began diffidently.

'Except what?'

'It is so trifling a matter, I hardly think it is worth mentioning.'

'Let me be the judge of that! To what precisely are you referring?'

'To a stain upon the bag in which the diamonds were kept.'

'Stain? What sort of stain?'

'I do not know. It was very small, Holmes; little more than a smear.'

'What colour?'

'Brown.'

'Light brown? Dark brown? Come, Watson! Be more exact.'

'Dark brown.'

Holmes sprang to his feet and resumed his restless perambulations, his brows contracted and his hands clasped nervously together.

As he paced up and down, he muttered to himself under his breath, 'A dark brown stain. Not ink. Paint, then? Unlikely. Or dye? As improbable.'

Suddenly he gave an exclamation of exasperation and struck himself on the forehead with his palm.

'Of course! What a fool I am! The answer is obvious. Boots!'

'Boots?' I enquired.

'Yes, Watson, boots. Or to be more precise, boot polish. What else could be found among a gentleman's effects which would leave behind a small, dark brown stain such as you describe? The Baron must therefore keep his store of stolen diamonds in a pair of brown boots, almost certainly in the heels, the only part of a boot which offers any place of concealment. It is an old smugglers' trick, I believe, to hide small items of contraband in a similar fashion. It is moreover safe from theft. No burglar is likely to make off with a pair of boots when there are more valuable articles worth stealing.' Clasping me by the hand, he added, 'My dear old friend, you have done sterling service this afternoon. I could not have bettered it myself.'

I was highly gratified by this commendation, for I knew it was sincerely meant. It was not in Holmes' nature to flatter anyone, not even the highest in the land, with undue praise. His approbation had to be rightly earned.

'And now, Watson,' he continued, 'for the diamond. I assume Baron Maupertuis presented you with one. May I see it?'

'Of course, Holmes,' said I, taking the little jeweller's box from my pocket.

Seizing it eagerly, he carried it over to the window where, having taken the stone from its container, he subjected it to a minute examination with the aid of a jeweller's eyeglass, turning it over and over between his fingers.

'Is it false?' I asked, assuming he was looking for signs it had been faked.

'No, it is perfectly genuine. The Baron deals only in authentic diamonds,' he assured me, replacing it inside its box, which he returned to me.

I could not be sure, but I thought I perceived an expression of disappointment pass over his lean features. However, it was gone in an instant and before I could enquire into its cause, Holmes had moved on to the subject of my interview with the Baron, about which he questioned me closely, congratulating me again on the successful manner in which I had conducted it.

For the next eight days, nothing occurred to forward the case and Holmes sank once more into that state of brooding melancholy which always overtook him in moments of enforced idleness. So low were his spirits that I feared he might have recourse to that artificial stimulant from which I had attempted to wean him.[10]

It was therefore a considerable relief to me when, at breakfast on the following Saturday morning, a letter arrived which Holmes had evidently been expecting, for he tore the envelope open and scanned the letter it contained with great haste.

'The stalemate is over at last, Watson!' cried he. 'And the game is once more afoot!'

Dashing into his bedroom, he emerged in less than ten minutes, fully dressed and carrying a small valise. 'You are going away?' I enquired.

'For four nights only,' he replied. 'I shall return on

---

[10] There are several references to Mr Sherlock Holmes' unfortunate habit of injecting himself with a 7% solution of cocaine. On occasions, he also took morphine. *Vide,* among others, *A Study in Scarlet*, *The Sign of Four* and 'A Scandal in Bohemia'. Dr John F. Watson.

Wednesday morning. Pray inform Mrs Hudson of my absence and try to keep Wednesday night free.'

'Why, Holmes?'

'Because, my dear fellow, by then I expect to have all my pieces on the board for the final move which will checkmate the Baron.'

The next moment, the sitting-room door had banged shut behind him.

I waited impatiently for Holmes' return, curious to know what exactly he had meant by his reference to chess and how precisely he proposed setting about the Baron's defeat.

In the event, Holmes failed to arrive as expected on the Wednesday morning. It was not until four o'clcok that I heard the sound of his familiar footsteps bounding energetically up the stairs.

'You are late, Holmes!' I declared as he entered.

'A thousand apologies,' said he cheerfully. 'I trust you were not anxious on my behalf. There was rough weather in the Channel and the packet was late in arriving at Dover.'

'So you have been to France again?'

'Not to stay on this occasion. I merely passed through on my way to Buda-Pesth.'

'Buda-Pesth? What on earth were you doing there?'

'Meeting a certain Mr Jozsef whose presence in London is essential to my plan. Mr Jozsef is a jeweller whose premises were burgled three years ago, presumably by Baron Maupertuis's confederate, and a quantity of uncut diamonds were stolen. Out of the sixteen jewellers and diamond merchants whom I interviewed during my earlier enquiries, he alone was prepared to swear that he could distinguish his stones from all others; or, at least, some of them.

'By great good fortune, Mr Jozsef, who designs and makes some of his own jewellery, had received an order for a bracelet from a wealthy client just before the burglary. It was intended as a coming-of-age gift for the customer's daughter. From his stock of uncut diamonds, Mr Jozsef chose twenty-one stones which most perfectly matched one another in weight and colour. These he set to one side, having first noted down their particulars. As an extra precaution in case they should, by some unlucky chance, become confused with his other stock, he marked each with a tiny scratch, invisible to the naked eye.

'However, before he could despatch them for cutting and polishing, his workshop was broken into and these diamonds, along with about a dozen more, were stolen. It is because of these tiny scratches that Mr Jozsef is certain he can pick them out from any others.

'I had great hopes, Watson, that the Baron might have passed on some of these marked stones to his shareholders, but of the few I have managed to examine without rousing suspicion, none bore that distinguishing sign, including yours. They must therefore still be in the Baron's possession. Consequently, I am left with no alternative. In order to retrieve them and so obtain the evidence I shall need to prove the Baron's guilt, I shall have to turn burglar myself.'

'But, Holmes, think of the risk you will be taking!' I cried.

'Oh, there is no risk, my dear fellow. The letter I received on Saturday morning was from the Marquis de Saint Chamond. In it, he informed me that, as I had requested, he had arrived in London and had written to Baron Maupertuis asking him to dinner tonight at his Mayfair house, an invitation the Baron has accepted. The engagement is for half-past seven. Therefore I estimate that by a quarter past seven at the latest, the Baron will have left the Hotel Cosmopolitan, clearing the way for me to enter his rooms and remove the diamonds.

'I have already taken the precuation of booking a suite in the hotel on the same floor as the Baron's and only a little distance from it. As soon as I have found the gems, I shall return to my suite with them, where Mr Jozsef will be waiting to examine them. If among them, he finds any of the marked stones, as I have every confidence he will, then the case against the Baron will be proved. If, on the other hand, none of the marked stones are discovered, then I shall simply return the diamonds to their hiding-place and the Baron will be none the wiser. I cannot see what risk I shall be taking.'

'I was not referring to the physical danger but the legal implications,' I replied. 'You will be breaking the law, Holmes. Do you not recall your brother warned you that he could promise you only limited protection, should you do so? You could be placing your whole career and reputation in jeopardy. I do beg you to reconsider.'

'I have,' said he most earnestly. 'For the past two

months I have thought of little else than how to bring the Baron to justice. I am touched by your concern, Watson. But believe me, there is no other way.'

'Could you not inform Inspector Gregson of your suspicions and leave it to him to make the search with an official warrant?'

'No, Watson; I dare not. Suppose I am wrong and the diamonds are not hidden in the Baron's boots? Or the marked stones are not among them but concealed elsewhere, possibly even on the Continent? Not only would the whole enterprise fail but the Baron would be warned of our suspicions. There lies the greatest danger. I must be sure of the evidence before Gregson can make an arrest. In this game the stakes are too high to risk a faulty throw.

'However, allow me to set your mind at rest a little. I have gone part of the way to make my scheme legitimate. Earlier today, I left a message at Scotland Yard for Inspector Gregson, asking him to call at the Hotel Cosmopolitan later this evening, bringing with him some of his colleagues and a search warrant but giving him no further information except that I hope to have evidence of the Baron's guilt and a witness to prove it. If I am right and the stones are where I think they are hidden, then Gregson will have the legal means to find them and arrest the Baron. If by any chance I am wrong, no action will be taken. I shall merely apologise to Gregson for wasting his time and some other method of entrapping the Baron will have to be devised.

'For this reason, I see no other solution than to break

into the Baron's rooms and steal the diamonds myself.'

'Then I will come with you,' said I.

'You shall do no such thing, my dear fellow. If you wish, you may accompany me to the hotel but you must remain inside the room and not set foot outside it.'

'You cannot force me to. I give you my word that, as soon as you leave for the Baron's suite, I shall follow at your heels.'

'What a stubborn fellow you are!' Holmes cried, looking annoyed. 'What can I say to dissuade you?'

'Nothing, Holmes. My mind is made up. You have often referred to me as your colleague, a title I have been proud to acknowledge. That same pride will not allow me to be merely your fair-weather friend.'

'Then I see there is no point in arguing,' said he, smiling and holding out his hand to me. 'You have won, Watson. We shall become partners in crime! Let us trust we do not find ourselves standing shoulder to shoulder in the dock at the Old Bailey! Now for the particulars of my plan. I shall leave here at six o'clock for the boarding-house in Chelsea where Mr Jozsef is waiting, together with Mr Melas whom you have met before[11] and who will act as interpreter, as Mr Jozsef speaks only Hungarian. From

---

[11] Mr Melas, a Greek by birth, knew nearly all languages and acted as an interpreter at the Law Courts and also to foreign visitors to London. It was he who, through Mycroft Holmes, introduced Mr Sherlock Holmes to a case, an account of which Dr John H. Watson published under the title of 'The Adventure of the Greek Interpreter'. Dr John F. Watson.

there, I shall take them both to Suite 206 which I have engaged at the Hotel Cosmopolitan. I suggest you join me there at half-past seven, after the Baron's departure. But first I propose we ask Mrs Hudson to provide an early supper, for it may prove a long and tedious evening.'

As soon as we had supped, Holmes set out alone for Chelsea while I departed for the Hotel Cosmopolitan a little over an hour later.

During that intervening time, I had the leisure to consider my own part in Holmes' plan and, while I had no regrets over my decision to accompany my old friend, it was with some trepidation as well as excitement that I contemplated the adventure to come.

Having met the Baron, I was in no doubt that he was a formidable and highly intelligent adversary with the wealth and power to strike back at anyone who opposed him. As Mycroft had said of him, he was an international criminal of the first order whose capture would avert a scandal of European dimensions. It was this latter consideration which afforded me the greatest thrill of expectation. Like a mountain-climber contemplating a high peak which he proposes scaling, my awareness of the dangers involved only served to whet my appetite for the challenge.

IV

It was little after half-past seven when I arrived at the Hotel Cosmopolitan and was shown up to Holmes' suite on the second floor, where my old friend opened the door to me.

'Come in, my dear fellow!' he exclaimed, drawing me into the room where two gentlemen were already seated. 'Mr Melas, of course, needs no introduction. My other guest, whom you have not yet met, is Mr Jozsef from Buda-Pesth. Mr Jozsef, Dr Watson, my colleague,' Holmes continued, smiling and putting a special emphasis on this latter word.

I shook hands first with Mr Melas, a short, stout man with an olive complexion, who interpreted Holmes' remarks for the benefit of his companion. Mr Jozsef, who was elderly and white-haired, seemed bewildered by his transference from his workshop in Buda-Pesth to a

London hotel. During these introductions, he kept casting anxious glances at Holmes much as a dog which, finding itself in strange surroundings, will gaze at its master in order to reassure itself by the sight of a familiar face.

Holmes, who was in high spirits, was eager for these social niceties to be completed. Hardly had I relinquished Mr Jozsef's hand than he had hurried on.

'And now, my dear Watson, if you are still intent on coming with me, we shall search for the Baron's boots, an amusing version of the old parlour game of Hunt the Slipper.'

He led the way out of the room and along the corridor to the door of the Baron's suite a little distance away where he paused and, having made sure no one was about, slipped a skeleton key into the lock and turned it.

The drawing-room beyond, where I had first met Baron Maupertuis, was in darkness apart from the glow from the street lamps shining in through the window. But a light had been left burning in the bedroom, where the curtains were already drawn.

Holmes crossed immediately to a large mahogany press standing against the far wall which he opened, revealing a pair of highly polished brown boots lined up side by side with other footwear below a hanging rail of clothes.

With a low exclamation of triumph, Holmes lifted them out and inspected the heels.

'You see, Watson,' said he, 'they are slightly higher than is usual. The Baron must have had them specially made. And look here! Can you see this line close to the soles where a layer of extra thick leather has been added and fixed into place by these tiny screws? They mark, I believe, the opening to the secret hiding-place where the stolen diamonds are concealed.'

Gripping the heel of the right boot firmly with one hand, Holmes twisted the lower section round in much the same manner as one might unscrew the stopper of a bottle. It yielded slowly to his grasp until at last the whole bottom section of the heel had pivoted stiffly on its retaining screw, revealing the hollow centre into which was crammed a small wash-leather bag.

The left heel was similary hollowed out and contained a second bag, as Holmes discovered when he had wrenched it open.

'A rich haul indeed!' he exclaimed, his eyes sparkling as he slipped both into his pocket. 'We are almost there, Watson. All that remains is to call upon Mr Jozsef's good offices to supply the final proof.'

Replacing the boots in the cupboard, he led the way out of the Baron's rooms, the door of which he locked behind us.

As soon as we had returned to our own suite, Holmes wasted no time in making use of Mr Jozsef's good offices, as he had termed them. Indeed, Mr Jozsef was already prepared for the role he had to play, for we found him seated at the desk in front of the window, the appurtenances of his trade set out before him in the form of a pair of tweezers, a jeweller's eyeglass, a pair of tiny brass scales and a square of black felt on to which he emptied with great eagerness the contents of the two little wash-leather bags which Holmes handed to him.

He set to work at once, picking up each glistening stone in turn which, after examining it with great care with the aid of the glass, he placed to one side, while we stood behind him, watching anxiously. From time to time, he selected one of the diamonds for special scrutiny and this, after the most rigorous examination, was weighed on the scales. Then, having consulted a small leather-bound notebook, Mr Jozsef would lay it down on the black felt, taking care to keep it separate from the other gems, until eventually they formed a little pile of their own.

There were, I judged, over three hundred uncut stones altogether and the task of examining each one was slow and laborious, made more onerous by the complete silence in which it was conducted. No one spoke and, as the minutes dragged by, first Mr Melas and then I, too, lost interest and quietly withdrew to the other side of the room where we sought the comfort of a pair of armchairs.

Only Holmes remained standing at the desk, still absorbed in Mr Jozsef's meticulous appraisal, although, as time passed, I was aware of an increasing tension on his part. On several occasions, he drew out his pocket watch and glanced surreptitiously at its dial and I guessed that he was anxious for the examination to be finished before the arrival of Inspector Gregson and his colleagues.

At last, it was over. Mr Jozsef removed his eyeglass and, looking up at Holmes, his lined features puckered up into a smile, the first which had crossed his countenance the whole of that evening, began to address him very earnestly and rapidly in Hungarian.

Jumping to our feet, Mr Melas and I joined them at the desk.

'He says that he is sure these stones are his,' Mr Melas said, interpreting the elderly jeweller's remarks, at the same time indicating the smaller of the two heaps of diamonds which numbered about twenty gems. 'They correspond in weight and colour to those stolen from him in 1884. What is more, they bear his mark.'

'And he would be prepared to swear to that in a court of law?' Holmes asked.

Mr Melas interpreted both the question and Mr Jozsef's assent.

'Excellent!' Holmes decared, his whole countenance lighting up. 'And now, Mr Melas, if you would be good enough to escort Mr Jozsef back to his boarding-house and to tell him to wait there, I shall call on him in a few days, by which time I expect the Baron and his associates will be under arrest.'

On receiving this assurance, Mr Jozsef beamed his approval and, gathering up the scales and his other instruments which he returned to the small valise he had brought with him, he and Mr Melas both took their leave.

As soon as they had gone, Holmes collected up the diamonds and replaced them in the two wash-leather bags with the exception of one stone from the little heap of marked gems, which he left lying on the desk.

'I shall now return these to the Baron's boots where shortly the good Inspector Gregson will find them when the official search is made. I should prefer you to wait here,

Watson, for I am expecting Gregson and his colleagues from the Yard to arrive at any moment.'

Within minutes, Holmes had returned and, shortly afterwards, a knock at the door announced the arrival of Gregson, a pale-faced, flaxen-haired man, wearing civilian dress, who was accompanied by two plain-clothes officers.

'I received your message, Mr Holmes,' said Gregson, looking about the room and acknowledging my presence with a curt nod of his head. 'Where is the evidence you said you hoped to have? And where is the witness you also mentioned?'

'The witness has already left but may be called upon at any time. As for the evidence, it is here,' Holmes replied, leading Gregson to the desk where the single diamond lay upon the square of black felt. 'If you care to examine it with the aid of this jeweller's glass, you will see a tiny mark scratched into its surface.'

As the inspector looked at the stone, Holmes gave him a brief summary of Mr Jozsef's acount of the robbery at his premises and how the diamond came to be marked in the first place.

'Well, that is proof enough for me,' Gregson replied. 'I have here a warrant to search the Baron's rooms, as you requested. All that remains is for me to present it when the gentleman returns.'

'Which should be soon,' Holmes informed him. 'The Marquis de Saint Chamond will so arrange matters that Baron Maupertuis will leave his house at approximately half-past eleven. It is now nearly a quarter before midnight.

I have tipped one of the pageboys to rap upon the door as soon as he sees the Baron enter the hotel.'

'Then we should not have long to wait,' observed Gregson. 'In the meantime, Mr Holmes, perhaps you would satisfy my curiosity about one aspect of the case.'

'Of course, Inspector.'

'It concerns that diamond,' Gregson continued, glancing down at the desk.

'What do you wish to know?' Holmes enquired casually, although I saw by the tightening of his jaw that he had anticipated the inspector's question and I felt my own mouth go dry in expectation.

Holmes would not lie in answer to a direct query. It was not in his nature to deceive deliberately when so challenged, although he might, when the occasion demanded, withhold evidence when he considered that to do so would assist an inquiry.

'How were you able to acquire it?' Gregson asked and then, to my relief and no doubt to Holmes' as well, he proceeded to supply his own answer. 'I understand the Baron handed out a number of these uncut stones to his various clients. I suppose you were fortunate in finding it amongst them. It's just a matter of luck, Mr Holmes. I don't mind admitting that there have been several cases I have been called upon to investigate in which, if Lady Luck hadn't been on my side, I should never have caught the villain. You may recall the Bermondsey murder?'

'I do indeed,' Holmes murmured.

'Now there was a remarkable instance.' Gregson, who

was evidently in a reminiscent mood, continued, 'If Clarke hadn't been seen by that costermonger climbing out of the bedroom window, I couldn't have proved his alibi was false and so brought him to the gallows.'

He was interrupted by a soft tap on the door, at which Holmes started up.

'There is our signal!' said he. 'Baron Maupertuis has arrived at the hotel. I propose, Inspector, that we allow him a few minutes to reach his room and then we confront him with the evidence.'

Inspector Gregson took this last opportunity to remind his fellow officers of their duties. Potter, the taller of the two, was to remain outside in the corridor while Johnson, a burly, heavily moustached detective, who was to accompany us into the room, would guard the door from the inside in case the Baron should attempt an escape.

Holmes, who had opened our own door a fraction in order to keep watch through the crack, now held up his hand and announced in a whisper, 'He is here!'

At this, Gregson nodded silently to his two colleagues and with the inspector leading the way, the five of us set off along the corridor.

I cannot speak for my companions but, as we approached the Baron's room, I felt my pulses quicken at the thought that within minutes the most accomplished swindler in the whole of Europe would be under arrest and that I had played a not insignificant role in his downfall.

When Baron Maupertuis opened the door to Inspector Gregson's knock, he was still wearing evening clothes, although his silk hat and cloak lay discarded upon the sofa.

It was evident that he was not expecting callers and, for a few seconds, his smooth, handsome features bore an expression of annoyance at our arrival at such a late hour.

But he was too intelligent not to guess the purpose of our visit. I saw his glance flicker across our faces and he gave a start of recognition as he came to mine. But it was on Holmes' countenance that it rested the longest and it was he whom the Baron finally addressed.

'I believe we have met before at a reception in Paris,' said he, smiling blandly. 'Mr Cornelius Spry, is it not?'

'Sherlock Holmes,' my old friend corrected him.

'Indeed, sir! I am honoured, for I have read about your exploits,' Baron Maupertuis replied. 'Then I may assume the gentleman with you is not Sir William Manners-Hope but Dr Watson, your colleague and amanuensis. Pray come in, gentlemen, and bring your companions with you. They are police officers, are they not? Their bowler hats betray their profession. No gentleman of any quality would wear such undistinguished items of apparel.'

'I am Inspector Gregson of Scotland Yard,' that officer announced, much piqued by the Baron's contemptuous tone. 'I have reason to believe that you have been engaging in a fraudulent enterprise. I have a warrant here to search your effects.'

'Search all you wish, Inspector,' the Baron replied, waving an expansive hand. 'You will find nothing incriminating either on my person or among my possessions.'

'Not even in the heels of your boots?' Holmes enquired.

'Boots?' Gregson cried, greatly astonished.

The Baron, who had retreated into the room as we advanced, came to a sudden halt, still smiling, although the manner in which he played with the signet ring upon his little finger, twisting it this way and that, betrayed an inner agitation.

'Yes, Inspector; a pair of brown boots which are in his bedroom press and in the heels of which is concealed a quantity of uncut diamonds,' Holmes continued. 'Among them, you will find more of those marked stones, similar to the one I have already shown you, which I can prove were stolen in May 1884 from Mr Jozsef's premises in Buda-Pesth.'

Before Inspector Gregson had time to recover from his surprise, the Baron began to laugh softly.

'Congratulations, Mr Holmes!' said he. 'You are indeed a worthy opponent! But if you think you will have the pleasure of seeing me behind bars, then I am afraid I shall have to disappoint you. I have spent too long mingling with the most illustrious society in Europe and dining at the highest tables to submit to eating prison fare or rubbing shoulders with the criminal classes.'

As he spoke, he continued to twist the ring upon his left hand; a mere nervous habit, I assumed.

Then suddenly, in one swift movement, he raised that hand to his mouth, pressing the ring against his lips. Before any of us could move or even cry out, he had closed his teeth with a snap and swallowed convulsively, the tendons in his throat straining like tightened cords. A few seconds later, a violent shudder passed through his entire frame and he fell lifeless to the floor as if struck by a thunderbolt from heaven.

Holmes and I ran across the room to his side.

'Prussic acid,'[12] said I, bending over the Baron's body and smelling the unmistakable odour of bitter almonds upon his lips.

'And here is the means of taking it,' Holmes added grimly. He had lifted the Baron's left hand and was pointing to the ring, the gold bezel of which was now open like a flap, revealing a tiny inner compartment. 'It must have contained a capsule of the poison. Oh, what a fool I am, Watson! I saw him toying with it but never guessed his purpose.'

'There was nothing any of us could have done. The poison acts too quickly. As soon as he bit upon that capsule, he was a doomed man,' I said, trying to reassure him, although I doubted if he found any consolation in my words.

'Indeed, Watson,' said he. 'But I should have liked the opportunity to return his compliment, for he, too, has proved an adversary worthy of the name.'

He had drawn himself upright and was gazing down at the Baron's inert form, his countenance so grey and haggard that I was deeply shocked, not fully realising until

---

[12] Prussic acid or hydrocyanic acid is the fastest acting poison known and can cause death within seconds. Cyanide is found in many plants, including bitter almonds. Hence its distinctive odour. In *A Study in Scarlet*, Mr Enoch Drebner was poisoned, probably by Prussic acid or one of its salts, sodium or potassium cyanide, for when Mr Sherlock Holmes gave his landlady's sick terrier one of the pills found in Joseph Stangerson's room, it died almost immediately. Dr John F. Watson.

that moment the intensity of the strain he had undergone during the course of the investigation.

Nor was it over with the death of Baron Maupertuis. There were certain formalities which had to be carried out, including the inquest at which both Holmes and I gave evidence, although, through Mycroft's influence, no reference was made to the means by which my old friend had acquired the proof of the Baron's guilt.

It was because of this same reason that I have decided not to publish a full account of the case.[13]

There were other duties placed upon Holmes' shoulders. On several occasions, he was obliged to travel to the Continent to assist the police authorities in those countries where the Baron had carried out his fraud in compiling a full report. This led to the arrest and subsequent imprisonment of the Baron's confederates, the two so-called experts who ran his laboratory at the Hague, and the professional burglar, a notorious criminal, Pierre Loursat, who had stolen the uncut diamonds. I understand that, after protracted enquiries, these stones were eventually returned to their rightful owners.

In the meantime, although congratulatory messages and telegrams poured in from all over Europe, Holmes

---

[13] In 'The Adventure of the Reigate Squire', Dr John H. Watson refers to the Netherland-Sumatra Company and Baron Maupertuis but gives as his reason for not publishing an account of the case that it is 'too recent in the minds of the public, and too intimately concerned with politics and finances, to be a fitting subject for this series of sketches.' Dr John F. Watson.

received little pleasure from these accolades and continued to sink deeper into depression.

I shall refer only briefly to the subsequent events. If this narrative is ever published, then readers will be aware of what followed, for I have given as full an account as I thought suitable in the opening paragraphs of 'The Adventure of the Reigate Squire'. In it, I refer to the complete breakdown of my old friend's health and how, on 14th April, I was summoned to Lyons, where Holmes was helping the French police. It was there that his iron constitution finally failed him, leading to his collapse from nervous prostration at the Hotel Dulong where he was staying.

On our return to England, I took him to stay for a week's recuperation at the house of an old army friend of mine, Colonel Hayter, at Reigate in Surrey, hoping that the rest and change of scenery would help to restore him to full health. It was during this visit that he became engaged in the curious and complex inquiry into the murder of William Kirwin, the Cunninghams' coachman.[14]

There is only one postcript I wish to add regarding an aspect of the Maupertuis case which was never resolved.

This concerns the number of the Swiss bank account in which Baron Maupertuis had placed the money he had obtained from the sale of shares in the Netherland-Sumatra Company. Although a full list of these investments, which amounted to the huge sum of nearly half a million

---

[14] William Kirwin was murdered by his employers, Squire Cunningham and his son, Alex. *Vide*: 'The Adventure of the Reigate Squire'. Dr John F. Watson.

pounds, was discovered among his papers, no record of where precisely they were deposited was ever found, apart from the enigmatic phrase '*Midas, le Roi d'Or*'[15] which featured several times in the documents.

Holmes is convinced that this is a coded reference to the name and number of the Baron's account in Switzerland. Despite strenuous efforts, neither he[16] nor any of the other experts who were called upon to give assistance were able to decipher it.

I assume the money is still there, accumulating interest, and must therefore, at the time of my writing this, have increased considerably.

If this narrative is ever published and if any reader succeeds in deciphering the code, then that person will have the key to a vast fortune which even Baron Maupertuis himself, for all his colossal schemes, could not possibly have anticipated in his wildest dreams.

---

[15] 'Midas, the Golden King'. In Greek mythology, Midas, King of Phrygia, was given the power to turn anything he touched into gold by the god Dionysus. However, when King Midas discovered that even the food he touched turned to gold, he prayed to Dionysus to help him and the magic power was removed. Dr John F. Watson.

[16] Mr Sherlock Holmes, who states that he was 'fairly familiar with all forms of secret writings', wrote a monograph in which he analysed one hundred and sixty separate ciphers. During his investigations, he solved four coded messages. *Vide*: 'The Adventure of the Dancing Men', 'The Adventure of the Red Circle', *The Valley of Fear* and 'The Adventure of the *Gloria Scott*'. In 'The Adventure of the Musgrave Ritual', he successfully interpreted a series of puzzling questions and answers which led to the discovery of the Musgrave treasure. Dr John F. Watson.

APPENDIX

An Hypothesis Regarding the Identity of the Second Mrs Watson

Students of the Sherlock Holmes canon will be aware of the mystery surrounding the identity of Dr Watson's second wife and the precise date when this marriage took place.

The only reference to it is made by Sherlock Holmes, not Dr Watson, in a terse and enigmatic sentence found in 'The Adventure of the Blanched Soldier'. In this narrative, recounted by Sherlock Holmes, the great consulting detective merely states that, at the time of this particular investigation, January 1903, 'the good Watson had . . . deserted me for a wife, the only selfish act which I can recall in our association'.

Dr Watson himself never refers to this second marriage, an extraordinary omission when one considers that he shows no such reticence concerning his first wife, the former Miss Mary Morstan. Indeed, the circumstances of his meeting with and courtship of Miss Morstan are fully described in *The Sign of Four* while in such subsequent accounts as 'The Adventure of the Stockbroker's Clerk' and 'The Man with the Twisted Lip', references are made to his domestic life which was evidently happy though childless.

The first Mrs Watson died between 1891 and 1894, when Sherlock Holmes was absent from England after his apparent death at the hands of Professor Moriarty at the Reichenbach Falls. On Sherlock Holmes' return, Dr Watson, now a widower, sold his Kensington practice and moved back to his former lodgings at 221B Baker Street, possibly in 1894.[1]

It was at some time after this date that Dr Watson met the young lady whom he subsequently married.

Although the exact date of the wedding cannot be established, there are certain clues within the published canon which allow an approximation to be made.

As already stated, the case of the Blanched Soldier occurred in January 1903, by which time Dr Watson was already married and had, as Sherlock Holmes implies, moved out of the Baker Street lodgings. However, as

---

[1] Dr John H. Watson's return to Baker Street is assigned by some students of the canon to the year 1894. However, in 'The Adventure of the Veiled Lodger', dated 'early in 1896', Dr Watson states that he received 'a hurried note' from Sherlock Holmes, summoning him to Baker Street, which suggests that by that date he had not yet moved back to his old lodgings. Dr John F. Watson.

Dr Watson was still in residence there at the 'latter end' of June 1902 at the time of the case concerning the three Garridebs, it may safely be assumed that he had not yet 'deserted' his old companion for a second wife.

But in 'The Adventure of the Illustrious Client', which is precisely dated to 3rd September 1902, Dr Watson states that he was then already living in his own rooms in Queen Anne Street.[2]

Although he gives no explanation for this change of address, it is generally assumed that this was on the occasion of his second marriage. It must therefore have taken place between the end of June and the beginning of September 1902.

This dating is confirmed in 'The Adventure of the Creeping Man', also assigned to early September 1902, in which Dr Watson receives a message from Sherlock Holmes summoning him to Baker Street where, as Dr Watson explains, 'he greeted me back to what had once been my home.'

Unfortunately, there is no such evidence available to

---

[2] Queen Anne Street crosses Harley Street where many important consultants and specialists had their practices, including Dr Moore Agar, Mr Sherlock Holmes' own physician. Situated in the West End, Queen Anne Street was more fashionable than Baker Street, Dr John H. Watson's former address. As Dr Watson gives medical treatment to Baron Gruner, including an injection of morphine, it may be assumed that, at the time of this adventure, he was continuing to practise as a professional doctor from the Queen Anne Street address, presumably among a more wealthy clientele. *Vide*: 'The Adventure of the Illustrious Client'. Dr John F. Watson.

help with identifying the lady who became the second Mrs Watson and any attempt to do so must rest on mere speculation.

It is, however, possible to make an educated guess, based on information found elsewhere in the canon, concerning Dr Watson's attitude to women and in particular to the type of young lady who was likely to appeal to him.

As he himself admits in *The Sign of Four*, he had an experience of women which extended over 'many nations and three separate continents'[3] and yet it was the charms of Miss Mary Morstan, later to become the first Mrs Watson, which finally won his heart. As he describes his meeting with her in some detail, the researcher is given valuable information on which to base an hypothesis.

Although not strictly beautiful, she was attractive in appearance and Dr Watson was particularly struck by the 'spiritual and sympathetic' expression in her eyes and the signs of a 'refined and sensitive' nature in her features. Always a chivalrous man, he was also deeply touched by her plight, indicated by her 'intense inward agitation', despite her 'outward composure'. In addition, he was impressed by her courage, for, although she was alone in the world, she had supported herself through her own

[3] In *The Sign of Four*, Dr John H. Watson compares the heaps of earth in the gardens of Pondicherry Lodge to the gold-diggings near Ballarat which he himself had seen, although quite when is unknown. Ballarat, a gold-mining centre, is situated in Victoria, Australia. Dr Watson's experience had therefore included the continents of Europe, India and Australia. Dr John F. Watson.

efforts as a governess. This had given her an experience of life which also appealed to him.

Moreover, he fell in love with her on first acquaintance.

In short, Dr Watson was attracted to women of a warm and sensitive nature who roused in him admiration for their courage as well as compassion for the difficulties of their circumstances.

It has been suggested that the second Mrs Watson was Miss Violet de Merville, the daughter of General de Merville, who featured in 'The Adventure of the Illustrious Client'. Young, rich and beautiful, she had fallen obsessively in love with Baron Gruner, a highly undesirable suitor with a criminal background from whom her family was trying to separate her. Through the intervention of Sherlock Holmes, the engagement was eventually broken off and the Baron left the country.

However, in my opinion, Miss Violet de Merville is not the type of young lady to appeal to Dr Watson. Despite her passionate attachment to the Baron, she is at heart hard, inflexible and self-willed. Besides, there is no evidence that Dr Watson ever met her, Sherlock Holmes having interviewed her in the absence of his colleague.

But there is one young lady whom Dr Watson met and who possesses many of the qualities which he would have looked for in a woman. As a candidate for the second Mrs Watson, she is much more likely to have won his affections than Miss de Merville. Dr Watson was immediately drawn to her, as he was to Miss Morstan, and felt towards her the same protective urge. She was, moreover, a governess like the first Mrs Watson, and displayed those same qualities of refinement and sensitivity which had attracted him to his first wife.

If my hypothesis is correct, then marriage to this particular young lady would also explain Dr Watson's unprecedented reticence over her identity.

The lady in question is Miss Grace Dunbar.

Dr Watson made her acquaintance during the investigation into the death of Mrs Gibson, the wife of Mr Neil Gibson, the American gold millionaire, an account of which he later published under the title of 'The Problem of Thor Bridge'.

Accused of the murder of Mrs Gibson, Miss Dunbar was in prison awaiting trial at Winchester Assizes and it was in her cell that Dr Watson was first introduced to her.

In a lengthy passage, as detailed as his account of his meeting with Miss Morstan, Dr Watson describes her appearance and the immediate attraction he felt towards her. He writes: 'I had expected from all we had heard to see a beautiful woman but I can never forget the effect which Miss Dunbar produced upon me.'

But it was not only her beauty which captivated him. As in the case of Miss Morstan, he was impressed by the sensitivity of her features and her 'nobility of character' as well as touched by the 'appealing, helpless expression' in her dark eyes.

Although the two women were physically very different, Miss Morstan being small, fair and dainty of figure whereas Miss Dunbar was a tall, dark brunette with a commanding presence, I believe readers will acknowledge the many striking similarities in the two descriptions, not least in the immediate effect both young ladies had on Dr Watson's susceptibilities.

Indeed, Dr Watson was so taken by Miss Dunbar that the short journey from Winchester to Thor Place seemed intolerably long to him, so impatient was he for Sherlock Holmes to begin the investigation which was eventually to prove her innocence.

At the end of 'The Problem of Thor Bridge', Sherlock Holmes comments that, now the case has been satisfactorily resolved, it is 'not unlikely' that Miss Dunbar will marry Mr Neil Gibson. It is a curiously negative remark, as if the great consulting detective himself had doubts over the matter. And indeed many readers would also regard such an outcome as highly improbable.

Of all the clients to cross the Baker Street threshold, Mr Neil Gibson is surely one of the most unpleasant. Feared by his household, he is described by his estate manager as a 'man of violence' and an 'infernal villain'. On Gibson's own admission, it is because of his ill-treatment of her that his wife, a passionate and neurotic Brazilian lady, was driven to take her own life in such a manner as to throw suspicion of murder on Miss Dunbar, the children's governess, to whom Gibson had transferred his attentions.

Far from welcoming his advances, Miss Dunbar had threatened to leave Thor Place and was only prevailed upon to remain at her post by her employer's assurance that his offensive behaviour would cease. In addition, she had dependents who relied on her financially and, according to Gibson, she was convinced that, by staying, she could influence him for the better.

This last consideration carries very little weight in the argument. All of this happened before Mrs Gibson's suicide when the question of a possible marriage between the Gold King and the governess would not have arisen. It seems highly unlikely that, after Mrs Gibson's death, Miss Dunbar would have agreed to the match, even after the charge of murder against her was withdrawn. She had too much nobility and strength of character to marry a man who through his own obnoxious behaviour had not only driven his first wife to commit suicide but had put her own life in jeopardy.

The year when this investigation took place is unknown. Only the month is specified, which was October. However, from internal evidence it can be established that it was during the time when Dr Watson was still living in Baker Street.

Any theory regarding the dating of subsequent events is therefore merely speculative. I suggest, however, that the case should be assigned to October of 1901 and that, after her release from prison, Miss Dunbar left Mr Gibson's household. As there was no opportunity at the time for Miss Dunbar to thank Sherlock Holmes and Dr Watson for the part they had played in proving her innocence, I further suggest that she travelled to London in order to express her gratitude in person. Nothing would have been more natural; after all, Sherlock Holmes had saved her from the gallows.

At this interview, Dr Watson renewed his acquaintance

with her, an occasion which was to lead to further meetings and to their subsequent marriage in the summer of 1902.

If this hypothesis is accepted, Dr Watson's reticence over his second marriage becomes perfectly understandable. He would hardly wish the public, particularly his professional clientele, to know that he had married a woman who had once been accused of murder. Social convention at the time would have inhibited him from making the truth known.

But there is a still more pressing reason for his silence.

Mr Neil Gibson was a man of a violent and revengeful nature. He even went so far as to threaten Sherlock Holmes when he seemed at first reluctant to take the case.

In Dr Watson's presence, Gibson told the great consulting detective, 'You've done yourself no good this morning, Mr Holmes, for I have broken stronger men than you. No man ever crossed me and was the better for it.'

How much more likely is it then that the Gold King would seek vengeance on the man who had won the affections of the young lady he himself had hoped to marry?

Under such circumstances, it is not surprising, therefore, that Dr Watson should have kept secret the identity of his second wife and have refrained from making any reference to her in the published canon.

John F. Watson, D. Phil. (Oxon)
All Saints' College, Oxford.
14th February 1932

If you enjoyed *The Secret Journals of Sherlock Holmes*,
look out for more books by June Thomson . . .

HOLMES AND WATSON

Sherlock Holmes and Dr John Watson, famous for their crime-solving capabilities, are mysterious figures themselves. What is known about their pasts, and the reasons behind their very different personalities? This detailed and enthralling account ponders answers to the many uncertainties and enigmas which surround the pair.

And there are other puzzles to be solved. Who was John Watson's mysterious second wife? And what is the real location of the legendary 221B Baker Street? A thorough investigation commences as Sir Arthur Conan Doyle's most famous creations are placed under the magnifying glass . . .

THE SECRET NOTEBOOKS OF SHERLOCK HOLMES

In Sherlock Holmes's London, reputations are fragile and scandal can be ruinous. In order to protect the names of the good (and not-so-good), Dr Watson conceals unpublished manuscripts in an old despatch box, deep in the vaults of a Charing Cross bank . . .

Now, outlasting the memories of those they could have harmed, these mysteries finally come to light. An aluminium crutch betrays the criminal who relies upon it for support . . . An Italian Cardinal lies dead in a muddy yard in Spitalfields . . . Can Holmes and Watson outwit the jewel thief who has the nerve to steal from the King of Scandinavia?

THE SECRET ARCHIVES OF SHERLOCK HOLMES

A mysterious veiled lady carries a counterfeit painting into an art dealer's office. A widow with three hands slips out of a church door. A farmer lies dead in a barn, his son accused of his murder, and a skeleton with a silver locket is unearthed in a back garden. Who can solve these mysteries? One man. He lives in Baker Street.

Accompanied by the faithful Dr Watson, Sherlock Holmes is back and brilliant as ever in this brand new series of untold adventures from June Thomson, packed with enigmas and enemies of old . . .